OLD TIMES

Old Times

Bill Brooks

First published in Great Britain by ISIS Publishing Ltd.
First published in the United States by Zebra Books

Published in Large Print 2009 by ISIS Publishing Ltd.,
7 Centremead, Osney Mead, Oxford OX2 0ES
United Kingdom
by arrangement with
Golden West Literary Agency

British Library Cataloguing in Publication Data
Brooks, Bill, 1943–
Old times
1. Western stories.
2. Large type books.
I. Title
813.5'4–dc22

ISBN 978–0–7531–8267–3 (hb)

Printed and bound in Great Britain by
T. J. International Ltd., Padstow, Cornwall

For Pat LoBrutto —
Who knows a thing or two about old cowboys
and fire in the blood

Prologue

They found the little bunch of cattle in Smiley's Draw at the foot of Bone Mountain. It was in the silver blue light of predawn and a cold wind was blowing off the ridge. The shod hooves of their ponies clattered over loose rock. It startled the small bunch of cows, which began to bawl their protest — first the mamas, then the calves.

"Jesus and Joseph," one of the riders said. "They'll raise up the dead!"

"Hush!" the other said. "We might as well dismount and go in there on foot and get one!"

A little white-face heifer stood down in the draw holding its ground and bawled at the approach of the shadowy figures. These were brush-popping cattle, half wild — mavericks — from a season on open range. They had broken off from the main herds farther south in the meadows. It was high country, and even though late summer, the nights still grew as cold as the inside of a well, and just as black.

The riders dismounted, ground-reined their horses, and started up the draw. One carried a needlenose gun and took the lead. The draw was boxed up at the far end with no means of escape.

"How you goin' to hit somethin' in the dark?" said the one, keeping his voice low.

"It'll be light in a few minutes, them cows ain't going nowhere."

"Whose cows you reckon these are?" the one without the gun said.

"Most likely J.D.'s. It's his herds back there in the meadows."

"Hell, I wouldn't be surprised. He owns nearly all the cattle in Judith County."

"Seems like, that's for sure."

"Well, he won't miss one or two, I reckon."

"Share the wealth," the one with the gun said. The other one grunted a short thick sound of agreement.

They worked their way farther up the draw, and as they did, the cattle retreated in a quick walk, their bawling carried on by only a few angry mamas whose calves stuck close.

Higher up the ridge, a silhouette against the skyline, sat a lone figure on a steeldust gelding. He listened to the two men speaking back and forth in the draw below. The first swath of light, gray as a pearl, seamed its way across the eastern horizon, bringing into view the wide sweep of the valley, the surrounding mountains, the splayed out herds of shorthorns in the distant meadows.

The rider upon the ridge dismounted, removed a long-barreled rifle from the saddle boot, and stealthily worked his way down the slope, through the tree line, and to a point just above where the draw was boxed in.

"Dawn's breaking," one of the figures in the draw said, the one not carrying the gun.

"Damned welcome as far as I'm concerned," the other said. "Hunting around in the dark and freezing my behind off ain't my idea of a good time."

"We'll need to be quick with our work," the other said. "J.D.'s cowboys will be out patrolling, popping the brush for strays soon's they've et breakfast."

"I think we'll take that one there," the other said, pointing with the needlenose at a large heifer. "She don't look like she's got any calves with her. Hate to kill a mama cow."

"Well, go ahead then and do it," the one without the gun said. "Go ahead and shoot her."

Just above where the heifer stood trapped, the man knelt on one knee and raised up the rifle, adjusting the rear tang sight, feeling the wind brush against the side of his face. Soon, the entire valley would flood with soft gray light and by noon the air would become still and hot, the sun a glare.

The figure with the needlenose took careful aim; the heifer stood there staring intently at him, its neck craned back across its wide brown body.

The needlenose cracked and the cow jolted sideways but did not go down.

"You missed!" the one without the gun said.

"Didn't!" the other said.

"Shoot it again!"

The heifer tried to scramble over a rock pile, staggered in the effort, a stain of blood leaking in a thin dark line from behind its shoulder. *CRACK!* The needlenose had little kick to it, but they could both see that the second shot spanked up dust in the rib area of the heifer. It bawled, took little side steps, then toppled over, still not completely dead.

"You should've brought your pa's bigger gun," the one said. "That big ol' Sharps! Now you're goin' to have to shoot her again!"

The one with the gun wiped sweat off his dark face with the sleeve of his shirt.

"Damn right!" he said in weak disgust. "This damn ol' gun couldn't knock down squirrel!"

The figure above brought the front sight of his rifle to bear on the one with the gun. The wind picked up a little, he adjusted the screw on the tang sight. *Left to right*, he judged. *A few more minutes, the light will be enough*.

The other cows clambered as far up the draw as possible, up to where the box end stopped them from going any farther, where the large gray boulders blocked their path. There, they bunched nervously, staring back, huddled with the calves between their legs.

The figures scrambled up and over the loose rocks to where the heifer had fallen. She lay there among the shale that had broken off the ledge above them, her sides heaving up and down like a broken bellows. Blood bubbled from her black wet nostrils. The second shot had gone through her lungs.

"She's damn near had it!" the one holding the needlenose said.

"Damn near, but we can't just wait for her to stop breathin' all together. J.D.'s boys might come ridin' up and find us here! You gotta go ahead and shoot her again!"

"You shoot her," the one with the gun said. "I already shot her twice!"

The other one took the gun without enthusiasm.

"It was your idea," he said.

"No, it wasn't."

"Was."

"You gonna shoot or not?"

The one now holding the needlenose raised it to his shoulder, sighted down the skinny barrel and squeezed the trigger. *CRACK!*

The heifer bucked its head and the eyes rolled up white there in the chill gray dawn. Her tongue rolled out, and she was finished.

"Well, you done it! Might as well start skinnin' her out," the one without the gun said.

The one with the gun swallowed and said, "Might as well."

The man above them on the ledge of rock had brought the front sight to rest just at a point between the shoulder blades of the one holding the needlenose gun. *Let them go ahead and start butchering up the cow so's everyone can know they're what they are: Rustlers. Cow thieves. When they find them, everyone will know they got what was coming to them. Got what I was hired to do: get rid of the bad element that was filling up the valley!*

They had blood up to their elbows, warm and sticky, as they cut into the haunches and cut out large slabs of beef. One had gone back to their horses and gotten a small canvas tarp to wrap the beef in, and they now had loaded up fifty or sixty pounds of heavy warm chunks of the heifer.

They were breathing hard from their labor, working fast before any cowboys came by and found them there in the draw butchering up a beef that wasn't theirs.

"How we goin' to get all this blood off us, Billy?" the one said, pausing to catch his breath, staring at the crimson on his dark arms.

"We can stop at Yellow Hat Creek and wash it off," the other said.

"It's all stuck to me, stuck so much I can't hardly close my fingers!"

"Stop jawing and cut up some of that hindquarter. Don't bother none with the ribs!"

"Sure, sure!"

The one who'd shot the heifer was on his knees cutting a slab of bloody meat, kneeling like he was praying, when the roar of the big rifle rolled down from above. He didn't even hear it. The slug tore through his spine and punched out the front of his shirt, taking with it all the life he'd ever had in him. A spray of blood and bone flew into the face of the other one, who raised up and said: "Sweet Jesus Christ!" He turned this way and that out of deep and awful confusion when the second slug plowed through his dark forehead and shattered out the back of his skull, knocking him over onto the soft white face of the dead heifer, flinging his arms out wide like a fallen angel.

With care, the figure kneeling in the tree line lowered the rear sight of the rifle, stood, and climbed back up to where he had tied the steeldust to a large leaning pine.

Sliding the rifle back into the boot, he placed a low-heeled boot into the stirrup and swung easily into the saddle. “Let’s go and have some breakfast and a little siesta,” he said, patting the warm, muscled neck of the horse. “We’ve done our job here. Those lads have learned the greatest secret there is to know: what death is.” He touched his heels to the flanks of the gelding and with hardly any effort rode up and over the ridge line and disappeared into the vastness of the Montana Territory.

CHAPTER ONE

The letter came General Delivery. There was a time when he'd have more to do than go down every afternoon to the post office and see if he had any mail come in, any catalogues. There was a time when mail was the least of his concerns.

Pete Opey glanced up with his one good eye working its way around the black patch he wore over the other and said, "Afternoon, Monroe. Got a letter for you," then held it out, his good eye looking over the black scrawl on the envelope and the Montana Territory postmark. *Ain't no one ever had an eye so curious as Pete Opey*, reckoned Monroe Hawks.

Monroe took hold of the envelope, studied it for an inordinately long time, doing so on purpose just to make Pete's eye worry over it, and to make him wonder all day what was in the letter that had come all the way from Montana.

"Well, ain't you going to at least open it?" Pete asked.

"No, I reckon I'll wander over and get me a beer and open it then," Monroe said, holding it up a little so the light could pierce through the envelope and show more scrawl on the inside. "I sort of like to read my mail over a glass of beer."

"Well, seems to me a letter come all the way from up there in Montana ought be something worth looking at right away."

"Reckon it took time to get here," Monroe said. "Reckon waiting to get read won't make it any less important."

Pete laid his good eye on Monroe, laid it on him wet and fierce, brimming with frustration. "Well, I ain't never knowed no one like you, Monroe. A man'd get himself a letter sent all the way from Montana Territory and not even the least little curious as to who it's from or what it has to say."

Pete had become Monroe's one good source of amusement late in life. Pete was by nature the most curious man Monroe had ever met. On hot slow days like this one, it was a special pleasure for Monroe to have the opportunity to stir him up so about a mysterious letter. Monroe wasn't in any hurry to end Pete's suffering as to what the letter contained.

He had known the civil servant ever since they had been boys, when Pete had been called "Peety-Eye" because of an unpleasant accident he'd suffered while keeping company with a girl named Sophie Sweet out at Sophie's daddy's barn one mild afternoon. Neither Pete nor Sophie ever admitted how exactly the accident had occurred. It wasn't until years later, when Monroe had gotten Pete drunk on tequila on a trip down to Del Rio, that Pete admitted the truth.

"We was foolin' around," he'd admitted. "Sophie wanted us to play married and I wanted to, too. It was the first time I ever kissed a girl or felt her chest."

Monroe hadn't been sure he wanted to know anymore about it than that, but Pete had been insistent with the drunkenness that tequila will bring. And now that the memory had been lit again in his mind, he wasn't about to have it banked.

"We was up in her daddy's hayloft, too close to the truth to ever turn back. I was kissin' her toes when we heard the barn door open. I got so scared I run into a barn post, only it had a nail sticking out of it. I put my eye out on it. And that's the goddamn truth if I have ever told it!"

It was a sad unwanted tale that Monroe cursed the liquor for, but at least he could now rest easy knowing how it had happened.

After that, Pete was called Peety-Eye because of his milky blind eye. He took it all his childhood life, then when he got old enough, he sent off to Dallas for a patch to wear over the eye. Most would've thought all the teasing would've turned Pete Opey into a sour man, but it didn't — just a curious one. It was as though he had to squeeze everything he saw around him into that one good eye, like he couldn't get enough seeing to suit him. And Monroe Hawks never let an opportunity pass to arouse Pete's curiosity about a piece of mail or anything else that would do the trick.

"You ain't much on curiosity are you?" Pete had asked him one day.

"No Pete, I ain't. Why should I waste my time being curious when you do enough of it for both of us?"

"Well, I just can't understand anyone who ain't interested in the mysteries of life," Pete had said. There seemed no end to the subject as far as Monroe was concerned.

Pete put his good eye up on the Regulator clock on the wall, saw that it was nearly three, and thought it just as good a time as any to take his afternoon break. He thought maybe he'd take it over at the saloon where Monroe took his glass of afternoon whiskey. He might just find out yet what news had come all the way from Montana Territory on such a warm day as this.

"You give me a minute, I'll lock up here and join you," he said to Monroe, who was already putting his hand on the doorknob.

"Suit yourself, Pete." Monroe thought it somewhat like a hound chasing after a meat bone, Pete and that Montana letter.

They walked down the street, Monroe tipping his hat this way and that to the ladies, grinning like an old opossum, especially to the young ladies. Pete thought his behavior lacking in the good graces. Pete thought Monroe somewhat disgusting in the way he took to the ladies so openly.

"Ain't you a bit old to be showin' your teeth to them young gals?" he inquired, his good eye staring straight ahead because of the way he thought Monroe was acting.

"Ain't never too old to stir sugar in the coffee, Pete. A man that thinks himself *too* old, usually is. I ain't. Might just well lay down in the middle of the street and have a beer wagon run over me as to quit looking at the ladies."

"I guess you learnt such things when you was still an active man with the Texas Rangers and such. I guess once a man gets caught up with the ways of whiskey and gay ladies and big cities and such, he just ain't never goin' to look right at the world ever again."

"Pete, you ought to go on up to Miss June's once in a while and visit her girls. It might take some of the vinegar out of you, give you a better disposition on life."

"Be the day I spend my hard-earned money on whores," Pete said, half wishing now he hadn't come all the way down the street with Monroe just to see what was in a Montana letter. "And besides, there ain't nothin' wrong with my disposition that a whore'd fix."

"You'd be surprised," Monroe said. "There's a lot worse ways of spending your money than on whores."

"Maybe in your book, Monroe Hawks, but not in mine."

They sat and had a glass each of whiskey in the cool confines of the Texas Cafe while commerce passed up and down the street and heads bobbed past the open door. Monroe laid the letter out on the table unopened, so Pete could stare down at it and get himself worked up over what was in it.

Pete kept checking the nickel-plated Waltham in his pocket for the time. He couldn't keep the post office closed all afternoon.

"Well . . ." he said after a time of waiting.

"Might be bad luck in that letter," Monroe said. "Not sure I should open it up and read it now that I think about it. Might be somebody I know from the old days went up to Montana and died and I'm just now hearing about it. Most everyone I know from the old days is already dead, killed, burnt up in fires, shot, drowned, or married off. Except for you. Don't knows I'd want to hear about another tragedy."

Pete tapped his forefinger on the table next to the letter. He knew Monroe could be as stubborn as a mule and a man of many superstitions, like the one he had about not laying a hat upon a bed or letting a rocker rock with nobody sitting in it. Superstitious and stubborn, that was Monroe Hawks.

"Well, maybe I was to read it for you, the news might not be so bad," Pete said. "You want, I could read it for you?"

"Well you might just have a point there, Pete. You was to read it, it might not be so bad." Pete started to reach for the letter.

"On the other hand, that don't hardly make a lick's worth of sense. Either it's bad news in there or it ain't." Monroe saw the fingers retreat.

"You goin' to open that dang letter or ain't you?" Pete asked, his irritation visible. "I can't sit here all day waitin', I got a post office to tend to."

Monroe figured he'd worked up Pete's curiosity all he could, and the truth was, he was curious himself about what the letter contained. He reached for it, thumbed open the envelope and pulled out the single page. It was a heavy black scrawl and somewhat hard to make out. Here and there, the ink had smudged, like water had dropped down on it.

He read it, then read it again. He laid it down on the table before him still staring at it.

"Well?" Pete inquired, craning his neck, cocking his good eye trying to read what he could upside down.

"It's from a fellow I knew in the old times," Monroe said. "We soldiered together, and later after that, did a little government work."

"Meaning the badge?"

"Yeah. Was a time we was both Deputy United States Marshals in the Western District, Judge Parker's court out of Fort Smith."

"Was that when you first grew your tastes for expensive liquor and fancy gals?" Pete offered him a smug glance, removing his good eye from the letter just long enough.

"No, back then, I was an honest man."

"Honest?"

"Married."

"When'd you ever get married, Monroe? I never knowed you to be married."

"It was old times, Pete. Long time back. Almost forgot her till just now. Blanche. That was her name. Blanche Pettigrew. Nice woman. Handsome. Kept me up at nights." Pete saw Monroe grin wide like a opossum that had come up on some eggs and was getting ready to eat them.

"Well, she either had to have been a saint or a desperate sort of woman to have been married to you, Monroe. I don't know of any decent woman that would marry a man who'd chase whores and drink expensive whiskey and gamble at cards the way you do."

"We lived in a little two-story house on Front Street and sometimes went over to dinner at the Judge's. She insisted I wear neckties whenever we did . . ."

Pete shook his head, the gleam of light from above reflecting itself in the bald sheen of his scalp.

"I sure would have liked to have met the woman that would've married you," Pete said with a tone that wasn't as much sarcasm as it was disbelief and envy.

"Well, you would've liked her, Pete. She was a lot like you in some ways. Curious and difficult to get on with. I've heard since that she married a dentist."

"Well, no doubt she will never have to worry about her teeth," Pete said. "So, what's this fellow in Montana have to say?" Pete's curiosity over the letter had renewed itself.

"His boy was murdered. He'd like me to come up and help him find the man that did it."

"You! Hell, Monroe! You're too damn old to ride a horse more'n a mile. And you probably couldn't hit the ground you're standing on was you to hold a pistol in both hands!"

"Well, I reckon that may be just *your* opinion, Pete!"

"You go up to Montana lookin' for killers, you might just as well go throw yourself in the Rio Grande and drown. It'd be quicker and save you a long horse ride besides!"

"You don't know a thing about it," Monroe said, calling for another glass of whiskey.

"About what? Gettin' killed?"

"About loyalty and friendship and such! That's what this is all about! Going to a friend in need!"

"He was any kinda friend, Monroe Hawks, he wouldn't be askin' some old boot like you to ride all the way up to Montana just to get himself killed! You ain't the man you once was! Chasin' whores and drinking pricey whiskey is one thing, catching murderers is another!"

"Aw, Pete! What would you know about any of that?" He sipped the whiskey, saw the large blue veins standing out in his hands, and noted that, even though they were old hands, they still didn't shake.

"Well sir, I guess I've heard all I need to about that letter and you," Pete said, rising from his chair. "I reckon you've taken it into your mind to go on up to Montana and get yourself murdered and there is not a thing more I can say about that. I guess I might just as well say good-bye to you now, Monroe, for I don't ever expect to see you again, not if you go to Montana I don't. I reckon there's anything more you want to say to me, you'll know where to find me." And having said that, Pete Opey turned and walked out of the cafe.

"Well, you just don't know a thing about it," Monroe said to Pete's absence. "You knew anything about it, you'd know a man that gets called by an old friend ain't much of a man, he don't go."

Monroe read the letter once more, folded it, and put it in his shirt pocket. It was too late in the day to start out for Montana. He figured on taking his supper, then maybe going over to Miss June's and visit that new girl of hers. Talk was, that the new girl was French. It sounded like just the thing: a warm supper and a French whore.

He figured he could start for Montana the first thing in the morning. Another whiskey was in order. He thought maybe he had heard it said that the French girl's name was Monique, or something close to it.

CHAPTER TWO

He heard the steel rims of the wagon's wheels rattle down the long trace long before he spotted it. He stood there in the late hour of day, the shadows reaching out across the yard, his own reaching clear to the corral.

He looked up from the wood chopping, his muscles ached, the ones in the shoulders and along the arms and down into the wrists. The ax grew heavy and stayed that way anymore.

He heard the wagon coming, then looked up and down the trace and saw that it was Cousin Ike coming. Cousin Ike's white hair stood out like cotton against the dark face. He reckoned he and Ike had picked plenty of cotton when they were boys and maybe Ike had picked so much cotton his hair had turned white because of it. His own had mostly just fallen out.

He took a red bandanna out of his back pocket and wiped the sweat off his face and waited for Cousin Ike to come on. Ike's old brown mule pulled hard on that wagon, getting it up over the little rise, its tall ears twitching round and round like crank handles helping to pull the old mule along. Nate Love couldn't help but smile. Cousin Ike was a mule man, always was and always would be.

Ike was slapping the reins over the mule's bony rump, "hawing" it this way and that, his raspy voice carrying out over the low hills and most likely clear to the blue mountains.

Suddy came to the door of the cabin and said: "Is that Cousin Ike I hear?" Suddy was big and plump and she could've carried jugs on her hips, they were so wide. Maybe it was because she'd had so many babies over the years.

"I reckon it is," Nate Love said to his wife as he leaned on the handle of the ax. "I don't know what the man is doing out this way so late of the day."

"Maybe he's come to bring a truck of melons from over to his garden," Suddy said, her brown face darker now because of the late shadows.

"Don't know why he'd come so late," Nate repeated. Suddy looked over at him, noted his gauntness, and thought: *You was such a fine handsome man once, now age has done got you, bent you over and taken all the meat off you. Lord! Has we all got that old already?*

They stood there like that: one plump from age, the other grown to flesh and bone leaning on an ax handle, watching the wagon come rattling down off the rise toward them.

Nate could see right away, as soon as the wagon drew near, that Cousin Ike had trouble crawling all over his face. The old man's eyes were large with trouble. When he had come all the way up to the cabin, he hauled back on the reins and called out: "Whoa there ol' mule!"

Suddy called out from the cabin door: " 'Lo mistuh Ike!" and Ike turned his attention to her but did not return her warm smile, his lips pressed tight over a ridge of teeth, the muscles of his jaw bones knotted, his eyes yellow and flecked with redness like a pair of bloody eggs spilled into a black skillet.

He then turned his attention to his cousin, Nate, standing there leaning on an ax handle, a crop of chopped wood all around his feet.

"Lawd Nate, but I has some bad news fo' you!" Then he saw how Nate stood up straight, or as much as he could with his poor back, and all the old pride and dignity creeping into his bony face, like a man ready to hear whatever bad news was being brought to him, a man ready to stand up to it, whatever it was.

"Go on, Cousin Ike. Go on with it."

Then the tight lips loosed themselves, quivered over the old man's horsey teeth as he craned his neck around indicating the back of the wagon.

"I brought Efrim, Nate. I brung you your boy!"

"What's wrong with him, you had to bring him, Cousin Ike?"

"You best come see, Nate."

Nate looked at Suddy who hadn't stepped out of the doorway. Suddy's brown face was now full of the same trouble as Ike's.

Nate dropped the ax and walked to the wagon.

"I sho' is sorry for this," Ike said, lowering his rheumy eyes to the tarp-covered corpse in the back of the wagon.

Nate reached in, removed the upper half of the tarp, saw the ashen face of his youngest boy, the only child of his that had not left home, Efrim Moses Love. A dark hole pierced the forehead. He turned the head slightly in his hands and saw the destruction out the back; almost everything was gone.

From a long way off, it seemed, he could hear Suddy's wail of heartbreak. But when he looked around, she was standing right there next to him, staring down onto the delicate dead face of their boy.

Cousin Ike sat there, his head bent down, his eyes nearly closed, staring down to the toes of his boots, listening to the sorrow pouring out of Suddy, listening to Nate say nothing at all except: "Help me get him out of the wagon, Ike, and carry him on into the house."

And when they had done that, they replaced the tarp with a clean white sheet and swathed his poor broken head in a pillow case. Nate told Ike to sit there with Suddy if he would until the worst of it passed for her.

Nate went and stood in the yard until he could no longer hear Suddy's voice coming through the walls of the cabin, then he went back inside and held her for a time and said, "I'll dig our boy a grave." Then he went out to the hill behind the cabin and dug Efrim a grave until the light failed and it grew dark.

Later, with his boy lying in one room wrapped in a sheet and Suddy in the other, worn out from her grief, he sat at the table with Cousin Ike and asked: "How did this happen?"

Ike's mahogany skin gleamed and shone in the yellow light of the whale oil lamp, his wet, worn eyes flickering.

"Efrim and another boy, tha' white boy he ran wid sometimes, Billy Sloan, was found murdered up in Smiley's Draw near the foot of Bone Mountain."

"Bone Mountain?"

Ike nodded till the top of his snowy head showed.

"Yes suh. J.D.'s cowboys found them this mornin'."

"Bone Mountain's clear to the other side of the valley."

"Yes suh, 'tis."

"What was they doing clear on over to Bone Mountain?"

Ike blew off steam from the coffee Nate had made them and sipped at it with tentative lips. He looked up at Nate's question into the gaunt face of his cousin, a man he had long ago picked cotton with and joined the Union Army with and fought in the war with and whose sister he had wound up marrying, only to see her die just seven months ago of what the doctor had said was heart failure. They had been married nearly forty years. He'd seen a lot of Nate in his dead wife's face. And what he saw now renewed and doubled his current sorrow.

"They say they was stealin' some of J.D.'s cattle. They was caught with blood on their hands and a bunch of meat cut up ready to be hauled away." Ike said it softly, slowly, hoping the words wouldn't be heard, or if they were, that they wouldn't mean anything.

"Stealing! My boy stealing cattle!"

"That's what they say, Nate. I don't believe it myself, but that's what them cowboys tol' me when they come and got me and said that I should take Efrim on to his daddy."

"They killed my boy over a *damn* cow?"

"Oh, no suh! It wasn't J.D.'s cowboys'd killed him. No suh! They said they come up this mawnin' and found them two boys that way. Shot to pieces! They come got me 'cause I ain't too far away from there. Come and got me and say I should take Efrim and bring him on out h'yea to your place."

"Well if they didn't kill him, who did?"

"No one said anythin' about who did. But you know Efrim and tha' white boy ain't the fust ones killed lately. Talk's been all over the valley about a stock detective been hired to clean up the rustlin'. 'Course, ain't no one sayin' who or who hired him."

They were talking like that, discussing the stock detective who might have been hired by one or several of the ranchers thereabout, when they heard the low mournful wail of Suddy rising from her room again.

Nate rose slowly from his chair and went to Suddy's room. He saw the bulk of her sitting on the side of the bed, her face cupped in her brown hands, her whole body shaking like she had the fever and chills.

He went to her, sat on the side of the bed with her, and put his arm around her. It had been a long time since he had put his arm around her, a long time since he had had to comfort her.

"Suddy, you just go on ahead and cry it all out of you, girl. Just go on ahead and let it out. I'll be here until you do." She shook against him, the warm softness of her, but he didn't say anything more to her, just sat there in the quiet darkness of the room with her with the warm yellow light coming from the kitchen lying in the open doorway.

Ike told himself not to listen in on their sorrow, told himself that this was practically the worst day of his life, having to carry Efrim, their boy, out here in a wagon destroyed as he was. No man ought to have to look at his own child that way, no woman either. He wandered outside to his wagon, reached in under the seat, took out a stone crock of red whiskey, and took a drink of it, a long hard drink.

His cousin Nate wasn't a drinking man himself but never did look down on another man because of it; still, Ike didn't feel right turning to the jug in front of Nate and Suddy with what they were having to go through now. *No suh*, he said to himself, *I'll drink my liquor in private and let 'em keep to their peace and sorrow with one another*.

Ike stood there drinking and looking up at a sky that was filling up with stars and wondering about what it was about life that sometimes made it so damn hard to live in, what it was about men that would cause one to do to another what that shooter had done to Efrim and that white boy, Billy Sloan. Just two boys not even full grown and shot to pieces over a little heifer cow, shot and left there in the draw like they weren't worth anything at all, knowing that the wolves and coyotes would scavenge on them.

What sort of life had it got to be anyway when one body would do such to another body?

Ike heard the door creak on its hinges and turned to see Cousin Nate standing there in the warm buttery light coming from the kitchen; the man had lost his size. Ike remembered when Nate had been a good-sized man, strong as a three-year-old mule, but age had worn him thin. And Suddy, who was once so thin, had gotten bigger and bigger. It was like they were each growing in different directions. *Funny how life does you*, Ike thought.

Nate came out into the yard, out by the wagon, saw the jug in Ike's hand and said: "I think I could stand a drink of your whiskey if you wouldn't mind." He drank some of it and gave it back to Ike and said: "I want to thank you for bringing my boy to me, Ike. I want to apologize to you for letting my anger and hurt get in the way of thanking you for bringing Efrim home."

Ike started to protest, but Nate stopped him with a wave of his hand. "No. You did a righteous thing bringing home Efrim and I can't tell you what that means to me. We're kin, Ike, me and you and Suddy. I know that once she gets over the worst of it, she'll thank you, too. Will you stay over the night and help me bury Efrim in the morning?"

"You know I will, Nate. He's like my own, that boy. S'pity to have to see how it turned out for him. To see him that-away."

"I reckon we'd best get some rest now. Put up your mule in the corral and come on in the house and I'll fix you something to eat before you go to bed."

"No need to trouble yourself, Nate. I'll make do with just this," he said, holding to the jug.

"No, Ike. Drunkenness ain't going to do it. If it could, I'd get drunk with you. You put up your ol' mule and come on in and eat something. We've plenty."

So Ike put up his mule and went inside and ate a plate of greens and some fried pork and a helping of molasses beans from a kettle heating over the fire. And he and Cousin Nate sat across from one another and ate with a silent solemnity that befitted a house where a dead boy lay in his room and where grief could be heard through the walls.

And when next he knew, he awakened sometime in the middle of the night to a great and terrible silence, and he reached a hand out and felt the rough wool blanket of his bed and thought to himself that he was only dreaming. But something that had settled itself inside his soul like a rock resting in the bottom of a clear cold stream told him the truth: Efrim was dead!

CHAPTER THREE

The news of the latest killings spread through Bozeman like a kerosene fire through a hay barn. It stirred a lot of talk.

Some were saying it was a good thing that the cattle rustlers were finally being taken care of and that the territory was finally being cleaned up. Others weren't so certain because they didn't know who was doing the killings. They were just young boys. Cattle thieves maybe, but young boys nonetheless.

J. D. LeFlors sat in the swirl of it, the hot talk running back and forth about the mysterious "stock detective" who had killed the boys up in Smiley's Draw three days previously. Once word got out, it had been all anybody could find to talk about.

In between the last killing of an itinerant drifter, more than two months previously, and this of the boys, the only thing people in Bozeman had to talk about was the weather and whether or not it was ever going to quit raining because whenever it was thought that the rain had finally ended, it would rain again, only harder.

J. D. LeFlors sat at his usual table inside the Bozeman Cattle Club and listened to all the talk about the killing swirl around him. Most who spoke their mind were all for law and order and the riddance of outlaws and thieves. Most were cattlemen and thought it was high time somebody did something.

There were those dissenting voices, however, who were not so certain as to the justification of the latest killings, and neither were their wives and neighbors.

He listened to Jake Childress say: "Goddamn man'd steal another man's cattle deserves what he gets!"

He listened to Al Freemantle say: "Damn straight he does!"

He listened to Ev Windlass, the second largest cattleman in the valley say: "It's a simple shame. They weren't nothing but boys got killed out there at the base of Bone Mountain. But, damned if boys don't grow up to be men, and damned if a man that would steal one cow won't necessarily steal a hundred!"

He listened to Karl Swensen, the only foreigner in the bunch, say: "It don't make it right even though they ver butcherin' a cow. It don't make it right to murder young boys, neither!"

Then several of the others hooted at Karl and told him if he didn't agree that the cattle stealing ought to be cleaned up, he could take his business to another valley or take white paint and label his cows as "Free" to anyone who wanted to ride in and take them.

And it went like that all day for several days. The mood could be felt on the streets as well and seen in the worried eyes of women who had boys about the same age as the two who had been murdered and in the eyes of their husbands, too.

Inevitably, the talk would wind up on J.D.'s doorstep since he was the largest stock owner in the valley and it was his cow that the boys had been butchering.

"I'm not saying what has or has not been done on my behalf to put an end to the thieving," he would say to the others who stood around with cigars caught between their fingers and tall glasses of whiskey in their hands.

"I'm not saying that I did hire a stock detective, and I'm not saying I didn't. There's lots of other cattlemen who have plenty to lose besides me. Maybe the fellow that done the shooting is my man, and maybe he ain't." There was that air of dreaded mystery around what J. D. LeFlors had to say to them; for some knew the truth, and some did not.

"I will say this," LeFlors spoke with the measured evenness of a man reading from a book, "that maybe it took something like this to get the word out that stealing cattle anywhere in Judith County is risky work!" Then, having stated and repeated his position on the issue, J. D. LeFlors took the liberty of ordering himself another glass of rye whiskey, which he favored more than bourbon or mash, and waited for those who sided with him to take up the cause once more.

After a time, J. D. LeFlors would take his leave of the club to make his daily walk down the street to the Bozeman Hotel for lunch, and the speculation would continue unabated as to whether or not he was the one who had hired the mysterious stock detective.

★ ★ ★

Orna Sloan was doing other people's laundry when the Bar JD cowboys came riding into her yard. There were two of them, one leading a bay horse. Slung over the back of the horse was a body, and she knew without thinking that the body was her son, Billy.

"Ma'am," said one of the cowboys, the one holding the lead rope. "I'm sorry to say, we brought you your Billy." She looked into their faces, faces that hardly knew a razor, faces that were no older than her Billy. They shifted their gaze from her.

The other one said to her: "It wasn't us that killed him, ma'am. We found him out in Smiley's Draw. He had been shot. Him and a colored boy, Efrim Love . . ."

She felt it impossible to breathe, the lye water scalding her hands and arms; she had forgotten to remove her hands from the laundry tub.

One of the cowboys, the one holding the lead rope, heard her say: "No!" He wished he hadn't been one of the ones to have been given the dreadful job. He knew the dead boy, so did Jimmy Jake, the cowboy with him. They had gone hunting together a time or two, had fished and swum naked in Yellow Hat Creek together. Now, he wished he hadn't been one of them that had had to bring Billy out here to his mother.

They had shovels with them.

"Would you like us to dig a grave for him, ma'am?"

She took her hands from the wash tub of hot water and lye soap and a man's britches and shirts and wiped them on the apron she wore. She did it all ever so slowly and Jimmy Jake found himself wanting to look off toward the blue mountains and so did Louis, his partner.

Without willing it, she went to the horse carrying the body, wrapped in a yellow slicker. From one end hung the pale, lifeless hands, from the other, a pair of scuffed boots.

"Take him down," she said. "Take him down from there." And they quickly dismounted and took him down and stretched him out on the ground, where she saw his bloodless face and the wide ears he had inherited from his father and that side of the family and the sandy shock of hair that was splattered with blood dried brown like mud.

"Why did you bring him to me like this?" she said, the hot dry wind sweeping the question out onto the valley, and neither of the cowboys understood what she meant.

"Ma'am," Jimmy Jake said, his blue, full-of-life eyes matched almost exactly the color of his faded denim shirt. "We was told to by Mr. Teal, our ramrod."

"It's not even decent!" she cried. "It's not a decent thing to bring a boy home to his mother slung over the back of a horse. Is there no decency in you?"

Jimmy Jake's face flushed red and so did that of the other boy, Louis. Their throats percolated as they tried to bring up words to console her. They knew hardly anything about women.

She placed her reddened hands along each side of her son's face, felt the cold smoothness come through her fingers, the death of him, and bit down on her lips against the anguish that flooded her chest. Jimmy Jake and Louis stood waiting for her to direct them.

She blinked back the blinding pain that had risen up within her and flooded behind her eyes. Chickens scratched in the yard and the wind blew against her skirts and the floppy-brimmed hats of the two cowboys so that it covered their eyes and half their faces. They weren't much older than Billy.

"Take him inside," she said at last. "I must bathe him and put on clean clothes. I won't have my only child laid to rest in a bloody shirt and pants . . ."

The two cowboys waited outside, squatted on their heels, stood and squatted some more while waiting for the woman to call them. They smoked cigarettes and stared off toward the blue ranges, toward the rolling land and tall grasses — the only land they had ever known. There was still snow on the blue ranges, always was. It somehow brought them comfort, the land.

"Who you reckon done it, Jimmy?"

Louis turned his face toward that of his partner.

"Reckon it was that stock detective we keep hearing about. The one ain't nobody knows who he is."

"Yeah, that's what I reckon, too!"

"Do you think maybe he's J.D.'s man?"

"J.D. won't say whether or not he has a man. Says maybe he might, then maybe he might not. J.D. says it could be anybody's man."

"Don't seem to me those two had it coming over one little ol' heifer. Wasn't nothing but a stringy maverick anyways. What'd get them to run the risk do you think, Jimmy?"

"Look around you, Louis. You see much here? Billy and his ma ain't got' squat, I'd say. Probably they did it 'cause they was hungry. Why else?"

The wind died, came up again suddenly, blowing dust across the yard, flapped at the dungarees on the clothesline and the shirts and long drawers.

"She takes in other folks's laundry," Jimmy Jake said, puffing on his cigarette. "But hell, how much can you make taking in other folks's laundry anyways?"

Louis hunched his shoulders.

"I wish to hell it hadn't been me and you Teal wanted to bring him out here," Louis said. "It gives me the creeps altogether. Wasn't but two weeks ago we was all swimming in Yellow Hat Creek, me and you and Homer and Billy and Efrim. Now them two's dead!"

"What's it mean, you reckon — to be dead?" Jimmy asked.

"It means you ain't never goin' to eat no more beans or ride no more horses or see your mama again," said Louis. Neither one of them had mamas they could recall. Still, it was a troubling thought, death.

She came out of the house at one point, walked to the clothesline, took down a pair of fresh dungarees and a cotton shirt, and went back inside. She didn't trouble to look at either of them. They stood, walked to the corral, studied the pair of shaggy horses within.

"Them's poor horses," Louis said. Jimmy agreed.

She came out of the house again, walked up to them, said: "My boy is ready to be buried. There's a good place up that way." She stared off to the west from where they stood. "There are plenty of wildflowers growing up there beyond that meadow. I'd like him buried there." They pulled the hats from their heads and said, "Yes'm," then went and got their shovels and headed up to the other side of the meadow.

It took them nearly two hours to dig the grave. When they finished, they walked back to the house and told her it was ready. She had hitched one of the shaggy horses to a spring wagon. She had changed into her one good black dress, the one she had purchased for Billy's daddy's funeral, and unpinned her hair and held a small Bible in her red hands.

Jimmy Jake and Louis picked up the clean and freshly dressed body, noticed how the corpse was beginning to stiffen, and carefully laid him in the back of the wagon, a bright red wool blanket wrapped around him. The blanket would have to do in place of a coffin. There was no money for a coffin. It didn't do for her, but it would have to do for him.

Then the two cowboys led the shaggy horse hitched to the wagon out to the meadow and on to the far side, where the wildflowers grew in patches of reds and yellows and blues, patches of columbine and Indian paintbrush and cowslip. They used their lariats to lower her son into the ground, and she insisted that she stay until their work was finished, until the grave had been filled in, until she knew that he was in a place where no one was going to get to him again.

The boys stood with their shovels still in their hands, sweat staining their shirts dark, their faces sheened from it, their eyes cast downward.

"Now that he is at rest," she said. "Will you tell me who is responsible?"

It took a long time to decide who was to say it, but at last, Louis said: "Ain't nobody knows for certain, ma'am. We just found 'em the way they was in Smiley's Draw early this mornin'."

"Was it the stock detective?" She saw how they traded looks with one another. She had not been so removed from the doings in the valley that she had not heard rumors of a stock detective.

Jimmy Jake shrugged his shoulders and Louis let his slump.

"Word is that maybe it was," he told her. "But truth is, nobody knows for certain."

"The stock detective is Mr. LeFlors's man as I've heard it said?"

"No ma'am, we don't know that." Louis tried to assure.

"Well, I know it!" she said. "J. D. LeFlors is the only man I know that'd put more value in a cow than he would a human. He killed my boy, he and his stock detective. You go back and tell him I will find justice for my boy. You tell him he can't just kill my boy and let it go at that. I'll find justice!"

"Yes'm," Jimmy Jake said. "I'll tell him."

The wind coming down from the mountains ruffled her long loose auburn hair and splayed it about her face like a veil. The two cowboys could see the glint of light from her eyes behind the veil, and it caused them to shift their weight and look off toward the blue mountains once more.

"You go on now," she said. "You go on and tell J. D. LeFlors that I will find a justice for what he did here this day."

And she stood for a long time by the new grave watching the two cowboys ride off in the distance, their horses throwing up clots of dirt in their wake.

When at last she could see them no more, she let herself weep.

The hour late, Nate Love sat at the table alone — Cousin Ike off in one room, his deep exhausted breathing sounding like the distant rumble of thunder, Suddy sleeping in the other room in a chair next to her child, Efrim, who lay on the bed in peaceful stillness.

He studied his mind, wondered how he was going to get justice for his boy, him an old man like he was. He knew it was J.D.'s man, the stock detective, that everyone said he'd hired to clean up rustlers.

First, there had been that man over at Bluestone Meadows they had found with a bullet through his back, and no one seemed to know who he was or what he was doing there, except that he had several running irons with him that didn't fit any of the brands in the valley. Then, a few weeks after that, there had been a killing along Ten Mile Creek, and it turned out that the fellow killed was a known cattle rustler and wanted in Nebraska for some other crimes as well.

It was J.D.'s man alright. There hadn't been any killing before all the talk got around about a stock detective being brought in. But no one seemed to know who it was, what the fellow looked like, his name. So many strangers came every year, drifters mostly, some looking for work, some looking to thieve and steal. It was hard to tell who was seeking honest work and who wasn't, the way the valley was filling up anymore.

He felt helpless thinking about it, thinking about all that men like J. D. LeFlors had and what they'd do to keep it and how were he and Suddy and men like Cousin Ike, old men and women, going to go up against men like LeFlors and the rest of them? How?

And, like always when the frustration of his age set into his mind, he took to thinking about the *old* times, the times when he'd been a fighting man, a time when he'd ride up to J. D. LeFlors's ranch and put a bullet in him for having his boy killed. It hurt to know that he would've done just that when he was a fighting man but now he was just an old man.

Should've never had another child so late in life, he thought, sitting there alone at a table he had built himself when his hands were still strong. *Had that boy too late in life, and now look what it has brought me!* He swallowed down the bile, the bone deep sorrow that had hold of him. And his mind wouldn't get off the old times any more than it would let him not listen to Cousin Ike's snoring or Suddy's hurtful breathing or the awful stillness of his dead boy.

Then, when the thought came to him, he rose, went to the place where Suddy kept her personals, found a piece of fresh paper, pen, and some ink, and set himself once more at the table. Then, he simply wrote it out: a letter to the meanest son of a bitch he'd ever known as a fighting man: Monroe Hawks.

He did not even know if Monroe Hawks was still alive or if he was yet living down in Texas or, if he was, whether or not he could even read. The first light thought he'd had since this morning: whether or not Monroe Hawks could even read. It was a subject that'd never come up between them the whole time they had been fighting together, and damned if he could remember.

It wouldn't surprise him if Monroe Hawks couldn't read. Monroe was a man about many things in life — women, card playing, whiskey drinking, and fighting. But he didn't know if Monroe had ever taken the time to learn to read.

Well, if he couldn't read and if he was still alive, he could get somebody to read the letter to him. Nate dipped the pen in the black ink and began to write. When he finished the letter, he studied it, studied the wide looping letters wet and dark against the primrose paper. Then, he folded the letter into sections and put it in an envelope and sealed it shut.

First thing in the morning, after they buried Efrim, he'd go to town and mail it, then he would ride out to Miss Sloan's and pay his respects to her and her boy, Billy.

He let his large brown hands rest on the letter as a way of feeling hope. Then, finally, he closed his eyes, his hands resting on the letter like that.

CHAPTER FOUR

It felt like he'd been bucked and kicked by the same horse. Monroe opened his eyes to a room full of white light. It took some little time to realize where he was and what he was doing in a room full of white light and curtains on the windows. Pain banged in his head like old pistols being shot off. He lay there thinking maybe the worst had come to him, maybe he had died, or was about to.

He ran a tally on his parts, found they were all there, sat up on the side of the bed, saw that he was naked as the day he was born, then remembered what had become of him.

She was there in the bed next to him — Monique, the new French girl of Miss June's. Craning his neck round to look at her, he could see now in the harsh light that she wasn't as young as he remembered her to be last night, nor as frail. Nor as pretty. But he reckoned it was the price a man had to pay for loneliness. One plump leg lay outside the covers.

It was a chore just getting dressed, pulling on his pants and shirt. And what was it in the shirt pocket? A letter? He took it out, moved closer to the window in order to read it, and remembered as soon as he had that he was supposed to have left already. *Montana. Go help an old friend, Nate Love*. Nate Love's boy had been murdered, and now Nate needed his help. He'd said he needed to kill a man, maybe several. Would he come help?

"*. . . your the meanest son of a bitch I know in a fight*," was how Nate had said it in the letter. It made him feel somewhat special that Nate thought of him that way: *The meanest son of a bitch!*

He stood in front of Monique's long mirror and looked at himself, the letter still in his hand. His beard was as white as the curtains, and so was his hair, but damned if he still wasn't built like a drover — rawhidy! Tough and hard as he was twenty years ago, only a little less leather and maybe a little more bone.

Monique stirred herself among the covers, and he caught her movement in the mirror. A little grin played at the corners of his mouth. *You ought not be such a haughty man, Monroe. Just 'cause you can still have a good time with the ladies, don't mean you ain't a sinner of the worst sort. And being the meanest son of a bitch that Nate Love knows sure ought not to be a point of pride*. But try as he might, he couldn't help but take pleasure in thinking those things — even if it wasn't all true.

Well, time was wasting, and Montana was about as far away as a place could get as he recalled it. He had helped drive a herd up that way a long time ago and remembered all the rivers a body had to cross just to get there, all the rivers a body could drown in.

It wasn't a comforting thought: a long trip with so many rivers to have to cross.

The thought crossed his mind as he strung his bandanna around his neck that maybe once he got to Montana, and if things went well, he might just stay up there rather than face a long trip back to Texas. He figured he only had so many long trips left in him.

Monique lay like a wilted flower amid the bed covers, her face a sad story of love and regret. Monroe hoped someday she'd marry and live a proper life like some whores were known to do. He took an extra dollar from his pocket and placed it on the nightstand before leaving.

In spite of his stiffness, he felt a little extra spring in his step as he descended the staircase, crossed the empty parlor, and stepped into the morning freshness.

A man ought not to be haughty with pride, he told himself. But damned if it sometimes could not be helped!

Come the next day, rain dripped from the sky in a steady endless fashion. The clouds had swung low over the blue mountains and skimmed along the valley so low that a cowboy on a tall horse could reach up and touch them.

Cousin Ike stirred from his sleep and came into the kitchen to find Nate still sitting at the table, a cup of coffee held between his bony brown hands.

"Mawnin', Nate," he said, then sat down opposite.

"Ike." Nate's eyes were flecked with red for want of rest. *Maybe for tears they'd shed*, thought Cousin Ike.

He had had dreams about the dead boy, Efrim, disturbing dreams that left him fitful throughout the night.

"Suddy up yet?" he asked.

"She's been up since daylight," Nate said. "She gone back in there with our boy, doesn't want to leave his side knowing that in a little while he'll be gone from her for good."

"Can't blame her," Ike said, his own eyes stark and white in his dark face. "How old was Efrim? Fifteen, sixteen?"

"Turned seventeen in the spring," Nate said, remembering.

"Time sho' fly," Ike said with a shake of his head as he poured himself a cup of the coffee and blew at the steam before putting his mouth to the cup.

"Seem like jus' las' week, Efrim wan't no mo'n a baby. 'Member how Marfa baked two pies an' had me bring 'em over, then she come 'long later and brung Efrim his fust suit of clothes. They was way too big for him, that's fo' sure." Cousin Ike smiled, his yellow horsey teeth appearing in the dark sheen of his face. He was happy for the memory.

"I had him too late in life, Ike," Nate said. Ike stared up from the coffee with a look of puzzlement.

"Me and Suddy was way too old to be having children. Least I was. Suddy's a whole lot younger'n me. I guess she didn't know. But I was way too old to be having anymore children."

Ike blew the steam away from his coffee, then said: "Ain't never too old to have babies if you love 'em."

Suddy came and stood in the doorway. She was wearing her good dress, the dark one with the lace sewn around the broad white collar.

Her cheeks were stained wet and her eyes so red and sorry that Ike couldn't look directly into them.

"It's raining out," she said, and both Nate and Ike nodded.

"It's like the Lord is crying for Efrim 'cause he knows what a sorry thing has happened to him."

Ike swallowed hard and stared down into his cup some more. Nate stood and went to her, put his arm about her shoulders, and spoke her name: "Suddy . . ." And she looked at him but all she could see was Efrim.

Nate and Ike carried Efrim out and put him in the wagon, and Ike's mule brayed and pulled against the load and the mud that clutched at the wheels as they climbed the little rise to where Nate had dug the grave the night before.

When they had lowered Efrim down in the grave, Suddy sang, "Swing 'Lo, Sweet Chariot" and "Bless'd My Jesus" in a soft rich voice that caused Ike's heart to nearly break in two and made him snuffle into a big hanky he pulled out of his back pocket.

After Suddy could find no more strength in her voice to sing for her dead child, Nate told Ike to take her back to the house while he finished up and then waited until Ike put Suddy in the wagon and left.

Rain dripped off him as he shoveled the heavy earth, filling up a hole that wouldn't ever be filled up, not in his own heart it wouldn't. And pretty soon, he couldn't tell which was rain and which were his own tears running down his face.

Orna Sloan sat on the porch, staring off beyond the meadow to where the freshly turned mound of earth rose a foot higher than the ground itself. She found it impossible to believe that it was Billy out there lying beneath that mound. She refused to believe it. Billy was off somewhere having a good time with his friends. It wasn't Billy lying out there all alone with the rain dripping out of the sky and the silence nothing more than what the rain was when it struck itself against something. That soft *splatting* sound of rain, dripping as steadily as a thousand tiny heartbeats against the land, the prairie, the small cabin, the freshly turned mound of earth, dripping off the eaves and wet green branches of the trees and off the horses' noses. The forever rain.

She didn't see the rider coming down the road from Bozeman until he was a hundred yards from the house. He rode a tall steeldust gelding and wore a rubber slicker that gleamed wetly in the pearlescent light. The legs of the horse were slathered with mud, as was the animal's belly.

She stiffened at the sight of him, not knowing what to do, for no stranger had passed this way since last spring.

John Henry Crow saw the way the woman started at the first sight of him, even at this distance through the dripping rain; he prided himself on his eyesight and abilities at observation.

He knew from inquiry that her name was Orna Sloan and he knew it to be her boy, the one he had killed the day previous up in that draw, where he and that other one, the colored boy, were skinning out the cow.

She didn't know what a man would be doing out riding on a day like this with the weather so poor and the rain cold as it was. He rode like he didn't seem to mind about the weather, rode like he was in no hurry to be anywhere.

He saw, as he neared the cabin, that she was wearing a shawl against the bad weather and that she had long brown hair and fit a dress pretty well. His observations told him that she was there alone, no man.

She had hoped he wouldn't turn in off the road, that he would not come riding down the trace to the house, that he would not stop in her front yard. But he did. He rode the steeldust to within a few feet of the porch.

"Ma'am," he said, and she could not see his eyes for the way the brim of his hat was bent down from the dripping rain. And when she did not speak, he said: "Might I offer to buy a cup of hot coffee from you, perhaps a biscuit or two?"

Now that he was sitting his horse there in her yard, he did not seem nearly so frightful a figure as he had out on the road when she had first spotted him. He had a soft, engaging manner of speaking and she had the feeling that if she turned him away, he would go easily, without protest. She was being foolish in her trepidation, she told herself. The terribleness of yesterday was still haunting her.

She had many times fed strangers who came through the valley on the Bozeman road past her house. She had accepted pay for the meals she prepared, and it helped to keep her and Billy sustained. The money didn't seem to matter so much now, but maybe the company would.

"Ma'am?" he said again, a question against her silence.

"Yes. Yes," she said at last. "I can offer you coffee; the biscuits won't be fresh."

"Oh, that's alright," he said. "Biscuits are biscuits in my book. I've not et since yesterday." She wanted to ask why he hadn't, but thought better of it.

He tethered his horse and stepped in under the porch, took his hat off, and shook the rain out of it. She could see then that he was a man of about her age, tall, dark-eyed, in need of a shave. And even though there was something wan in his appearance, he was not an unhandsome man.

When he removed his slicker and hung it on a nail on the outer wall, she could see he was wearing a large pistol on his right hip. His spurs rang when he walked. He ducked partway entering the cabin. He seemed to fill up a room.

She indicated that he should sit at the table while she heated coffee and took leftover biscuits from the pantry. She noticed his hands resting atop the table, they were large and bone smooth, the fingers long, almost delicate. They were not working hands.

He watched her move about the kitchen, watched her in a way that was no way at all, none that she could see or that he could be caught at. He watched the way the gingham dress held her, clung to her hips. Once, she caught him looking and was given the immediate impression that he wasn't looking at her so much as within her.

She watched him run those delicate fingers over his long moustaches, sweeping out the moisture, then along the chaps he wore, as she handed him the coffee and biscuits.

He didn't speak while eating, but he didn't look away from her either. She busied herself in the kitchen, then gave up and sat opposite him.

"You're not a local man," she said.

He had fleckless dark eyes that seemed to pierce her soul when he looked at her.

"No ma'am, I'm not from around here."

She knew it improper to ask him his business or where he'd come from, or what he was doing in Judith Valley, but it didn't stop her from wanting to ask.

And then, as though to ally her fears, he said: "I've come here looking to buy a ranch, perhaps. My name's Crow. John Henry Crow, from Oglalla. You've heard of Oglalla? It's in Nebraska."

Truth was, he did not look like a rancher or a man about to become one. The thought darkened in her mind that he could be the stock detective that everyone was talking so much about. He could be the man who'd murdered Billy. She felt a coldness climb her back and prickle the skin at the nape of her hair.

"I guess I didn't quite catch your name," he said. He spoke openly and easily, revealing nothing. *You're being spooked for nothing*, she told herself. *What sort of man would murder my boy then ride into my yard and ask for coffee and biscuits?*

"I hadn't said, Mr. Crow. But it's Orna Sloan."

"Orna," he said, as though tasting the name. "Orna is unusual, but I like it. I'd say it fits you."

His gaze fell on her in soft, immeasurable ways, ways that both disturbed and dispelled her uncertainty about him.

He stood from the table and went to the door.

"The rain's about let up," he said, the size of him taking up most of the doorframe. Watching him standing there in the doorway, looking out at the land, she was reminded a bit of Henry: the man had died on her four years previously. Henry had brought her west from Ohio, had given her Billy, and had built her this cabin. Henry had loved her at nights and made her feel safe and wanted and he'd proved a good father. Henry had lulled her into believing that her life was always going to be that way, then he had died, toppled from a wagon that had rolled across his neck and killed him. And the world for her had changed forever.

Now Billy was dead as well and it felt like she was dying like Henry and Billy, only not as fast. Not as fast as she wanted to now that they were gone from her.

He saw the wagon coming down the road, driven by a black man, and decided he had shown himself enough for one day.

"Now that the rain's let up," he said, stepping onto the porch, "I reckon I'll get on my way." He turned and held a dollar out. "For the coffee and biscuits, ma'am."

She shook her head. “Not necessary, Mr. Crow. Not this time.”

He looked at the dollar, then at her, then smiled slightly and said: “Maybe I’ll find my way back here and let you know how I come out on buying that ranch I was telling you about.”

“Yes, perhaps,” was all she could manage, then watched him mount his horse and turn back up the road to Bozeman. It struck her then that he had come in that way and was now returning in the same direction. She wondered if he had ridden out to see her on purpose, and if so, for what purpose?

She watched until he was nearly out of sight, then turning to go back inside the house, she saw the wagon coming up the road in the opposite direction. She saw that it was being driven by a black man and knew, without really knowing, who it was.

CHAPTER FIVE

He watched through the smoke-smudged window of the rail car the land rushing past; his reflection was ghostlike. All the way to Denver, it was the long sweeping plains, tan under the cloudless sky, tan and endless. Nothing more than sage it seemed, sage and yellow grass and openness. He grew weary just looking at the endlessness of it all.

He settled back in the upholstered seat of the rail car and stared across at a youngster, who was giving him the face. The child had dark ringlets of hair and so did the woman in whose lap he stood. The child aped him and stuck out his tongue in a sly manner that the mother could not see, or refused to.

You don't know that Nate Love thinks me the meanest son of a bitch he knows, he thought in wry reflection of Nate's letter, while unable to take his attention off the surly little monkey. *You knew what Nate Love thinks of me, you wouldn't be sticking out your tongue at ol' Monroe Hawks!*

"Mama, that man looks like gran'pa!" said the boy, poking a finger into his mother. "Hush!" she told him, and offered the stranger across from her a benign but apologetic expression.

Grandpa! He felt the press of the big Smith & Wesson against his ribs underneath the greatcoat he wore. Two hours of sitting on a train and already he was cramping up and feeling uncomfortable. There was a time, he'd ride a horse till he wore it out, then change and ride a second until he wore that one out as well. He'd ride seventy, a hundred miles a day chasing down bandits and border ruffians; now, he had trouble sitting in a cushy seat for two hours at a time.

He left his seat, went to the rear of the car, and stood out on the platform. The rush of wind felt strange and refreshing, and he could smell the cindery smoke rolling overhead from the engine.

It was a smooth stretch of track, and the steady vibration coming up from the floor, up through his legs and hips, helped ease some of the cramps he suffered from having sat too long. Montana seemed a terribly long way off, forever away.

The rear door of the adjoining car opened and a short, thick-set man stepped out. He wore a bowler and a brown suit, of which the pants were too short and the coat too tight. His cravat suffered the stains of something having been spilt on it. He had the soft wet eyes of a hound, a hound that looked sad and tired, as though he had seen too much of life.

He gave a start at the unexpected presence of Monroe standing on the car's platform across from him. His luminous eyes blinked several times.

"Oh! Excuse me, sir, I hadn't expected —"

"Riding in them cars gets a man stiff," Monroe said.

"Yes sir, they certainly do. Allow that I might introduce myself: Junius Bean, correspondent for the *Denver Post*."

"Writer?"

"Ah . . . a bit more than that, sir, but basically, yes."

"Well, I've known a few writer fellows in my time," Monroe said. "Most interesting breed of people, writers."

"Well, some of us, I suppose, are considered different by the very nature of our work," Bean admitted, a crescent smile spread itself within his moon face, a face that suffered the pitting scars of acne along the lower jaw and neck.

"Most writers got more whiskey in their veins than ink," Monroe said. "Most I know wouldn't be caught more'n a short walk from a drink." Monroe had no urge to be subtle about his need for a drink. All the hot smokey air within the rail car had given him an enormous thirst.

The journalist offered a quizzical look, then allowed the crescent to spread his mouth enough so that short blunt teeth revealed themselves. Reaching inside his suit coat, he pulled out a small silver flask, unscrewed it, and held it forth.

"I catch your drift, sir. Care for a drink, Mr . . . ? I didn't catch the name."

Monroe took the flask, tipped it up, and swallowed enough to cut the dryness out of his throat. It seemed top shelf. He admired a man who drank good whiskey as much as he admired a man who rode a good horse or wore good boots. It was a common thing with him to study what sort of whiskey a man drank or the quality of the horse he rode or the boots he had on his feet.

He studied the engraving on the flask for a long solitary moment, then handed it back to the reporter.

"Name's Monroe Hawks, Mr. Bean, and that's good whiskey."

Tentative, stubby fingers took the flask and held it unsteadily while the moist hound eyes of the correspondent studied him. The name sounded familiar, an old name from the distant past. Of that, he was certain. But right off, the name's meaning escaped him. He repeated it in his mind until he could come up with the answer.

"Monroe Hawks! Not the Texas Ranger? Not the man that killed Spanish Bob outside of Dallas and China Jim in the Nations? Emporia and Hays . . . ? You the same Hawks that marshaled in Emporia and Hays?"

"I was only in Hays three months," Monroe said. "I got fired from there. I guess I didn't fit the bill. They hired Haycock, then he come in and done the job and they fired him, too." Monroe was still irritated by the fact he had been fired from the Hays job and replaced with the dandy Haycock, a man who was more vain than even Monroe. Up until that time, Monroe had never figured he'd come across another man more vain than himself, but Haycock sure took the prize, with his fancy pistols and long golden curls.

Bean took a hasty sip of the whiskey and offered it back over to Monroe, who took a turn and handed it back over.

"Haycock's been dead way over ten years," the reporter said. "It was widely rumored that you were as well! I read where you were killed in Fort Smith?" Monroe had heard that Haycock had been killed up in the Black Hills — now it was confirmed. He took no cheer in the news, then or now. But it sure did not hurt his feelings any that the world was shy one less vain man.

"I read that, too," Monroe said referring to the reporter's query about his own death. "It was supposed to have been a shoe salesman that'd killed me in a fit of jealous rage over his wife and me. Shot me with a derringer in the face as I read it in the *Dallas Telegrapher*."

"Unbelievable!" Junius Bean said.

"Well, now that you've seen me for yourself," Monroe said. "Maybe you could write in your paper that I ain't dead yet. It sorta hurts to have folks think of you as passed on to the other world when you are still here in this one." Monroe's real concern was that several women he had been intimate with over the years would have read the story as true, and it hurt him deeply that they would think him no more. Vanity!

"Sure, sure, Mr. Hawks. I'd be happy to. In fact, I'd be happy to write an entire piece on you if you'd consider it. A man with your vast reputation ought to be written about. We've too few colorful characters left anymore. The world is becoming dull!"

Colorful characters! Monroe liked the term nearly as much as he liked what Nate had said about him in the letter. He found himself warming to the company of

Junius Bean almost immediately. Some men were just easy to like. Not many, but some. Bean had the air about him of a friendly hound.

"My sentiments exactly, Mr. Bean. The world has become a dull place."

"Then it's agreed, you'll let me write about you?"

"Well sir, that's a problem, you see, for I am on my way first to Denver and then north on up to Montana to aid an old friend. After that, if all goes well, I reckon I could stop back by in Denver and look you up. And if you're still interested in telling a story about me, I reckon I could oblige, considering the accommodations were right. I enjoy a good bed and a quality restaurant on occasion, and I hear Denver has some of the finest."

Bean understood Monroe exactly. "I'm sure my paper would be willing to accommodate you in those matters once I sold them the idea of your story, Mr. Hawks."

Junius Bean was doing his best to contain his excitement at having encountered the famed lawman. He had once met Buffalo Bill Cody on one of his many trips through Denver but had found him too dramatic and too drunk at the time to conduct a decent interview. It had been a great disappointment, his meeting with Bill Cody.

"Well then, I'll consider it," Monroe said, satisfied with the prospect.

"Yes. Ah. Do you mind my asking just what sort of business it is that carries you to such far-flung reaches as Montana, sir?"

"Already told you — to aid an old friend."

"Would you mind being a bit more specific? Perhaps it might be of added interest to the story I would be writing about you."

"Well sir, I wouldn't mind, exceptin' that my stomach is crying out for a good meal, and that little daub of whiskey of yours is already beginning to wear off. I suppose was I to discuss my Montana business over a good steak, I'd be more up to it."

"Have you ever eaten at the Denver House?" asked the journalist.

"No, but I've heard about it."

"Well, if you have a few hours to spare before departing Denver, I'd consider it an honor to buy you the biggest steak you ever ate."

"I suppose I could spare an hour, Mr. Bean."

"Good, good."

Nate Love was still a quarter-mile from the house when he saw the man ride off on a tall steeldust horse. He reckoned it was someone come to pay their respects, like he was coming to pay his. He didn't know the widow well. He didn't know her at all if the truth were known. He'd heard Efrim speak of her, how she always invited him to stay for supper whenever he was around that time of day. Mostly, though, it was her son Billy Efrim talked about.

The rain had mostly let up, and for that he was grateful. He watched the muddy road between the mule's ears. He had bought the mule in Arkansas on his way to Texas. He and Ike had each bought one of a pair of mules from a man named Fike, who'd said he had to sell his mules in order to feed his family, things had gotten that bad. Feeling sorry for the man and his family, they'd paid the man's asking price of forty dollars apiece — a high price to pay for a mule, rather than bargain him down like they normally would have done. The man's children looked starved.

Orna Sloan saw the black man coming, riding in a spring wagon that did not appear to have any springs left in it. She did not have to guess why he had come, and now she felt a twinge of shame that here was this poor old man riding out in the rain, even though it had mostly now quit, coming to her when his own boy was also dead and he had his own grief to suffer just as much as she had hers.

The wagon rattled to a stop, he took his floppy hat from his head, revealing a smooth brown skull. His eyes shone clear in his dark face, though tinged red from grief.

"Mrs. Sloan," he greeted.

"Mr. Love. Won't you please step down and into the house? I've fresh coffee made. We can talk in the house."

He craned his neck, looked around this way and that, his sacrificial eyes studying the surroundings. She knew instantly why he hesitated. He was a black man, she was a white woman alone. It wouldn't matter to some why he had come or why she had invited him in.

"No need to fuss with what people might think, sir. Our boys have been murdered. There can't be nothing worse than that to concern ourselves with."

"Yes'm, I reckon that's true." She waited until he stepped down and scraped the mud from the bottoms of his boots on the low step, then stood aside while he ducked in under the doorway, his floppy hat still in his hand.

She poured him coffee and sat across from him and encouraged him with her gaze to drink it. His clothes were wet through from the earlier rain. It was clear across the valley from her cabin to his. "I could make a fire," she said, thinking how uncomfortable his damp clothes must feel.

"Needed to come," he said, after several sips of the coffee. "Needed to pay my respects to you over your loss." She saw how the sadness drew down his face, how it tried to leak out of his eyes.

"I am sorry, too," she said. "I am sorry, too, that your boy was killed." She thought something inside her might break and struggled to maintain her composure in front of a man she did not know.

"Yes'm. I reckon we are both sorry for ourselves and for the other," Nate said.

"It was kind of you to come such a distance."

"Felt I had to." The coffee was burning the chill out of his bones and blood. She saw his cup was nearly empty and refilled it, for which he was grateful.

"I understand," she said. "I understand the need to . . . to tell someone."

"I didn't know your boy none too well," Nate said. "Efrim and him was friends, but me and Suddy never got to know him too well."

"I know. I only got to meet Efrim a time or two. He was always a polite boy. He and Billy seemed to strike a strong friendship."

She saw the knots work up in his jaws and knew that he was suffering, knew exactly how. His hands were as bony as the rest of him, only big and knuckly as though they had done all the work there was for a man to do. He had big hands and big feet, but the rest of him seemed average, except that his back seemed somewhat bent. He had probably known more work than that old mule he had hitched to his wagon.

"It'd help to talk about them," she said. "To remember some of the good times, I suppose. It drives me nearly insane to think of my boy dead and buried when just two days ago he was so alive."

"Yes'm," I know. I wished I'd known Billy better. I wished I'd known them two boys better."

"Can't know everything, Mr. Love. They were nearly men already. Hard to keep at home, hard to know much about a child that's nearly grown and gone from the house all the time."

"Efrim, he always was close to his mama, Suddy. Always was respectful to her. Me and him was struggling some. Suddy, she'd just say, 'Nate, you got to let him grow up, got to let him go on and be a man. Can't be holdin' on so much. Efrim's almost eighteen.' Suddy and Efrim understood one another."

"I know how she feels, Mr. Love. I know how Suddy feels."

"Yes'm, I reckon so. Women understand things in that way that I guess a man never can."

And for a long time they sat there in the mute light and stared at their hands spread upon the table, each thinking the unthinkable, each seeing a child's face, each remembering old laughter and old hurts and old moments full of love and sorrow, such as the whooping cough and the first ride on a horse.

Nate suddenly looked up and asked: "Where is your boy buried? I'd like to go and pay my respects directly."

"Across the meadow. I will show you."

He followed her outside into the freshness of air that comes after a good hard rain, the grass still wet from it. He watched as she picked wildflowers along the way and carried them to the place where he could see a new grave had been dug. A grave that was already beginning to settle down under the weight of time. In the spring, the ground would renew itself, and unless she marked the grave, it would be lost.

He watched as she laid the wildflowers on her boy's grave. Once more, he removed his hat and stared down at the burial place, his jaw working at the knots along it, his eyes blinking. He said a silent blessing for a boy he'd never known too well and wished he had.

If it had been possible, he would have asked: "What happened out yonder? Who was it that shot you and my boy Efrim down in an ambush over one poor ol' cow?"

It was, for him, one of the cruelest fates: not to be able to speak to the dead. A dead boy ought to be able to tell who it was had killed him. There ought to at least be that kind of natural justice in the world.

The wind gathered itself along the shelf of land. It had rolled down from the blue mountains in the distance, swept along the grasses, and gathered itself along the shelf of land, the slight ridge where they stood. And now it worried their clothes and troubled their already troubled spirits.

"I sent for a man," Nate said.

"What sort of man?"

"A man that will help me see this trouble through," he said. "If he is still alive and gets my letter, I think he will come."

She thought she understood what he was saying to her. "A man that will come and find the murderer of our boys?"

"Yes'm. A man that will do just that." But the truth was, Nate Love was not at all sure that Monroe would come. There were far too many odds against his coming. More so than the other way around. But still, he wanted to give the woman hope, and himself some, too.

"It was the stock detective. Mr. LeFlors's man that did this," she said.

"I reckon that, too," he said.

"J. D. LeFlors's cowboys brought my Billy on the back of a horse. That is no way for a mother to see her son, draped over the back of a horse. I told them to tell Mr. LeFlors I'd see justice done to him for what he'd done. Now, if your man comes, maybe I will."

"I don't know no other way to go about it," Nate said. "Was it ten years ago, I'd see it done myself. But look at me now. I'm old bones, just one man, and Mr. LeFlors could call all the guns he wants against me.

Nobody would side with me, or you neither I'm regretful to say. This is something I can't do by myself." He looked so frail to her that she thought a good wind might come and blow him over.

"But this man you sent for, he can?"

"Yes'm. I believe he can. The two of us together, I believe, can."

"Do you mind if I ask you how you know he'll come and see justice done?"

"He's an old friend of mine. We fought lots of times together. Old times, I admit, but he's about the best man I know when it comes to a fight. And if anyone was to see it done, it'd be him. He puts stock in such things as friendship. Not many do these days. That's how I know."

She felt the sudden stab of hope pierce her marrow. More than anything, she wanted justice done for Billy and for herself.

"I have a little money saved," she said. "I could give it to you to offer your friend . . ."

Nate Love put his hat back on, turned his sorrowful gaze to her, and shook his head.

"No ma'am. I've already taken care of everything. You keep your money. Buy this fine boy of yours a marker and have it put up or soon the prairie'll come and cover him up and he'll be lost. A child should not be a thing easily forgotten or lost to the wilderness."

She felt her eyes brim over for this unexpected kindness, this unexpected hope that justice would be done.

“What is your man’s name, Mr. Love? I want to be able to think his name and pray for him until he arrives.”

“Monroe Hawks is his name.” And the wind seemed to snatch the name from the lips of Nate Love and fling it out across the valley.

CHAPTER SIX

J. D. LeFlors waited, seated in the protection of the cabriolet, the air chill and still hanging with rain, the mountains obscured by the clouds. He wore a heavy beaver coat and a new bowler and kid gloves on his hands. Even though it was summer, the weather had turned cold. He looked for all the world a gentleman, a man of money and promise and power. He thought of himself in those ways. It angered him now that he was having to wait out in the elements for his man to show.

He produced a small black cheroot from an inside pocket and struck a match to it. The bay that was harnessed to the buggy cropped at the tall grasses. He had paid three hundred dollars for the horse, just to have it pull his cabriolet, mostly to the Presbyterian church on Sundays, where he was a deacon, and about town. It suited his image.

He was sitting, smoking the cheroot, feeling the anger rise up through his chest, when he saw the man riding out of the mist — ethereal. *An angel of death*, he thought, then stiffened at the thought.

"LeFlors," said the rider. He had a grayish pallor about him, as though some old illness clung to him, but with the darkest eyes Jipson LeFlors had ever seen on any man.

J. D. LeFlors pulled a gold pocket watch from his vest, snapped open the lid, looked at it, then said: "You are late."

"Time is a relative thing," said the man.

"Don't try to impress me with your education, Mr. Crow. I'll have none of it."

The dark eyes showed little expression over the slight rebuke. John Henry Crow had known many such men as Jipson LeFlors; men of wealth and holdings but not necessarily of intellect or class. Men who paid others to do their bidding, their killing, as casually as they paid to have their laundry done.

"You owe me one thousand dollars, LeFlors."

"You have created a controversy, Mr. Crow. You have murdered two boys . . ."

"Cattle rustlers," interjected the rider, droplets of mist clinging to his heavy moustaches. "They were butchering one of your cows."

"I know that. I ain't the one raising any hell about it, but some of the others are. Some of the others are saying that the boys was murdered outright! They're trying to drop this thing at my door! Saying that the stock detective is my man! A thing like this could get out of hand!" Jipson LeFlors harbored thoughts of politics, a governorship perhaps, maybe a United States senatorship. All of that could become clouded if the connection were proved between himself and John Henry Crow and the murder of the two boys in Smiley's Draw.

John Henry Crow dismounted, working at tightening the cinch of his saddle with strong sure movements.

"It was agreed," he said with his back still turned toward the man in the buggy. "You offered me five hundred dollars for any man I stopped from stealing your cattle. I stopped two of them. I didn't take the time to ask their ages."

He finished his work with the cinch, lowered the stirrup he'd hooked over the horn of the saddle, turned, and leveled his gaze at the man in the buggy.

"If you are to dance with the devil, Mr. LeFlors, you'd better be ready to pay his price."

"Then you keep what's between you and me private, Crow! That understood?!"

"Discretion is the main reason you hired me as opposed to a lesser man," said the stock detective. "Our business is that way and shall remain that way as long as you honor the bargain. You owe me one thousand dollars."

LeFlors dug a hand in his sidepocket, produced a weighted pouch and handed it over to the rider. "Count it," he said.

Crow hefted the poke of twenty dollar double eagles and said: "No need. I expect they are all there."

"I'm thinking maybe your work the other day has put an end to any more rustling in this valley," said LeFlors. His voice was thin with hope.

"What you are thinking, Mr. LeFlors, is that the crime is heinous enough that maybe you won't require my services any longer."

J.D. LeFlors leveled his gaze at the man, detesting his arrogance while fearing what he knew to be true: that the killing would be over when John Henry Crow determined it to be over and not when the rustlers quit coming to the valley, or when J.D. LeFlors decided.

"Don't kill when you don't have to, Crow. It ain't necessary!"

"You are a man that knows about ranching and acquiring land and water rights and such, Mr. LeFlors. I am a man that knows about the habits of other men, of *lesser* men, you might say. I'll not attempt to tell you how to conduct your business, please don't tell me how to conduct my own."

Now the anger rose white hot in LeFlors, for he was unaccustomed to such impertinence.

"Goddamn your soul should you cross me, Mr. Crow!"

"No, Mr. LeFlors, goddamn yours." And with the slightest of movement, there was a parting of the rider's slicker, just enough to reveal the ivory grips of a large pistol worn at his side.

John Henry Crow saw the man swallow back the words held ready in his mouth. LeFlors felt the tingle crawl up the inner part of his thighs, into his groin, like the feeling of having stepped down on a snake hidden in the grass.

"I doubt . . . if there will be . . . any more trouble from thieves," said LeFlors. "I think this thing has sent a message."

"Like I said, LeFlors, I know the habits of men. I don't think the job is yet complete. Oh, it'll die down for a short time, the rustling will. But then it'll start back up again. No, you let me be the judge of when your troubles are over here in this valley. I don't enjoy seeing a job only half done. We made an agreement that I should clean up your troubles and that you should pay me for it. Let's stay the course, Mr. LeFlors."

The man in the buggy watched the rider mount his horse and turn its head into a cloud, watched as both were swallowed by the mist, a silent vanishing that left his guts churning. He realized then his mistake: men who would kill for money would not allow themselves to be held to the same standards as other men; they were without reason.

His hands trembled as he held the reins. He had, as they say, gotten cold feet.

Suddy was waiting for Nate when he returned home. Sitting in her rocker, her large brown hands folded in the lap of her dress, her eyes red from crying.

"How was Mrs. Sloan?" she asked.

" 'Bout the same as us," said Nate, removing his hat and hanging it on a peg. "All tore up inside. They brought her boy to her laid over the back of a horse. That had to be a hurtful thing. She had him buried on the edge of a meadow full of wildflowers."

"I spoke to Efrim this morning," she said. "He come to visit me while you was gone. Sat right there at the table."

Nate lowered his eyes from hers. Suddy always was a superstitious woman, just like her Mama. Her mama kept contact with the haints, talked to them whenever she wanted to, or so she claimed. Suddy was somewhat that way, too. Only not as much.

"Suddy . . ." he started to say, then thought better of it, poured himself a cup of coffee and sat down at the table, his clothes still damp from the earlier rain.

"He said, 'It'll be alright, Mama, where I'm at now. It ain't so bad a place.'" Suddy's round brown face was caught in the oyster shell light coming through the window, her cheeks sheened with old tears.

"Then he smiled, Nate. Lord, you know how Efrim could smile so sweetly nothin' could keep your heart from meltin'. Efrim smiled and asked how you was doin', and I tol' him you was doin' fine," but that you missed him as much as I did. And he said how sorry he was that you and him had got on poorly lately and that he wanted you to know he was sorry for his end of it . . ."

He listened to her go on like that, knowing that she needed to talk, even if what she was talking about was all in her head. All she had left of Efrim was what was in her head. It was alright that she talked. He went to her, touched a hand to her moist cheek and said he had to go out and do a little work before supper, chop up some wood for the stove.

But what he needed to do was go to the old shed and get something he had put there a long time ago.

CHAPTER SEVEN

"Let me eat my steak in peace," Monroe Hawks said, hoping to avoid the persistence of Junius Bean's questions about his many exploits in the old times. "Let me eat my steak, then afterwards we'll talk. I can't hardly listen and chew at the same time and enjoy both, except was you young and pretty and female."

Junius Bean crinkled his moon face from across the table. Ever since he had met the old shootist, he had been anxious to learn firsthand all he could about what it was like to shoot men and have them shoot at you. It was something that he himself could never imagine doing — shooting at men or having men shoot at him.

Monroe held up one of the water glasses and studied it against the light. "Crystal," he said.

"It is indeed. This is one of the finest eating establishments west of the Mississippi."

Monroe could see that; all the waiters were dressed in boiled shirts and had their hair combed neatly and showed clean fingernails whenever they put anything on the table, such as a dish or fresh ice water.

"I'll have my beans on the side," he told the waiter who attended them. The man wore waxed moustaches and smelled of rosewater. He cast a cold glance toward Monroe over the request.

"To the side, sir?"

Monroe offered him an impervious look. "And several stalks of onions, you don't mind!"

Junius Bean offered to buy them a table wine, but Monroe said he'd prefer beer if it was all the same to anyone.

"In a pitcher!" he said. "And cold if you got it!"

The reporter smiled hugely and told the waiter to bring "Mr. Hawks whatever it was he'd want," which suited Monroe to no end. Being treated like a swell had its good points.

Monroe noticed the diffident glances from the other patrons, figured it to be his manner of dress, his rustic appearance — the large spurs that rang loosely as he walked all the way across the dining room to the table Bean had reserved for them. He had taken the spurs off a Mexican bandit named Felipe Gomez he'd shot down in Del Rio on a hot afternoon. He figured the bandit owed him the spurs since he had had to pay for the bandit's funeral expenses, which came to fifteen dollars. It seemed an even exchange — the spurs for the burial. After all, what would a dead Mexican bandit want with spurs?

He ignored the curious glances of the other patrons. However, he did remove his hat and place it on the empty chair to his right.

"I could have the waiter hang it up for you," said Bean.

"Not this hat," Monroe said. "It's been with me longer than a wife and several girlfriends."

Bean had taken the liberty to order appetizers — fresh mussels served on a platter of chopped ice. Monroe eyed them with interest as Bean cracked open the first and plucked out the contents.

"Care for one, Mr. Hawks?" he said.

"No, they look too much like river slugs. I'll pass."

The analogy did not seem to affect Junius Bean in the least. Working his way through the pile of mussels, the reporter took the liberty to ask: "Do you always go armed?" He pointed with his nose toward the butt of the pistol revealed in the parting of Monroe's coat flaps.

"Always, except when asleep or otherwise engaged with a gal. Women don't like cold iron up against them. I don't blame them for that."

"It seems an interesting affair, that pistol of yours. Are those stag grips?"

Monroe looked down at the pistol. "It's just a six-shooter."

"Have you owned it long, like the hat?"

Monroe shook his head.

"Well, ever since I took it off of Spanish Bob. It used to be his. But, he didn't own any other possession except a saddle horse, which was gaunt and not worth bothering with. I figured Bob wouldn't mind me having his gun." Now that the subject had been raised, Monroe realized that almost everything he owned of value he had taken off of men he had killed.

"*That* is Spanish Bob's pistol?"

Monroe took it out and laid it atop the table.

"Go ahead and look at it if you want. But be careful not to drop it on the floor. Many a man has been killed from having dropped pistols on the floor. I'm surprised Bob didn't shoot himself with it instead of allowing me the privilege. It's said he robbed the Southern Pacific with that very same pistol and shot a deputy down in Las Cruces. I personally find it hard to believe though. Bob didn't have that much gumption to rob a train; he had lazy and slothful ways. But I can believe he'd shoot a deputy if given the right set of circumstances. As long as it wasn't something that called for hard work."

It was a .44 caliber Smith & Wesson with a seven and a half inch barrel. It had scroll work on the cylinder and yellowed stag grips. Bean picked it up with both hands and was surprised that it weighed so much.

"Whoa!" he muttered. "This is quite a weapon!"

"It'll see the job done, that's a natural fact!" Monroe said, amused at the writer's capacity to be so easily entertained.

"It's a single-action," Monroe said. "You have to thumb back the hammer in order to fire it. Once you do, you don't have to hardly touch the trigger to set it off. I'd be careful, I was you!"

The waiter brought their steaks, cast yet another disapproving look at the firearm the reporter was holding in his hands, then set their meals down in front of them. "May I get you gentlemen anything else?" he asked.

Monroe said: "You can bring them beans anytime you get ready."

The steak he had ordered covered his entire plate and was bloody enough to remind him of his days as a Texas drover and the long trails to Kansas and the pretty girls who'd awaited them in Dodge and Abilene to steal their money and their hearts. It was amazing what something so simple as a bloody steak could cause a man to remember.

They ate in the silence that Monroe had requested. Junius Bean found himself amazed at the rapidity with which his companion devoured the meal. He was struck by the amusing thought that the old man ate as though his steak might grow legs and run off before it could be finished.

Monroe washed his food down with several glasses of beer, then sat back and admired the T-bone on his plate. He was a man who took great satisfaction in eating everything put before him. Too often, he had had the bad experience of going hungry. The longest he had ever gone without eating was once on the Staked Plains while under siege from a band of Kiowas, who had chased him and a pair of buffalo skinners into an abandoned adobe. Normally, Kiowa braves weren't much on patience, and if they couldn't get their man right off, they'd give up. But this particular bunch must have had nothing better to do than sit around in the shade of mesquite bushes and wait for their quarry to die of thirst and starvation. It had taken three days and nights before the Kiowas had disappeared. Monroe had chewed on his leather belt and had even eaten some of it, he'd gotten so hungry. A good steak had it all over a leather belt in his book.

"Now, we can talk if you care to," he said.

"While you were seeing to your quarters," Bean replied, "I was able to obtain by wire an agreement from my newspaper to do a complete story on you, a serialization if you will. I convinced them that men like yourself are a rare and vanishing breed, that you are exactly what the public would want to read about. They agreed."

"To what exactly?"

"To immortalize you, sir! And for that, they are willing to pay you five-hundred dollars if you'll agree to be completely forthright as to your exploits as a lawman and a shootist!"

"Five-hundred dollars!"

"Yes. Spread, of course, over a period of time, the several months it might take me to complete the endeavor. We figure to publish a segment of your life every other week, say over a period of six months or thereabout."

"You mean something like they did with Haycock in those dime novels?"

"Yes, something like that indeed."

"I don't have several months, Mr. Bean. I don't have even one month. I have to get on up to Montana and see my friend."

"Yes, yes. I understand exactly so. I wanted to ask you more about that. Would this be one of your exploits, your assisting this friend of yours?"

"I don't know about an exploit. I just recently got a letter from him requesting I come on up and help him kill a man, maybe several. If you call that an exploit, then that's what I am on my way to do."

Bean reached inside his coat pocket, produced a wad of bills held together by a rubber band.

"One hundred dollars for the first installment," he said, his moon face gleaming. "I shall accompany you to Montana, write the details to this new challenge — it will be the opening piece of our serialization of you, Mr. Hawks! I want to see you in action firsthand!"

"A hundred dollars to watch me go kill a man?"

"Yes sir. Exactly!"

Monroe reached for the old hat that had been with him longer than one wife and several girlfriends and said: "I guess this ain't going to work out, Mr. Bean. You paying me a hundred dollars to watch me go to Montana and kill a man."

Junius Bean spread all eight fingers and both thumbs of his hands in front of him, a look of confused disappointment gathered in his eyes.

"But I thought we agreed?"

"No sir, I ain't no circus! You want to write about my remembrances, that's one thing. But I won't be paid to perform gun tricks and shootouts for your entertainment!"

Thinking fast, the reporter said: "Then what if I don't pay you, but come along anyway? Would you mind so much that I come along anyway?"

"You do what you want, Bean. It's a free country. But don't expect me to perform for you. And don't interfere!"

Monroe Hawks stood, placed the old hat on his head, and said: "I reckon you can get the bill on this," then turned and walked back across the dining room, his Mexican spurs causing people to lift their heads from conversation and plates of food to stare after him.

The air outside the Denver House was cool and fresh, the sky black and filling up fast with stars. His hotel was seven blocks up the street; he'd counted them on the way down. He made himself a cigarette, struck a match to it, then started on his way. The walk would settle that chunk of meat he'd just eaten and give him time to forget about reporters and soft-handed men who were easy with their money and didn't mind paying to watch a killing or two.

In spite of it all, though, he still liked the little writer Bean. He figured the man was just doing what it was he was naturally called for. All men were naturally called to do some particular thing in life, Monroe was convinced of that.

He figured Bean had been born to the pen, just as he had been born to the gun. Some men were born to go to sea on sailing ships, others were born to the pulpit or to dig around in the earth for gold.

He was thinking about such matters when two shadows stepped from an alleyway directly ahead of him. They were poorly dressed, and he could see they were young, hair instead of whiskers growing on their faces. He had seen it before in Emporia and Hays — street ruffians, slothful boys always waiting for an easy mark.

"Hey there, dad!" said one, a tall skinny boy whose voice whined through his long, thin nose. "Wonder you might have a taste of whiskey on you. Night's gettin' awful chill out here!"

"Step aside, son." Eating such a big meal had made him tired, and he was in no mood to be troubled by poor trash such as these.

The other, the shorter muscular one, offered him a brooding grin; he spoke in a dull, slurred manner as though his mouth was too heavy to say much.

"Aw, you wouldn't hold out on us now, would you old feller?"

Monroe looked them in their faces, saw their meanness, saw, too, they were stupid and mean — a bad combination for anybody to be born with. The steak was beginning to ache in his belly. As much as he enjoyed eating, he could no longer eat as much as he once could. He figured it had something to do with the magnetism in his body having changed. He had once heard a traveling professor talk about the magnetic fields a body has and how, depending on such things as disposition and the phase of the moon, the body's magnetic fields would change. And when they did, such things as appetite and mood could change, too. Monroe figured that maybe his magnetic fields were off kilter for one reason or another. And though he still enjoyed a meal as much as any man, he could no longer eat until the cows came home, which he once could!

The professor could also read the bumps on a man's head and tell a lot about his future, which Monroe had also found interesting.

Once more he ordered, "Step aside. Get out of my way!"

The taller one raised a hand, tapped a finger on Monroe's chest, and when he did, Monroe brought Spanish Bob's three pound pistol out and struck the thug alongside his ear with it. The would-be mugger sank to his knees, grabbed at his ear with both hands, and screamed "The ol' bastard's split my head open!"

The shorter one with the dull mouth raised his fists in a fighter's stance, his hands looked like a pair of little hams.

"You're askin' for it, mister, and I'm goin' to give it to you good!"

Monroe swung the Smith & Wesson in a short quick sweep, thumbing back the hammer in the same instant.

"I pull the trigger now, it'll set your clothes on fire. You know what it feels like to be shot through and through and be on fire at the same time?"

And when the thought of being shot and being set afire at the same time caused the fighter to blink, Monroe struck him hard across the collar bone, which collapsed him alongside his friend.

"Hurts, don't it?" He declared as he stepped around the pair and made his way the other six blocks to his hotel room. He was ready for a good night's rest. Montana still seemed a long way off.

CHAPTER EIGHT

Amid the low hills, a campfire's light flickered in the pastoral blackness of late night. Yellow flaming tongues licked at the surrounding darkness that was as smooth and black as velvet. There was only the fire to disturb the night, the popping of pine pitch trapped in the chunks of wood, the showering sparks as log fell upon log, collapsing downward in the small heat.

Dismantled upon a blanket were the oiled pieces of a rifle's mechanism, the fire's light trapped within the sheen of oil upon blue metal.

The yip-yip-yip of a coyote barking across the valley was soon answered by the long mournful call of another. John Henry Crow listened. He listened as intently as though being told a dying secret; his mind was full of dying secrets.

He held a spring between thumb and forefinger and examined its cleanliness, its tensile strength, there in the fire's light; the light was trapped as easily in his dark morose eyes as it is in the sheen of the oiled metal parts.

Earlier, he had come across an encampment across the Yellow Hat River. Four or five men, two women, and several children. Possibly others he had not seen, who may have been out of camp, hunting game. It was nearing dusk and no time to study the situation. *Squatters*, he figured.

Yellow Hat River ran through LeFlors's land. *Squatters have to eat something*, he reasoned. *Cows are the most abundant, the easiest to hunt. Eating cows is a whole lot tastier than eating jackrabbits. Anyone with any sense would know that much*.

He blew dust from the rifle's breech, wiped it with a piece of flannel damp with oil, then set about putting the pieces back into working order. The slight sure clicks of metal fitting metal were pleasant sounds to him, like ice tinkling in a glass on a hot afternoon or like rain tapping on a window pane.

Across from him, sat the mute boy who he had named Joshua. The boy stayed in camp and kept it orderly for him, preparing his meals and caring for the stock: the steeldust and a mustang pony of brown and white that the boy rode.

John Henry looked across the fire at the wet glistening eyes of Joshua and said: "Few can appreciate the engineered intricacies of something like this." And he held the assembled rifle in both hands, showing it off.

The mute boy uttered mysterious sounds, then offered a look of understanding.

He was of slight build, the mute boy, as though his inability to speak had affected his ability to eat and kept him small. He was waif-like in his appearance: large wet eyes filled up most of his face, a slight thin nose, small mouth, as though small because he did not speak.

Joshua uttered a sound and pushed a green twig he was holding into the fire, stirring up embers that glowed and blinked like pulsating cat's eyes.

With the flannel cloth, John Henry made a final effort to wipe off the excess oil so that it didn't collect dust and dirt and risk jamming the mechanism that he so admired.

Joshua had prepared them a mutton stew, the bloody wool of a lamb laid nearby, the unneeded parts — the lamb's offal — flung far out into the darkness, where the coyotes would discover them and carry them away to hidden dens.

Mixed in with the mutton were wild onions and a few carrots, and several handfuls of salt. The mute boy was an uncommon cook. He ladled out a bowlful of the stew and handed it across to John Henry along with a pewter spoon and watched while the man took the first careful bites.

"Excellent!" John Henry announced. "A fare fit for a king."

Joshua smiled, exposing small sharp teeth, then ladled himself a bowl of the mutton stew. There was only the silence of the chill night and the knock of pewter spoons against wooden bowls and the crackling fire. But to the boy, it was all silence.

The wind shifted, and they could smell the horses hobbled nearby.

"Where did you find the lamb?" asked John Henry.

The boy read the question on John Henry's lips, lowered his eyes at first, stared into the oily waters of his stew, then looked off toward the nothingness of night and nodded.

John Henry wondered if the lamb belonged to the squatters he had seen earlier. They had had a few sheep and one or two milk cows among them.

John Henry saw such lovely tragedy in the boy's urchin eyes. His dark hair hung limply about the edges of his face. *He is an angel without voice*, thought John Henry. It was a mystery of nature to him how someone so delicate could hear but not speak. What would render a beautiful boy unable to speak?

In the morning, he will ride to where he saw the squatters along Yellow Hat Creek. He has not fully decided yet what he will do about them. He finished his meal of mutton stew and handed the bowl over to Joshua to be cleaned. A small trickle of a stream ran near their camp. It was a pleasant camp.

The boy ate without urgency, thoughtful, as though each mouthful had meaning to him. He had baked shepherd's bread in a large black skillet and now ate a chunk of it with his stew in the same deliberate process.

He watched John Henry ease himself up from his ground blanket and go off into the bushes. He stared into the fire as he ate, the dancing flames mirrored in his gaze like two tiny campfires trapped within his skull, behind his liquid eyes.

He finished eating, pulled a blanket over his shoulders, and stirred the collapsing embers with the green switch, feeling the heat on the back of his hand.

He was sleeping by the time John Henry returned.

Thin gray clouds swept across the morning sky. John Henry was already up and saddling his horse. Joshua rose and made a fire to brew coffee and reheat the pan bread.

"I'll be gone most of the morning," he said to the boy. "Move camp to that far ridge over there." He pointed west to a line of low green hills speckled with wildflowers. Joshua uttered a sound and brought him coffee.

The squatters were still camped where he had seen them the afternoon before. They were up and about, the women had placed wet clothes they'd washed in the creek on bushes and the low branches of trees to dry. More discreetly, they had hung up their undergarments on some low mesquite branches. The men squatted on their heels around a smokey little fire; they had corncob pipes clenched between their teeth, and the few children ran back and forth and in among the wagons. The men were four in number.

There was something in him that detested such people of low station, people with gaunt faces and thin bodies and poor clothing. His headache began, a small white fire behind his eyes.

He judged the hour to be between eight and nine in the morning. It had taken him more than an hour to ride there. He sat the steeldust on a rise and observed them below in their little encampment. It had already taken on the air of permanence, their little camp. Besides the hanging clothes, there was a large camp kettle set up over the fire. They had oxen bedded down on the dewy grass. A chest of drawers sat out behind one of the wagons. Then he saw it: the patch of green corn a little taller than a man's knees sprouting out of the ground beyond the wagons.

The squatters were having their breakfast when they noticed the lone man riding down from the ridge; he rode a gray horse. The men were hunkered about the fire warming their hands, waiting for the women to fill their plates, placidly smoking their pipes when they saw him.

"Rider," said one of the men, tall and thin as though there were only bones under his clothing. His name was Ezekiel and he and his family had come all the way from Iowa just to be there.

The others stood when Ezekiel stood — all brothers and Ezekiel's sons.

"Martha," Ezekiel said to one of the women, his wife. "You and Adeline gather up the children and go stand by the wagons." Adeline was the wife of the eldest son, Nathan. She was young and plain, with modest green eyes and a small dark mole on her right cheek.

Martha raised herself from where she was bending over the camp kettle and looked first at her husband and then out beyond the camp to the approaching stranger. She was broad of face, Martha. Broad-faced and big-boned and had the look of weariness about her.

They watched the rider work his horse down off the ridge in short switchbacks, cutting through the swales of grass, leaving a dark green trail from where the grass was bent over behind them.

"Silas, might not be a bad idea for you to get your breech loader, just in case," said Ezekiel to the middle boy Silas, who was hobbled from a permanent limp that he'd suffered long ago in a fall from a hay mow, a limp that had ever since burdened him in ways the others could not know. For what girl would want a boy who was half crippled? And what man would hire him on, except his own father? And who would not stare at him if he even so much as walked down a street, except his own kin? He hobbled off to get the rifle.

The brothers stood side by side like curious ravens in their black coats. *Mormons*, thought John Henry. *Goddamn Mormons come west to squat land*.

As he neared the camp, John Henry saw one of the men hobble off toward one of the wagons and retrieve a long gun. He saw, too, the women gather up the children and take them behind a wagon.

When he rode down among them, John Henry saw that the men resembled one another in their looks and guessed them to be kin. He brought the steeldust to a stop not ten feet away, removed, for an instant, his large hat, and wiped his forehead with the sleeve of his shirt. Already it was growing hot. The headache throbbed behind his eyes. The weather in Montana was most unusual, for yesterday he was wet and cold and today he was near removing his coat.

Ezekiel waited until the man had finished looking them and their camp over before putting forth a greeting.

"Welcome to our camp," he said. "You are welcome to step down and share our morning meal."

John Henry leveled his gaze at this man.

"Your camp?"

The man nodded uncertainly.

"This cannot be your camp," John Henry said. "This land is owned by Mr. J.D. LeFlors. Everything you see around you is owned by Mr. J.D. LeFlors. The fact is, you'd have to ride three days solid without ever once getting off your horse not to be on land owned by Mr. J.D. LeFlors."

The brothers had stark, bland faces that stared at him in the whiteness of the morning sun. The headache caused him to squint.

"We've seen no fences," Ezekiel said. "Nor have we seen any homestead or other sign of habitation hereabouts. Could it be that you are mistaken about the land already being owned?"

"No mister. You are on private land here."

Ezekiel turned and looked into the faces of his sons, then turned his attention back toward the women and children, who stood peeking out from behind one of the wagons.

"How were we to know?" he asked, raising the palms of his hands heavenward.

They saw the man on the gray horse sigh deeply, roll his dark eyes slightly.

"How many beeves have you killed and eaten?"

He saw the slightest nervousness in their eyes, the grave uncertainty. The eldest boy, Nathan, standing next to the one carrying the rifle, was first to defend: "We've killed and eaten no beef." And when he said that, he saw the man on the horse curve his lips into a soft smile.

"No, you've killed one or two, I know that."

The man shook his head, looked round toward his kin, those standing on either side of him, and saw the protest in their stark faces.

"No, we've killed a deer and a few rabbits. We've shot no cattle!"

"I think you're lying. I found the remains of a butchered beef north of here. A day's ride. I saw wagon tracks, like the wagons you've got there. There's no other squatters in this valley but you. What am I to think?"

The man shook his head in innocence and so did his sons.

"This is a difficult thing we are faced with here," John Henry said. "You have squatted on another man's land, killed his cattle, and now are forced to lie your way through it. Do you see how it becomes, this lying business?!"

He saw the storm of their resolve gather itself behind their eyes, their gazes now moody with uncertainty and anger at having been challenged in such a manner. He saw the one holding the rifle lift it up to aim at him. The glint of morning sun danced off the nickel-plated barrel of John Henry's pistol as it flashed for an instant in his left hand.

He shot Ezekiel's son, Silas, through the chest just above the heart collapsing him, spilling him into the dirt, his hat landing in the campfire.

The other men jerked about in fear and in surprise at the shooting. The women cried out in anguish and terror at the sudden unexpected brutality, and the children wailed their fright. The women and children were screaming and crying and the men stood there jerking their bodies as they stared from the dead man to the one on the horse.

"You see how it becomes, this lying?!" John Henry said, feeling his own blood hot from the moment, from the sudden violence, the headache growing, spreading like a fire in his brain. It was different, killing a man up close, different from a great distance with the rifle. It brought the blood hot.

"You have been warned," he told them. "Is there anyone else who wants a taste of it?" His blood was hot now and he was ready to kill them all. He looked into the eyes of each one.

In a grave and quivering voice, Ezekiel said, "You have murdered my son!"

"Yes, and you and you and you will be next if you do not leave this valley!" And looking into their eyes, he knew he had broken their will to stay.

And when he saw they had lost their resolve, saw the way it washed out of their faces, he turned the head of the gray horse north and rode up toward the ridge where he had instructed the mute boy to make camp. His blood was still hot from the killing and the headache was near to making him ill.

They watched him for a long time, too afraid and uncertain to turn their attention to their dead man — their brother and son, Silas, the one who had the permanent limp but would no longer be burdened by it.

CHAPTER NINE

The woman's dress was sour with her sweat. She was sitting across from Monroe Hawks within the tight confines of the Denver to Cheyenne stage. She was a woman of ample proportion, and the white salt lines of old sweat stained her black dress. She had small eyes for a woman her size. Small eyes like a pig has small eyes for a creature its size. He did not trust a woman with small eyes. His wife had had small eyes, and she'd proved to be untrustworthy about certain things.

Her name had been Blanche and he had married her young, while still a drover. And at the time he had married her, Blanche was no bigger around than a sapling. But marriage did something to her and she grew big in small ways: an extra meal here and a cake there. He had quit droving and tried clerking, reasoning that clerking was a better occupation for a married man than droving. Besides, he reasoned as well, it would give him and Blanche more of a time to stretch out the honeymoon if he was coming home regularly every evening and not leaving for long months on a dusty trail somewhere.

But clerking seemed to be no kind of an earnest endeavor for a man, being stuck indoors all day and sweeping floors and wearing an apron. And all the while, Blanche had seemed determined to increase her bulk, seeming to enjoy her own cooking much more than he did. He could have sworn the woman did not know what salt was.

In less than six months, Blanche had put on a good forty pounds and the clerking job had lost all its attraction, if there ever had been any to begin with. The bloom was off the rose. And so when Monroe had announced to her that he was going back to being a drover, she had made her own announcement: "You do that, and I might not be here when you return." And when he did return after six months of trailing a herd of a thousand cattle up from the Brazos to Abilene, he found that Blanche had kept to her promise: she had left with no further explanation or apologies. He also found out she had run off with a traveling dentist and she had taken their meager bank account with her. After that, he did not trust women with small eyes or dentists who would let a woman with small eyes clean out her husband's savings account without his knowledge or permission. From that day forward, he avoided conversation with small-eyed women and most dentists. Rather than save his money, he'd spend it.

Next to the woman, the reporter, Junius Bean, sat fairly squeezed between her and the coach door. At least he could lean his face out the window on occasion and breathe in the dusty air without being obvious about it.

Sitting next to Monroe was a tubercular young man of not more than twenty, whose cough was near constant, disturbing what little peace there was inside the coach.

"Going to see my sister up in Cheyenne," he had said almost immediately to the three of them soon after the stage left Denver, as if apologizing for his condition. "I am dying in slow ways, coughing up blood and most all my strength. I figure to stay up there in a shed she has fixed up for me."

"I thought most folks went to the desert for your condition," Monroe said.

"I got no sisters that live in the desert," the man said. "My only kin lives in Cheyenne."

It didn't make much sense to anyone, what the young man was telling them, but just looking at him, Monroe could see that he was quite right about the dying part. His eyes seemed to be trying to escape from their sockets, and every time he coughed, his neck veins stood out like small blue ropes. He couldn't have weighed more than a hundred pounds. About the size of one of the woman's legs, Monroe calculated.

Junius Bean made it a habit of raising his own bandanna to his mouth every time the sick man, who said his name was William, coughed up the bloody phlegm, as though to keep the consumption from entering his own mouth.

Monroe simply smoked a cigarette whenever the woman's sourness or the young man's coughing got to him. It was going to be a long ride.

In twenty mile intervals they would stop to change teams and give everyone a chance to stretch their legs.

At one stop, Monroe bought a basket of fried chicken from the wife of one of the stage hands. She was nearly as big and plump as the woman who sat across from him on the stage. He sat down on a stump to eat part of the chicken while the stage hands changed horses.

"Will you have some to eat?" he asked Junius Bean.

"Gladly," said Junius, who took a drumstick.

They watched the woman from the stage march off to the privy and the consumptive man stand outside the door to wait his turn.

"I'm afraid that man will make me sick with his disease before we reach Cheyenne," Junius said. "It's passed through the air, you know."

"This is good chicken," Monroe said. "I ought to buy another for down the way. You never know about the victuals you'll get in a stage stop."

A slight girl wearing a man's rough shoes came and stood in the doorway of the stage dugout and stared at them.

"Would you look at her," Junius said. Monroe did, then went back to concentrating on the piece of chicken he was eating.

"She doesn't look like she has all of her wits about her," said the reporter. The girl had wide-set eyes that gave her the appearance that she was looking in two different directions at once. One of the eyes was looking at the two of them eating chicken.

"Don't reckon I would either," Monroe said, without looking away from his chicken. "Clear to hell and gone in a place like this with nothing more to look at than them stage hands and the wind."

"Do you reckon she's married to one of those men?"

"What difference does it make?" Monroe said, and then they all boarded the stage once more.

Monroe felt the butt of his Smith & Wesson pistol bang up against his lower ribs with every jolt and jar of the stage, and he was sorry he was wearing the thing instead of having packed it in his warbag along with his hand mirror and straight razor and fresh shirt.

The streets of Cheyenne were deeply muddied from a week of rain. The sick man's sister was waiting at the stage depot when they arrived. She was a big-boned girl with yellow hair and a shy husband and two little children who couldn't take their eyes off Monroe as he stood there waiting for the reporter to get his valise down from the boot of the coach.

What is it with me and youngsters? Monroe wondered when he saw the sick man's sister's children staring at him like he was a circus elephant.

The woman with the sour dress was met by another woman and they hugged and kissed one another on the cheek, then trundled off down the sidewalk talking all the while, their heads bobbing like corks on rough water.

A cold rain hissed from the sky and boiled up in puddles in the cold muddy street. It was as gray and gloomy a place as he'd ever been to, Cheyenne.

"I'd say it's time we warmed ourselves with a whiskey," Monroe suggested to the writer.

"It will be my pleasure to buy the first round," Junius Bean said. "I still have the odor of that woman's dress in my nostrils and the taste of that man's sickness upon my tongue."

It did not take long to find a place to drink, just two doors down the street. Monroe was relieved to see that there was a saloon in nearly every other building, and between saloons there were sporting houses and restaurants. Cheyenne couldn't be all that bad a place with so many saloons and sporting houses and restaurants in spite of the evil weather.

They drank their whiskey standing by a woodstove and watched a man feed boiled eggs to his bulldog. Three fellows were playing a game of Chuck-a-luck at one of the tables. One man sitting by the stove said: "Cold for a summer's day, ain't it?" Junius replied that he thought so, too. "Ain't usually this cold," said the man, "but sometimes it is."

A tall man wearing a rubber slicker came in and stood by the bar and never took his gaze from them.

"That man is staring at us," Junius said, speaking surreptitiously from the side of his mouth.

"Yes, well, let him look," Monroe said, his attention had fallen upon a young slatternly girl casting him coy glances; she was sitting on the lap of a cowboy. Monroe knew she was a working girl of the first rate. She had blond hair and a mole next to her mouth. The tops of her milk white bosoms were revealed in the low-cut velvet dress she wore. He'd seen enough whores to know that this one was first rate.

I have seen that son of a bitch before, thought the man in the rubber slicker, who stood at the bar watching the two strangers. His name was Harry Walker and he'd been the city marshal of Cheyenne for the last two and a half months, a position he had come by when his predecessor, a man named Henry Tree, had been shot in the mouth by the town butcher, whose wife Henry Tree had been carrying on with, or at least that was the local talk. It had proved a sad day all around when vigilantes had hung the butcher from a telegraph pole, not caring to wait until the man could have a trial. There were those who were disgusted by the act, for the butcher had always been an honest man and kept his thumb off the scale.

It had been a good break for Harry Walker, for he had been near quitting his position as a deputy and was determined to head for the silver mines in Tombstone, where he'd heard that a man could pick up enough silver out of a miner's hair to get himself rich. But like most such talk, it couldn't be entirely believed. In a way, he was glad the new job had been offered to him, and he would not have to go all the way to Tombstone to just be disappointed.

The girl's name was Belva Spain, even though everyone called her Little Parakeet or The Belle of Cheyenne. She was not having much luck with the cowboy. He was near broke by his own admission. "I only got fifty cents left and that has to last me till the end of the month," he told her. Her interest at once turned toward the new arrivals, the old man and his companion. The old man threw her looks and she threw him some back. She just had to figure out how to get rid of the cowboy without him raising a fuss. She saw Harry Walker come in and knew that he would not tolerate her or the cowboy having a public fuss. Harry could be as hard as winter!

The more the lawman stared at the old man, the more worked up his guts were getting. There was something familiar about the fellow.

"He keeps looking over here," Junius said nervously.

"Who?" Monroe asked; the girl was being openly flirtatious with him now, even though she was still sitting on the lap of the cowboy. Monroe was remembering Monique, the French girl back at Miss June's, and thinking to himself that it had seemed like a long time ago since he had had the opportunity to "air out his grievances" as he liked to call it.

"That fellow at the bar, that one standing in the slicker," Junius indicated. "He's staring at us like he knows us."

Little Parakeet told the cowboy, whose name was Jim Rope, that he'd either have to buy the both of them another drink or she'd have to go sit with someone else.

"Why?" the cowboy asked, his eyes as innocent as those of a cow.

" 'Cause them's the rules, honey. Fat Karl don't allow us girls to just sit freely with cowboys if'n they ain't buying drinks. He sees you not drinking, he's liable to throw you on out of here and fire me in the process."

"Well, I told you I ain't got but fifty cents left," Jim Rope said, his face long with disappointment.

"Fifty cents!" Belva said, her breath hot and sweet against his ear. "Honey, fifty cents won't get you far, not in this world!"

"I don't know why Fat Karl would treat me thataway," the cowboy said. "After I spent all I had in here yesterday and last night!"

"He's just that way, honey," The Belle of Cheyenne said. "He's a businessman! I'm going to go on over to that fellow standing over there by the stove before Fat Karl comes out and sees you an' me just sitting here without drinking and raises a fuss. You known Marshal Walker won't put up with no fusses. You want to come visit me again when you get your paycheck, I'll be happy to keep you company."

Jim Rope cast a forlorn glance at the old man standing next to the stove. Women could be fickle, especially whores. But in spite of his great disappointment, he could know only one thing with certainty: he was in love with The Belle of Cheyenne.

Monroe was feeling the tickle in him when he saw the girl stand up and start across the room toward him. Then, a voice as cold as old ashes said: "You look like some sort of trouble to me!"

Monroe turned and saw a face he hadn't seen in a long time: Harry Walker!

Junius felt the urgent need to make water, but his reportorial instincts caused him to stay still; the man in the slicker was challenging the presence of Monroe Hawks. Either way it turned out, he reasoned, it would make a good story.

The man in the slicker stood so close, Junius could smell the bay rum he was wearing. There seemed something brutal and overwhelming about his stature. He was terribly big-boned and had a large head with close-set nervous eyes under brushy brows.

For a long full moment, the two men stood eyeing one another like two dogs that had met on the street and were sniffing each other, deciding whether or not to have a go at it.

"Mr. Bean," Monroe said, breaking the silence. "This here is Harry Walker. I'm sure you've heard of him in your travels." The man in the slicker twitched his head at the recognition.

"Harry is a natural killer of men and stray dogs," Monroe continued. "He's killed more stray dogs in Emporia, Kansas than any other man I ever met. Ain't that a fact, Harry?"

The lips parted until they revealed uneven, blunted, brown teeth and the thickness of a large tongue pressing against them.

Harry squinted at the mention of Emporia and the time when he was a deputy constable under Monroe Hawks. City council had paid twenty-five cents to its constables to shoot stray dogs on the streets, but ol' Monroe had said he wasn't going to shoot any damn stray dogs for twenty-five cents or even a dollar, that it was a waste of time and good cartridges and didn't bring any pride to the job. But Harry had seen it as some sort of bonus plan and had gladly taken up the offer.

"Mr. Bean here is a writer with the *Denver Post*, Harry. He likes writing about pistoleers and shootists, says there ain't many of us around anymore. I guess that would include you. Mr. Bean, maybe you could get Harry to tell you about his exploits."

"I'd heard you was kilt down in the Cherokee Nations, Hawks," Harry Walker said, his voice thick with bad emotion. "I can see now that the good news was wrongly told! I heard a pimp shot you in the face!"

There was silence between them again. Junius was not so sure that at any second one might not draw his pistol and fire it into the body of the other and felt his need to make water grow even greater.

"No. No I wasn't killed in the Nations, Harry, and if you'll excuse me, I'd like to have a word or two with that young woman standing over there."

"The Belle of Cheyenne!" declared Harry, most of his brown teeth now exposed in a sort of flat smile. "I can see that whores is still your weakness!"

Monroe gave him a level gaze that Junius was sure would take the heart out of anyone.

"You leave off now, Harry. You know I draw the line when it comes to insulting ladies. You go on out and find you some strays to shoot and leave off with me now."

Junius saw Harry Walker stiffen, saw the gathering of bulk underneath the slicker. Even he knew that there was a pistol carried underneath the slicker. The question was, would he reach for it? Would he have the nerve to draw it on Monroe Hawks?

Harry turned his attention to the reporter.

"You get him to tell you about Cora McDuffy, sometime," he said, then turned and was gone through the doors of the saloon.

Junius looked into the faded eyes of Monroc Hawks for an answer to the question, but none was forthcoming.

"Is she someone from your past?"

"It's nothing I care to talk about," Monroe said.

"But why would he say — ?" Monroe cut off the question with a wave of his hand.

"I said it's nothing I care to talk about. Leave off!"

The need to make water could wait no longer. The relief and privacy of the privy gave Junius a chance to mop the sweat from his forehead. He wondered if he had not made a grave mistake in traveling with a man so full of potential danger as Monroe Hawks.

Grave mistake, indeed. A grave might be where he would end up. The thought made it hard for him to make water; it seemed to stop up all his plumbing.

CHAPTER TEN

It was an old Schofield .44–40 wrapped in a piece of oily burlap that Nate Love had gone to the shed for. It had been twenty years or more since he had last held it with any intention of using it. Why he'd ever kept it around in the first place was beyond him. Once he'd left off going into the Nations for the Judge, he pretty much figured he had no more use for it. He and Suddy'd had three babies by then, and he already losing his hair and some of his step. Suddy'd said: "Time for you to give it up ol' man. Time for you to help me raise these young'ns and settle down and plant a garden." The truth was, it seemed like sound advice.

He was nearly forty when Suddy'd said that, and he'd known it was true. He held the Schofield in his hands and remembered the men he had killed with it: white, brown, red, and black ones, too. *Every man's got a history*, he thought. *This damn ol' Schofield's got one, too*.

He turned it over in his hand, its walnut grips dark as his own skin. He couldn't remember where he had gotten it, didn't even know if it would still fire or maybe blow up in his hands if he did try and shoot it. Cartridges couldn't be good after so long a time. He'd have to go into Bozeman and buy cartridges for it. He thumbed back the hammer and the cylinder clicked around.

Evil piece of work, he thought.

He did not recall it being so heavy.

He took it out and put it in the saddlebags; he'd saddled ol' Preacher, and the horse stood there patiently, dull-eyed, its head hung down. Ol' Preacher hadn't hardly been ridden at all in two years, having been mostly relegated to pulling a plow or Suddy's spring wagon. Nate Love wasn't so sure how Preacher would take to being ridden again. So he simply had put the saddle on him and tied him up out front and let him stand that way getting used to the saddle while he had gone and found the Schofield.

Suddy came to the doorway just as Nate was stuffing the pistol down inside his saddlebags.

"What you doin', Nate? Why you got ol' Preacher wid a saddle on his back?"

"Going to town." But Nate didn't look at her when he announced his intentions, and because he had not, Suddy knew that he was up to something.

"Town? What it is you be needin' in town we ain't got already?"

"Things," Nate said.

"Things that got to do wid Efrim?"

He looked at her then, saw the hurt still hadn't gone out of her sore red eyes.

"Not to worry," Nate said. "I just got to go on in to town is all."

"You sorry ol' man," she said in a tired way. "All these years we been married, an' you thinks you can still pull a fast one on me."

"I'm going to town to get some cartridges," he said.

"Cartridges!"

He nodded in a way that the light gleamed off his smooth hard skull. She wished he wouldn't go about without his hat for fear that someday he'd catch his death from a cold. She'd once had a cousin who'd never worn his hat, and sure enough, he'd caught pneumonia and died one winter. Everybody was agreed it was because of not wearing a hat.

"Well, I reckon you goin' to town for cartridges," she said, "you best be wearin' your hat. It looks like it might come some mo' rain."

"Yes'm," he said, and put the hat on his head. The hat was old and floppy-brimmed and had a tall round crown; she didn't know how long he'd owned it, but it seemed like he'd owned it for quite some time. She wished he'd purchase a new hat.

With a little effort, he was able to get his left foot in the stirrup, and with a little more, he was able to pull himself up and swing his right leg over the cantle. It all felt so unfamiliar to be sitting a horse again. It looked to him like he was ten feet off the ground.

He fixed the hat a little lower on his head in case ol' Preacher decided to get rambunctious; he did not want to have to chase his hat halfway across the valley. It was a foolish thing for a man to have to chase his hat.

"I'll be home before dark," he offered, and Suddy said she'd have his supper waiting, then fussed with her hands, one against the other, and swore to herself she would not let him see her spill tears over his leaving, even though she knew as soon as he was out of sight, she was going to break down and bawl.

"You ride that ol' horse careful, Mistuh Love. He ain't used to no man up on his back. And the truth be known, you ain't rode no horse in a long time neither."

"I will," Nate said. He was thinking that maybe he would buy her a bright blue bolt of cloth — her favorite color — to make a new dress.

Off to the east, the sky was clearing so that the sun sparkled through a crack in the parting clouds. Nate touched heels to the horse and started off toward the valley and toward Bozeman. He had to stop several times before reaching Yellow Hat Creek because his legs and feet grew numb and tingly from the ride. He would stop Preacher, climb down, walk around and stretch a bit, then mount up once more and ride a little farther. By the time he reached Yellow Hat Creek, he was ready to forget about going all the way into Bozeman just to buy cartridges. He'd do it another day, a day when he took Suddy into town in the wagon.

When he topped a grassy rise, he saw them camped down below along the creek: a family of white squatters. He saw another thing, too: a freshly turned grave. Maybe he would stop in for a cup of coffee, give himself a chance to rest a spell before turning back.

They saw the rider coming down the slope and Ezekiel said: "Oh Lord, he's returned!" And the women turned their frightened faces toward him, the children gathered in the folds of their wind-swept skirts.

"He'll kill us all!" announced Ezekiel's wife. "He killed young Silas, and now he's come back to kill us all!"

"It ain't him!" one of the brothers declared. "It's a black man!"

When Nate reached the creek, he sat on the other side of it and called into camp. "Mind I come across?"

"No, you come on ahead," Ezekiel said. The brothers weren't so sure, neither were the women. The children stared wide-eyed and clutched the women's skirts in their small fists.

Preacher was balky at stepping into the water (the sorrel never had cared for river crossings and a creek in his mind was the same thing as a river) but Nate urged him across. And when he had splashed out the other side and climbed the grassy bank, he announced: "Name's Nate Love. I live on up the other side of that ridge." Nate saw their long faces and figured he represented some sort of trouble to them.

"Mind I step down?" asked Nate; he was smelling the squatters' coffee, and it was making him near weak with desire for a taste of it.

"You're welcome to," Ezekiel said, who, when Nate did dismount, extended a long bony hand and said who he was, then spoke the names of each of his two sons. "These are my boys, Nathan and Jediah." Then looking back toward the two women, he said: "That's Josie and the other one's Fredricka. Fredricka is Nathan's wife. Josie is mine." He didn't bother with naming the children or saying whose they were.

"Pleasant to meet you," Nate said. They saw him looking beyond the camp to the grave.

"Young Silas," Ezekiel said. "Murdered yesterday." The announcement caused Nate to blink. *More murder*, he thought. *Another boy killed*.

"Who done it?" Nate asked. "Who murdered your boy?"

"A man that come riding over the ridge same as you," said Nathan, a tall hollow-eyed man with thick dark hair that was wild and uncombed. "Rode down here and accused us of stealing and butchering cows! Said the cows belonged to a man named LeFlors. Said he knew it was us that did it. Silas was holding a Sharps and the man shot him because of it and warned the rest of us to leave!"

It was a piece of news Nate had not counted on.

"You got a good look at him, did you?"

"Standing as close as you to me," said Nathan. "Christ almighty!"

"I am sorry about your loss," Nate offered. "But I must know what this man looked like!"

"Rode a gray horse for one thing," the other brother, Jediah, said. He had a soft way of speaking and averted his gaze from looking at the rest of them.

"Had dark eyes, Mr. Love. Real dark, and pale-skinned, like he never was too much out in the sun, sorta sickly almost."

"Did he say whether or not he was LeFlors's man?" Nate asked, feeling his heartbeat quicken over the news.

They exchanged looks with one another, the brothers did, trying to remember and finally agreed that the man on the gray horse had not laid claim to being LeFlors's man, but it seemed to them that he must have been or why else the interest, why else would he have killed poor little Silas?

Nate Love tried to think hard if he had seen a man in the territory like the one being described to him now. He could not.

"Which direction?"

"Back the same way you come from."

Nate glanced over his shoulder, back toward the low hills and the long ridges and the far blue mountains. *Hell, it was a big country!*

"You fixing to take revenge for your boy's killing?" Nate asked.

"No sir," Ezekiel said. "We're fixing to clear out! We're just farmers come from Indiana, come to settle some land and raise a few things and maybe some milk cows and a few sheep. You can see we ain't gunfighters!"

"You'd leave it like this?"

They nodded their heads in a slow, sad way. Nate wanted to be angry with them because they were going to leave it like it was: their dead kin unavenged. He didn't understand it, didn't want to understand it. Another dead boy! He didn't want to understand it. But, looking into their sad, troubled faces, he knew he couldn't be angry with them. He shifted his gaze back toward the grave. That boy's grave would be gone in less than a year, the grass grown up over it and the piece of plank they had stuck in the ground as a marker blown away, or someone would come along and use it for firewood. There wouldn't be anything more left of that boy's existence than there was of all the others that would die out on the frontier.

Their sadness became his own, transferred over into him through their watery eyes and soft words and beaten down postures, and through the stares of dismay and fright from their little children. And he said: "It's alright. It'll be taken care of." And they did not understand what he was telling them.

"What do you mean?" Ezekiel asked.

"You go on and clear out before that fellow comes back and shoots more of you," Nate said. "You go on." And they looked at one another and back toward the women.

And while they were still looking at one another, Nate mounted his horse and rode away.

Suddy was waiting supper for him just like she said she would be, and when she heard Preacher's exhausted whinny as he neared home, she stepped out into the fading light and saw the old man riding into her yard. Her heart filled with so much relief and gladness it fairly took her breath away.

"I see you has come back," she said. "I see that ol' Preacher ain't throwed you off in a briar patch somewheres and lef' you."

"He might just as well have for all the grief it done give me to ride all the way to Bozeman and back," Nate said, sliding down from the saddle and spending several seconds getting his legs back. The last time he had felt so unsteady, it was whiskey that had done it; and that was a long time ago, back in the Nations when he and Monroe had been after a woman outlaw named Madam Cherry, whose specialty was seducing wealthy gents and then having her paramour, a man named Albert Fly, knock the gents on the head with a lead sap before robbing them of their bank notes. It seemed hardly the type of crime worthy of sending U.S. deputies into the Nations for, but Judge Parker had expressed special concern over "crimes of passion" as he'd put it and therefore had ordered Nate and Monroe to capture Madam Cherry and her lover.

Twenty-two days of riding in freezing rain and snow looking for the pair had brought him only the chilblains — his hands and feet so swollen and sore he couldn't ride a horse or hold a fork in his hands. Monroe had said the only cure was his Indian-bought whiskey, and lots of it. Nate had accepted the diagnosis and for several days after had floated somewhere between the pain and the vaporous effect of Monroe's Indian-bought whiskey. It had left him feeling about like he did now, having ridden all the way to Bozeman and back just to get some cartridges for his Schofield. The sad part was, he remembered standing there holding onto his saddle horn, they never did catch Madam Cherry and Fly. He wondered if they were still knocking gents in the head.

"I brought you something."

"What in the world you done gone and brought me that I need?"

"Ain't nothing you need, I expect, but something you might just want to have. A bolt of blue cloth."

He saw her shake her head as though disappointed, then her eyes spilled over with tears that coursed her brown cheeks.

"Lawd," she said. "You rode tha' ol' hoss all the way to Bozeman to buy me a bolt of blue cloth?"

"I was going in anyway," he said, finally finding the strength to undo the cinch and remove Preacher's saddle before turning him out into the corral. The horse fluttered its lips and shook its mane when Nate removed the bridle and bit.

"I don't know who's more glad to be home," Nate said. "Me or him."

Suddy took the bolt of cloth, kissed him on the cheek, and said: "You better go wash up your face and hands and come on in and eat. I cooked us up a nice plump hen and some dandelions."

Afterwards, he found himself dozing in his chair in front of the fire while Suddy laid out some of the cloth and cut it into sections on the table. Soon, he was snoring in a light rhythmic way that brought her comfort. She had lost all her children, some to the world and one to death. She didn't want to lose him. It was a comfort to hear him snoring in his chair. The snoring she didn't mind. It was what would take place the next day and the day after that and the one after that that she minded.

For come the next morning, he commenced to target practice with the Schofield. He would go way out back of the house with that big pistol she remembered him as always having owned ever since she'd first laid eyes on him but had not seen him carry in years, and he would set up cans on the side of the hill and shoot away with the pistol held in both of his hands until she thought he might cause himself to go deaf from the *BANG! BANG! BANG!*

And each time he fired the pistol, she flinched.

CHAPTER ELEVEN

Three more men were shot dead in the valley during the time Nate Love practiced shooting cans with his Schofield. As far as anybody knew, they might have deserved it, they might have been cattle thieves, or worse. They were all impoverished in their appearance, even more so in death to those who were witnesses.

J.D. LeFlors fretted inside his big house. John Henry Crow was a man of his word: the killing was not over yet.

John Henry Crow presented himself at the house now and then, demanded payment for his work, came like a ghost, went like a ghost. J.D. LeFlors fretted, paced through the house in his stockinged feet, peered out windows into the night when the moon was full, expecting at anytime to see John Henry Crow sitting outside on his gray horse. And sometimes he did.

"Killed a man on that little branch of water that runs beyond the high meadow," John Henry said on just such a night when J.D. spotted him sitting near the wrought iron fence that he'd had sent all the way from Pennsylvania. J.D. came out and stood on the wide porch in his stockinged feet and John Henry told him about killing the man.

"He cut up two or three good beeves, even skinned them out for their hides," John Henry said, shaking his head in disbelief that a man would want the hide of a cow.

"Can't imagine why any man would skin a cow," said John Henry.

"Son of a bitch even boiled the hooves and ate them!" He seemed deeply amused by the man's actions; his flat smile showing in the moonlight all the way to where J.D. stood on the front porch. It caused him to shudder, hearing John Henry talk about the man and the killing.

"He moved just as I shot him, the lead went through his neck; cut an artery I believe because the blood shot out in spurts three feet long. Damnedest thing!"

J.D. LeFlors tapped his teeth with a fingernail out of nervousness, a habit he disliked in himself.

"I want to end our agreement," he told John Henry.

"No sir, not just yet," John Henry said. "There is still work to be done. I've seen this happen before. I know my business."

Then John Henry would say he was owed five hundred dollars and wasn't that the agreement: five hundred dollars for every rustler he got rid of? And J.D. would disappear inside the house and return with the money that he kept in a small black safe in his bedroom.

"This must stop," he said.

"No," said John Henry. "You are wrong and I will prove it to you."

"I am convinced already," J.D. LeFlors said desperately.

"If I were to leave now, the job would only be partway done. The trash would fill up this valley and steal your cows and you'd be sorry that I didn't stay and finish the job. Please don't argue with me about this LeFlors, I know my business."

Then John Henry would ride off into the night, or whatever hour it was that he'd come to visit in his infrequent manner, and J.D. would fret and fret over this business that John Henry Crow would not leave undone.

Ten days of riding a horse across country as empty as the bottom of a drunkard's glass had just about taken the heart out of Monroe Hawks. It had reminded him of the time he'd had his horse shot from under him on the Staked Plains by a small band of Kiowa; whatever they had been doing that far north was a wonder to him, but they had shot his horse from under him and had kept him lying in an old buffalo wallow for two days and two nights before finding something else that interested them more than one poor white man with a repeating rifle.

He had had to walk nearly a week to reach a settlement. It had about taken the heart out of him, that walk, much like this ride had nearly taken the heart out of him. Only in a way it was worse than the time with the Kiowas. Then, he had been young and full of fight. It was different now.

"I used to do this all the time," he told Junius Bean as they camped late one afternoon and sat and watched the sun slide down beyond the blue mountains. "Used to could ride a horse till it'd give out on me, then I'd get another and ride that one till it'd give out, too." Junius Bean could not imagine riding a horse so long that it would give out on him.

"This friend of yours, this Nate Love," Junius said. "He must be a very good friend for you to come all this way."

Monroe watched the way the grass waved under the wind and said: "Friends are few no matter which life you live. I guess it ain't too much to ask for me to come all the way to Montana."

"I envy you that," Junius said. "I've no friends like what Mr. Love seems to be to you, or you to him. None I could ask to come such a great distance . . . especially for the purpose of killing a man! It seems to me it would be a most difficult thing."

"Well, the killing part I reckon will be easy enough. It's the traveling that's gotten hard."

"Perhaps you could tell me, Mr. Hawks, what sort of man is your friend? Was he with you when you killed China Jim in the Nations?"

Well, that brought back a memory. The memory came back clear and bright, like a good morning.

"Nate was there alright," Monroe said, seeing it again in his mind. "It was a damn good thing, too! Me and Nate was sent out from Fort Smith. The judge said for us to be wary because ol' Jim was about the meanest son of a bitch there was to deal with. He cut a woman's throat and stole her savings. I guess he *was* a mean son of a bitch."

"It wasn't just China Jim though, he had others with him: Cherokee Red and Slim Miller and Roy Thourgood. Now, Roy Thourgood was a mean son of a bitch in his own right. He was a gambler and a whiskey peddler and a sure shot with pistol or rifle. In addition, he was rumored to have killed several men by strangulation. Big ol' boy, Thourgood was. Had big hands and feet, could track him through a swamp with those big feet."

"Nate's wife was about due to have a baby, I remember that. It was near Christmas and she stuck out to here. Nate wasn't too up on going into the Nations with his wife about due to make him a daddy one more time."

"Said to me, 'Monroe, you best go on with someone other'n me, 'cause I ain't leaving Suddy alone to have that child by herself.' But the judge come by and talked Nate into doing his appointed duty and said Nate's woman could stay with him in the big house until the child was born and he'd see they was both taken good care of until Nate got back."

"You've got to understand that in those days, a man done his job without a lot of question. Not like a lot of these boys today that question everything and run out at the first sign of trouble. Nowadays, a lawman is more politician than anything — a handshaker and baby kisser. Not back then. We beat the bushes dry looking for the trash and bloodletters, stayed out weeks on end, stayed out and drowned in the rain if we had to. Always found our man or run him clear out of the territory looking."

Junius was scribbling as fast as he could to get it all down, and the sky over the blue mountains was turning brassy and the *THUCK! THUCK!* of a prairie chicken blowing up his breast could be heard off in the distant grass.

"Well, we went, Nate and me, even though Nate had his doubts because of his woman being so pregnant. But the judge had a way about him and convinced Nate to see his sworn duty done. We knew that China Jim liked to hang out near Cherokee Red's people over by Webbers Falls. China Jim, it was said, had a fondness for one of Red's sisters. So, in that way, tracking them wasn't any big deal."

"We found them easy enough, right where we thought they'd be, living the lazy, no-account life that men like them live, liquored up on corn whiskey and slothful in the ways of the wicked. Proves out that Cherokee Red had more than one sister and was sharing them with the boys at a cost of two dollars a head. China Jim, Slim Miller, Roy Thourgood — they all had themselves a sister keeping them company. Cherokee proved a good businessman in that way."

"They was about as sweated out and uncaring as hogs on a July afternoon when we arrived. Nate went in one way and I went in another and rousted them out. That's when China Jim's girlfriend shot me through the ribs. Stepped out of a privy with a pistol in both hands and called me a red-faced bastard, then shot me!"

"Shot you!"

Monroe pulled up his shirt and showed Junius the puckered scar where the bullet had gone through. "See around here," Monroe said. "Come out this side taking with it half a lower rib; near knocked all the wind out of me." And there was yet a second scar where the bullet had gone out.

"I guess China Jim thought if his woman could shoot me, he could shoot me, too, and took up the cause, drunk as he was. He missed me with all five shots. That's when I killed him. I was lying on the ground with half my blood pouring out these two holes when I let Jim have it. He died with a surprised look on his face, having been murdered by a man bleeding bad as I was."

"That's also when Slim Miller and Thourgood got into the act. Nate shot them both so quick they died at the same time. Then he shot the girl as she was fumbling with the pistol, for it was a single action and not a double and she was having trouble thumbing back the hammer all the way. She was a frail girl to begin with and I guess that big Starr .44 she was carrying was just too damn much for her to handle. Some can't function in the heat of battle, I guess she was one.

"Cherokee Red threw himself on the ground and begged Nate and me not to kill him. We wouldn't and didn't even though our blood was hot with the fighting. A man's blood will near boil in his veins in a pistol fight. We took Red back to Fort Smith and he was given twenty-one years in the prison up in Detroit for his sins. I reckon he's an old man by now and knows better, if he's not died of one cause or another."

Junius finished writing and put the pencil down.

"That is some story, Mr. Hawks. Is it the exact way that it happened?"

"Most of it is," said Monroe. "About all of it."

Looking into the weathered countenance of Monroe Hawks, the writer could not see the truth one way or the other; for the old pistoleer continued to look out to the swales of grassland in a pleasant manner, as if he were looking upon the company of a young attractive woman, or several. In the end, Junius decided that whether or not Monroe was telling the complete truth about the incident with China Jim was not necessarily all that important. The story had a certain flair of the dramatic, and what it lacked he was sure he could invent in order to round out the tale.

They figured to arrive in Bozeman within the next day or two. Once there, he would go to the telegraph office and file the story with his editor. He would entitle the piece: "Blazing Death, Or, China Jim Dealt His Due by The Knight of Justice!"

He figured to wait until the actual publication before presenting Monroe with his new appellation: The Knight of Justice. Why take chances?

The light was growing dim and the long shadows of the trees encroached upon their little camp. A cool wind blew in from the north and feathered through the topmost branches of the pines.

"This is damn pretty country," Monroe said. "Even if it is to hell and gone. I wonder how deep the snow gets and whether a man could stand the cold in winter?"

Junius was feeling weary from yet another long day of riding horseback. He was unaccustomed to riding a horse to begin with, preferring instead the comfort of a buggy or a railroad car. But when given the choice between horseback and a stage, he had felt the horse was the better choice. He could still smell the woman's sour dress. At least he didn't have to smell another person's odor when riding a horse.

"You married, Mr. Bean?" The question was a casual one and took the reporter by surprise.

"Why yes, I am."

"Long time?"

"Nearly twenty years."

"You miss your wife?"

Junius sighed; it was a good question. He had not thought much about Earnestine since having left Denver. Now, in that moment of question, he did. He could see her plain square face there in the shadowy light above the camp fire. It seemed like he had always been married to her, that there never was a time when he had not been married to her. But as he thought about it, he could not properly remember why it was they had married in the first place. It had just sort of happened without either of them willing it.

Earnestine was a good woman, who kept a clean house and set a good table. They had never had children, never even discussed it. It just seemed like the two of them lived together for no particular reason. She was always there when he came home and when he left home. In lots of ways, Junius knew he did not know much more about her than that.

"Yes, I suppose I do miss her in a way," was his answer to Monroe's question.

"Well, having been married myself," Monroe said. "I can understand missing a woman. A man that's married well has done himself a good service. On the other hand, one who ain't has himself hell to pay! I suppose was the right opportunity to present itself, I'd do it again." Monroe smiled like he knew a secret.

"I suppose what you say is true, Mr. Hawks," Junius said. "But I could hardly understand why a man who was married once would ever want to try it a second time."

"Hell, that's easy, Junius: a lusty man never gets tired of the mystery of a woman. The mystery of a woman is the greatest mystery there is on God's green earth. It's what keeps a man young, the mystery of women!"

Junius wasn't sure he quite understood what Monroe was speaking of. Earnestine had never presented any mystery to him; she was as plain and open as the prairie. He remembered their wedding night when she had stood before him in a high-collared night gown and said: "Do you want me to take this off before I turn down the light?" And when he hesitated in his answer, she went right ahead and removed the dress, revealing whatever mystery she had had about herself up to that moment. And after that, there was nothing about her that he figured he had not seen or known. Even though now, he realized, he did not know much about her beyond the plain and simple facts of her as she presented them. It was like knowing himself, knowing Earnestine.

Something stirred in the dark, beyond the tree line, the cracking of a twig, both men looked up, looked out into the darkness, listened.

"Critter," Monroe said, finally.

"How can you be certain?"

"Same way you know whiskey's going to burn when you drink it and a horse never can be trusted completely. It's just something you come to know."

Still, Junius listened a long time there in his bedroll for whatever murderer was lurking about in the dark. He went to sleep listening.

CHAPTER TWELVE

It was Sunday. A day of rest. If a body listened long enough and hard enough, he might be able to hear the pealing of church bells coming all the way from the Presbyterian church in Bozeman.

Sun shone over the blue mountains and glowed in the grasses, deep green under a flowing wind. The same sun shone upon the water of the stock pond, gray and metallic like a smooth pewter dish lying on the prairie.

A dozen cowboys raced down to the pond, leapt from their saddle ponies and undressed, some to their underdrawers, some completely, and plunged themselves in the water, wild as otters.

Jimmy Jake said: "Damn if I couldn't do this all day long!"

Louis Butterfield said: "Feels like I got a month of dust to clean out of my hair!"

Homer Teal, their ramrod's boy, did a belly flop from off a large rock and the others ducked out of his way, for he was a fat kid, as big as his daddy was skinny. Everyone guessed that Homer must have gotten his size from his mother, though none of the cowboys had ever seen her or knew for sure if he even had one since neither Homer or his daddy ever talked about her and they'd both showed up in Judith Valley without her.

Jode Pierce sat on the sloping bank and read silently to himself from a pocket Bible and smoked his pipe.

Wayne Brazos timed how long he could stay under water and not come up for air.

"We get spit and shined," skinny Calvin Pruitt said, "we'll be all the sight for the whores in Bozeman!"

It was a thought that grabbed everyone's attention, even Jode Pierce, who looked up from his Bible reading. *The whores in Bozeman*. It was something a fellow could not ignore, even a righteous one. Women were a great and rare mystery, their charms unavoidable. And even Jode had to fight off the temptation to think about them.

It was a payday, the end of a long month of days, and they all had their earnings stored among their belongings.

Jimmy Jake was thinking about one of the whores in particular: her name was Bess Beauford. She seemed sweet on him. She called him Jolly Jim and held his hand and her hair smelled like primrose and her eyes were as beautiful as violets.

Bess had been Jimmy Jake's first time with a woman; it had happened six months before, in the late winter before the work had begun and there was plenty of time to go to town if a cowboy had the money and inclination, the latter of which most had but not the former. Jimmy didn't know what else to do that first time but to fall straight away in love with Bess, even though she was an older woman. He guessed her to be close to twenty-five and worldly. He'd spent his whole paycheck in one afternoon.

"You plannin' on seein' Bess?" Louis Butterfield asked as he stood chin deep in the warm pallid water; his hair was wet and dark and hanging down over his eyes.

Jimmy Jake felt a flush of embarrassment. Homer came up out of the water and spit a stream of it from his mouth.

"Well, are you?"

"Thought I might."

"You sweet on that gal?" Homer Teal asked, the water sheeting off his thick smooth flesh. Again, Jode Pierce looked up from his Bible waiting to hear the answer along with the others.

"You got titties like a gal yourself, Homer!" Louis shouted with a gaping laugh that pealed across the pond and back and got some of the other boys laughing as well. Homer shot Louis a hard look then dove under water to try and tackle his legs.

John Henry Crow sat a quarter-mile off on a slight rise and watched them there in the stock pond, the steeldust cropping grass under the loose reins.

He felt a darkness come over him as he watched the slender bodies falling and climbing back out again from the stock pond, reclining along the slopes of the wallow; some still wore their hats, even though they were naked or nearly so. He wanted to go among them and enjoy the day in their company. Something urgent and desirous swept through his veins. He thought of Joshua, the mute boy back at camp. And then, he closed his eyes against them and felt the throbbing in his temples begin.

They swam and washed and scrubbed their hair. They climbed out of the water and lay upon the grass and let the sun warm and dry them and their clothes. They rubbed down their horses with bunches of grass and some led their ponies down to the edge of the pond and washed their backs with yellow bars of lye soap and curry brushes.

They bragged about their horses and some got up to run races.

Jode Pierce was the oldest among them, nearly twenty-two, and some of them called him "Dad" out of their affection for his kindly and peaceful manner. He didn't mind, even took some little pleasure in it; he thought it a degree of respect.

"Watcha readin' in the good book, Dad?" Calvin Pruitt asked. He had a long scrawny neck that matched his limbs, and when he spoke his Adam's apple bobbed up and down like a fish cork.

"The prodigal son's return," Jode said. "How he went off into the world, and when he'd tasted of its sinful nature and seen it wasn't all that great, he come home."

"You mean like how we're gettin' ready to go off to Bozeman and visit the whores?" Homer Teal said, his small dark eyes darting within the folds of his round face; his belly jiggled over the girth of his underdrawers.

"Yes, exactly so, Homer. Just like the prodigal son. And when your money is all spent and your head is busting from hard spirits, you'll come home, too. Only your daddy might not be so kind to you and you'll still have to get up at four in the morning and chase cattle and work all day in the hot sun."

Calvin Pruitt was giving Wayne Brazos a haircut and was open for anyone else who wanted one, charging them each a dime. He thought of himself as enterprising and felt that such talent as being able to give haircuts ought not to be wasted or given away for free.

Jimmy Jake sat cross-legged polishing his worn-down boots and wishing he had new ones.

"What if Bess has got herself a new fella when you get to town, Jimmy?" Wayne Brazos asked, looking up from where his head was bent over while Calvin snipped at the hair along his neck.

Jimmy could see by the way Wayne was grinning that he was trying to kick his goat around the yard, but he thought he'd be cool-headed about it and not give Wayne the satisfaction.

"Bess and me is sweethearts," Jimmy said as casually as he could without looking up from the boot he was working on. "New fella, if there was one, would just have to get on down the road, or I'd make him."

It sent faces grinning and heads shaking all through the camp. Louis Butterfield said he was going to try and catch himself a fish out of the pond because he'd felt something nibbling his toes while he was swimming. Wayne Brazos said he'd join him as soon as Calvin finished cutting his hair.

As the sun twinkled golden and cast long shadows down the main street of Bozeman, the cowboys rode their ponies at a hard gallop, hooting and hollering and waving their hats in the air.

The whores stood in the upper windows of the Valentine House, a hurdy gurdy two stories high with a balcony all across the upper level. It was the fanciest whorehouse in the territory, or so the spinster sisters who owned it claimed. There were no cowboys willing to argue, for it was the only one they knew about without having to ride a hundred miles to the Rye River Settlements, which would make no sense at all. Louis Butterfield claimed he knew a cowboy who had ridden all the way to the Rye River Settlements just to see what the whores there were like but never did come back to tell anyone else what he'd found out. So it was still a mystery as to what the whores in the Rye River Settlements were like. No one else seemed to want to go.

The girls demonstrating their wares on the balcony called down to the cowboys, who slid their ponies to a stop just below them. And when they heard the girls calling their names the cowboys responded with hoots and yells like young hungry coyotes who had just caught a rabbit in the bush.

The whores lined up in all sizes and shapes leaning over the balustrade. They wore little more than their cotton undergarments that exposed their shoulders and most of their breasts and their bare legs in such a brazen fashion that the boys almost fell off their horses. Some were ugly, some were plain, and none were beautiful by anything but cowboy standards. But cowboy standards were all that really mattered.

Bess Beauford stood on the end of the line of girls. She was suffering one of her headaches that always came with her monthlies and was hardly in a mood to see cowboys or any other customers at such a time.

The one cowboy, Jimmy she recalled his name as being, sat astride a painted pony and stared up at her with wanting eyes. *Oh God!* she thought in silent regret. *That boy's gonna want romance and I'm in no position to earn a dime!*

"Howdy, Bess!" Jimmy Jake whooped, seeing the object of his affection staring down at him with her violet eyes. He remembered the last time and the time before that and every other time he had been to visit her.

She waved her hand weakly and figured she'd think of something if the boy had brought his money. There was more than one way to earn a cowboy's money.

"Well you boys climb down off them hosses and come on in!" shouted Geneva Lars, a fat woman from Minnesota with carrot red hair and bosoms as large as feather pillows. Skinny Calvin Pruitt took an instant liking to her and whispered his observations as to the size of her "pillars" to Louis Butterfield, who immediately flushed red from the neck up.

Edna and Edith Valentine, spinster sisters from Dark County, Ohio, owned and operated the Valentine House. They were well into their sixties but still believed that there was good money to be made in the entertainment business and that cowboys were the easiest of all men to entertain. The sisters had left home when they were not yet twenty, and worked their philosophy in several towns starting west of the Mississippi. Having started out themselves as working gals in a St. Louis brothel (they were known locally as the Tempting Twins), the sisters plied their trade until they reckoned they understood the business well enough to become proprietresses of their own entertainment company.

Now, they appeared as frail, fine-boned women wearing prim black dresses, whose high collars were pinned with garnet brooches. Their iron gray hair was pulled back from their narrow faces and set in buns at the crowns of their heads. They could have been mistaken as Lutherans. Severe-appearing in every way, the only evidence of their past was to be seen deep within their gay, green, demonstrative eyes, eyes that if a man were to take the time to understand, would quickly reveal that the twins still had a bit of fire in their furnaces.

"You boys scrape your boots off before you come in," ordered Edna, the more practical and business-minded of the two. "And make sure you use the spittoons if you chew."

Edith, the more romantic-minded one, could only stand by and watch as her sister laid down the house rules; her own memory of handsome eager young men lay vivid and shining in the back of her mind like old jewelry kept in a drawer. She remembered one particular boy, Alvin Greedy, who had overlooked her chosen line of work and had professed his love for her the first time they'd met.

Alvin had courted her in all the ways of a gentleman and proposed marriage to her while bent before her on one knee in the very parlor where she had conducted her business.

His ardor had purchased her heart. They were all set to go to San Francisco and marry, only to suffer tragedy before they could: Alvin died in a fire the week before their scheduled departure.

She had never felt the same about anything or anyone in life since.

They were called the Brides of the Multitudes and they came down the staircase and aligned themselves in the front parlor so that each of the young cowboys could pick and choose his own "bride."

Calvin Pruitt went straight over to fat Geneva and took her hand in his and said: "Which way, darlin'?" And Geneva wrapped a large arm about his neck and said: "Follow me, sweetness!"

Louis Butterfield blushed beet red when one of them, a woman named Obeth, came and stood directly in front of him with so little on she would have caught a cold in July, and said: "Do you like me well enough to pay money for me?"

Homer Teal was disappointed that Calvin had beat him out on Fat Geneva, but chose instead a thin frail girl with dark hair, a mole on her right cheek, and wide-set eyes. She said her name was Eliza.

"How about me an' you?" Calvin said, and she smiled broad enough to show she was missing a bottom tooth. But Homer was already set on her in his mind, and the missing tooth had no effect whatsoever on his determination or the fire that was raging through his blood.

Wayne Brazos was having trouble choosing between a bowlegged chippy named Sweetbread Sue and a somewhat mannish-looking gal named Dora Hand. Dora had the bigger bosoms, but Sue had the wider hips. He decided Dora after a long consideration. Why, he didn't know exactly. It was just something in the way her hips were so wide.

The others offered themselves up to the remaining cowboys, and soon the room was all but empty except for the Valentine sisters, Jimmy Jake, and Jode Pierce on the one side and two or three remaining brides on the other, Bess being one.

"I reckon I know which one it is I want," Jimmy said, his gaze resting on Bess. "You gonna choose one, Dad?"

Jode Pierce, a tender man in voice and spirit, felt the awful need to flee, to stay, to run, to choose one of the remaining girls. He had fought with the devil every time he and the others rode to town. And it seemed like some of the times he won and some of the times he lost.

The devil was a powerful force in Jode Pierce's book!

"No, I reckon I'll pass," he said, at long last turning back toward the door, his resolve weakened but still intact.

Jimmy Jake said, "Maybe just this one time you could let yourself have some fun, Dad. You've come this far. Heck, the Lord was to forgive anybody, it'd be you."

"No, I reckon I'll just wait outside for you and the others," Jode said and nodded toward the spritely sisters, one of them thinking how much this boy reminded her of another boy named Alvin Greedy. They both had the same color hair — light brown.

"Okay then, we'll catch up with you later," Jimmy said as he went and stood before Bess, his hat held in both hands.

"Bess, I've come back," he said expectantly.

"I can see that," Bess said as politely as she could manage, for the white hot light behind her eyes was exploding inside her brain. She would figure out something to entertain the boy. Just looking at his eagerness, she figured it wouldn't be hard.

And afterward, they rode home along the Bozeman road. The moon radiated among the rocks and trees and washed out silver over the rolling landscape and cast the far mountains in black jagged shadows. All along the road from Bozeman the boys could be heard singing and telling and retelling the praises of the women they had been with, reliving the delicious minutes of their manhood. And those whose first time it had been talked the most and sang the loudest and were the drunkest.

Jimmy Jake felt dreamy and hardly noticed all the hooting and hollering, all the raucous, whiskey-soaked banter and laughter and craziness of wild young cowboys coming back from a payday in town.

The only victim among them was Homer Teal, who was retching up the busthead whiskey he had purchased for fifty cents on the quart and then had proceeded to try to drown himself and the wall-eyed girl in. No one paid him much attention, and no one offered even a scintilla of sympathy.

Jode Pierce's thoughts were deep in confusion. Now, after all was said and done, he was more than a little sorry he had not participated in the revelry; he could still see the plain little face of one of the working girls who had laid her eyes on him in an obvious and wanton manner. He did not know her name, only that she was one of the whores — a girl who sold her flesh for money. It was a flesh he was fighting hard not to crave as he rode farther and farther from Bozeman.

Except for Homer and Jode, the others were as happy and uncaring as candy-fed children.

John Henry heard them coming down the road from where he had been waiting. He heard their hot breathless voices rising and falling in laughter and whiskey-stained jubilation. His own veins sang with the tension of tightly strung wire, his temples throbbed with the warm blood of passion.

And when they came within view of where he stood among the clutches of boulders, he fired a single shot into them.

CHAPTER THIRTEEN

The worst of the pain had eased off, and occasionally Suddy and Nate could go about the duties of living without thinking of Efrim every single moment, without thinking the terrible thoughts of the cold silent grave that was already settling back into prairie under the buffeting wind and warm sun and occasional hard rains. Fresh grass had already sprouted from the spaded soil, and Suddy, and sometimes Nate, went out and kept the little weeds and bull thistles pulled so that the wildflowers would have a chance to grow.

Nate had fashioned a nice headboard out of a piece of plank siding and had burned in Efrim's name, the date he was born, and that on which he died. He had heated up a piece of angle iron in a charcoal fire and burned in the details. He figured it to last two, maybe three years before he would have to replace it. He had heard of a place in Oglalla that made headstones out of granite and marble and figured that as soon as there was spare money, he'd take Suddy down to Oglalla and buy one for Efrim's grave and haul it back in the spring wagon. There wouldn't be anybody around to see that a new board was put up in a few years when he and Suddy were gone. He didn't want his boy forgotten.

Nate figured that maybe next spring he and Suddy would go to Oglalla — sell most of the hogs, take the money and go and buy Efrim his headstone.

The hogs called to him now, grunted and snorted and squealed wanting to be slopped. He had eight sows and two boars, mostly Durocs and Chester Whites, and twelve piglets, not counting the one that was ailing and surely would die soon; the piglets were small and pink and about ten pounds each. Every winter, he'd butcher a sow and have cured hams made from it and bacon and sow belly. Suddy'd pickle the feet in brine and cook up the brains into sweetbreads. Some of the hams he'd sell, and some of the bacon, and some he'd keep for him and Suddy.

He went to slop them now, their snouts pressed up to the rails of their pen, their grunt's and snorts renting the air.

"How long you reckon it is we've et hog meat?" he called to Suddy, who was sitting on a high-backed chair snapping beans into a pan, her broad brown feet resting on the warm floorboards of the porch where the sun had reached. The shelled beans sounded like rain hitting a tin roof when they struck the pan.

"Long's I can remember," she said, her dark, moon face looking up from the handful of beans she was working with her fingers.

"You ever get tired of eating hog meat?" he asked.

She wasn't at all sure of why he was discussing the subject of eating hog meat, but then, it was such a pleasant warm day that she didn't mind at all the idle talk. It was just good to have some normal conversation again, and she didn't mind one bit.

"No Mistuh Love, I reckons I nevah have got tired of hog meat."

Suddy watched Nate dump the buckets of slop into the trough and the hogs jostle their slab-sided weight against one another to get their snouts down in the sickly sweet-smelling slop.

When he had finished, he dropped the empty buckets and took a handkerchief out and wiped his forehead, then his skull, and finally his hands before replacing the rag in his back pocket, all the while standing there watching the hogs fight for position at the trough.

"Why you ask me 'bout eatin' hogs, anyway?" Suddy asked, puzzled by Nate's question.

"Just that as a young man, I never once thought that I'd ever be an old man raising hogs for my keep. It seems a long way from Louisiana and a whole lot of other things."

"She could tell when Nate was feeling melancholy. Her sister Jodyce suffered from the affliction, and so did Mistuh Lincoln, as she recollected hearing; clear up till the time that poor man was murdered in his rocking chair. Only with her husband it was just every now and again that he suffered from the affliction, and it never did last long, something she was grateful for, remembering how Jodyce would mope and cry for days on end."

"You rememberin' ol' times that don't exist no mo', Mistuh Love."

"Well, maybe I am," he said. "But what's wrong with that?"

"Nothin', I reckon." It was something she had never learned to understand fully, Nate's penchant for thinking of the old times. Sometimes he'd be an hour lazing about with what her mama had called "wistful" eyes. She recalled her daddy as having wistful eyes on occasion, and her uncle, too. Maybe all men got wistful eyes now and then. Maybe it was just something born in them. Something no woman could take out of them.

She did not recall ever having seen any women in her family with wistful eyes. Even Jodyce never got wistful eyes, not even when the melancholy come on her. She just cried a lot and lay across her bed and wouldn't hardly eat.

He was caught up thinking of a strong young man, of a man who had fought in a war and survived it, of a man who had hunted down killers in the Nations and survived that, too. Where had all that time got to? It was already two, three weeks since he had buried Efrim. Where'd all that time get to? It seemed like time ran as fast as a six-legged dog anymore.

Having finished clopping the hogs, Nate took the buckets to the lean-to, then Suddy saw him tucking the Schofield pistol down inside his belt like she'd seen every day for the last three weeks. Then he turned to go far out back, where a pile of old cans lay in a heap, jagged holes punched through them, shards of glass, catching the sun's light like winking eyes.

"How long you 'tending to shoot tha' ol' gun?" she said.

He stopped walking and turned to look at her. *He's still a handsome ol' fool*, she thought, *but an ol' fool nonetheless*. She knew what he was thinking.

"Long as I please," he said, and straightened up as tall as he could, for the arthritis had got down in his back and wouldn't let him straighten up all the way. It was just another thing about having gotten old, arthritis. *Maybe if I hadn't fallen off so damn many horses when I was younger*, he thought. And Suddy could see he had wistful eyes, standing there looking at her.

"I know what you is up to, Mistuh Love, an' I won't have none of it. No suh!"

"And what would that be, woman?"

"You's 'tendin' to go find Efrim's killer."

"Yes'm, I reckon I am."

Suddy stopped shelling the peas, her thick fingers trembling.

"I ain't got nothin' but you left, Mistuh Love. Could be I can't take no mo' heartache. Could be I can't stand to keep the weeds off 'n two graves." He could find no comfort waiting for him in her face.

"You 'tending to rob me of what little I've left?" she asked.

He hadn't told her about Monroe Hawks and the letter he'd sent asking him to come. He hadn't heard anything back in all that time. Maybe Monroe was dead or too old or too sick to come. Maybe Monroe had moved away and was lost somewhere in the world. He had thought to wait until he'd heard something back before saying anything to Suddy. But every day that passed without having heard from Monroe was one more day put in Nate's book, the book that said he'd have to take care of matters himself.

He'd gotten the old Schofield out and begun practicing with it and found out he couldn't even hit a can at twenty paces, except once out of every three or four tries. His eyes had grown dim. But there wasn't any other way around it. Efrim had to be avenged. And he'd promised Mrs. Sloan that justice would be done. Now, he wasn't as much sure as he was just plain determined.

"I reckon I still know how to shoot a pistol, Suddy Mae. I reckon I still remember what it is to fight a man, to see a justice done."

She saw how Nate stiffened with the remark, an old look she hadn't seen in a long time flashing up in his eyes. It pained her to see him thus, old and bent and full of sorrow. It made it feel like a fist squeezing her heart to know that they both knew he wasn't a young man anymore. Time had become an unkindness to them.

She refused to see him as he was. Instead, she saw a strapping young man with plenty of dark hair and a quiet charm flowing out of his eyes. She saw the man who'd ridden to her daddy's place three days out of five on a lop-eared mule, pretending he was coming round looking for work when everybody knew what he was really coming round for. And finally he'd gotten what he was really coming round for and they had married and she but sixteen and him all of twenty-four. Time had been a kindness to them then.

"You know I wouldn't have no reason to be goin' on, if'n you wasn't here no more," she said at last.

He stood there for a long time in the yard like a tired old dog catching its breath, unsure of whether to go chasing rabbits in the woods or crawl up under the porch and rest in the shade.

"I sent for Monroe," he said.

He saw the way the announcement worked its way into her brown face, the way the eyes widened and the lips parted and the shoulders slumped as though suddenly weighted down.

"Monroe Hawks!"

He nodded.

She fully understood then just how far things had gone.

She didn't say anything for a long time and neither did Nate. She knew how terrible and awful a man Monroe Hawks could be when it came to a fight. She knew him to be of cold blood and unforgiving ways. She knew that if he came and Nate went with him, someone surely was likely to be murdered because Monroe Hawks wouldn't stop until someone got murdered; and most assuredly, it would be one of the two old men, one of whom couldn't even hit a bean can at twenty feet! She thought of how aged Monroe must be by now, easily as old as Nate himself. An instant prayer formed within her that maybe Monroe Hawks was either dead or too old to ride a horse all the way to Montana or otherwise incapable of coming such a distance.

"You didn't mention nothin' 'bout sendin' for Monroe Hawks," Suddy said.

"Didn't think it necessary, not knowing if he'd come or not. So far, I ain't heard a word from him, so I reckon he ain't coming? Hate to think it, but he's most likely dead by now, hard a life as he tended to live."

"Like ol' times," she said.

"Huh?"

"You was hopin' it'd be like ol' times when you and Mr. Hawks would go off huntin' thieves and bloodletters out into the Nations."

He didn't own up to it; he didn't have to in her book. She already knew the truth.

She picked up a handful of beans and her tears dropped into them like a warm gentle rain at sunset.

"It ain't like that," he said. "It's about Efrim and what's right by him. Maybe I am just an old man with a backful of stiff bones and poor eyes and a damn gun that weighs more than it used to. But, I can't let it rest, Suddy. I can't walk out there to Efrim every morning and pick weeds off his grave and just say to him, 'That is it, ain't nothing more I can do for you, boy. Just pick the weeds off your grave.' I can't do that Suddy!"

His voice was full of broken tones that hurt her ears in a dreadful way. How could she deny him what he thought he must do? How could she say: "Don't go off an' git yourself murdered like our boy, Efrim!"

"I'll go git your supper ready," she said.

He watched until she went into the house, until everything around him was silent and still. Then, he marched out to where the tin cans lay scattered, picked up several, which he sat upright on rocks and along the ground, and marched off twenty good long paces.

He drew out the Schofield and held it with both hands, trying hard to steady it against his irritation with what Suddy had said about him and Monroe Hawks and the whole business of what lay ahead of him.

She was right! Damned if she wasn't. But, it didn't really matter this time.

BANG! The can just set there.

BANG! The bottle didn't move a whit.

BANG! The ground kicked up two feet beyond anything.

The sound of pistol shot rolled off toward the blue mountains and disappeared in a sea of sky, only to be followed by another and another.

Then, every once in awhile, one of the tin cans went flying or a green bottle shattered into a shower of glass, and when that happened, Nate Love felt an old certainty creep into the back of his mind. But it didn't happen often enough; he knew that.

He knew, too, that tin cans and liniment bottles didn't shoot back.

BANG! BANG! BANG!

He'd hit one out of six and was reloading when someone said: "Well, I've seen lots of sorry sights in my time, but I never figured I'd see the fellow that shot Roy Thourgood and Slim Miller so quick they both died at the same time standing out here busting cans with his shooter and raising hogs!"

Nate pulled his head around to see who it was, even though he already knew.

CHAPTER FOURTEEN

Foreman Ray Teal knocked hard on one of the doors of the big house. He stood and waited, then knocked hard again. It wasn't just a single door he stood before, it was two doors of heavy oak with leaded glass panels and brass knobs. Expensive. Like everything else J.D. LeFlors owned. There was also a bell ringer that could be pulled, but Ray ignored it. J.D. enjoyed telling everyone who cared to listen how he had sent to Omaha for the doors, and Ray remembered that they had arrived during a snowstorm and he and Jimmy Jake had taken a wagon down to the stage depot to pick them up. They were some of the heaviest doors he had ever carried. Fancy and expensive and heavy — he wasn't going to indulge J.D.'s wealth by pulling his bell ringer.

Finally, it was answered by Minnie Bluefeather, a plump Mandan woman who kept house and made meals for J.D. and his wife. Where J.D. ever found the woman to begin with was a mystery to everyone. He simply came home one day from Bozeman and she was sitting there on the wagon next to him. She spoke English as well as most of the cowboys and better than most Mexicans he knew. J.D. raved about her biscuits and the way she could cook a rabbit and that she was neat as a pin when it came to cleaning and washing clothes. One day Ray had spotted her through an open window spitting water on a shirt of his and then running a hot iron over it. It gave Ray a small amount of satisfaction to know that Minnie Bluefeather took such liberties with J.D.'s dress shirts. And for that reason alone, he sort of liked her more than he did most Indians and most woman.

"She keeps everything bright as a new penny," J.D. was fond of saying. "And you never saw a better hand at caring for a man's shirt."

Ray stood before her, his long face framed under great shaggy brows and long iron gray moustaches. His hat was dusty and sweat-stained and so were his clothes, and Minnie Bluefeather stood there looking at him like he was a dirty sock placed before her nose. Ray suspected strongly that before she had grown plump Minnie must have been an attractive woman but that most of her attractiveness had got lost under her plumpness. He was always unsure how to be around her.

"Need to see Mr. LeFlors, Minnie," he said. His words were so slanted and weighted under his Texas drawl that she could hardly understand a thing he ever said. Such a way of talking was strange sounding to her ears. But she understood the name of her employer and she knew that Mr. Teal did not come to the house except when he needed to see Mr. LeFlors. She stepped back enough for him to enter, making sure that he removed his hat by shifting her gaze to where it rested on his head.

"You wait," she said. Teal's mossy gaze fell upon the swell of Minnie's wide hips as she left to get Mr. LeFlors. He didn't know much about women. He found them to be more tricky to understand than a horse or any other sort of creature. He'd known a few in his time and was even married once to one for just a short period, but he'd never felt all that comfortable with a woman, not even the one he had married. Still, it did not prevent him from looking whenever the opportunity presented itself. Looking at women was something that he privately enjoyed.

He waited in the cool confines of the big adobe ranch house; he'd never gone beyond the foyer, had never been asked and had never made the request. He stood on smooth tile that J.D. said he had sent to Mexico for. Ray didn't know why a man would send all the way to Mexico for something to put down on his floor.

Far off to the rear of the house, he could hear the muted voices of Minnie Bluefeather and J.D. LeFlors speaking to one another; he stood there turning his hat in both hands.

There were footfalls on the tiled floor, the clomp of bootheels.

"Ray?" Teal nodded his presence.

"What brings you?" LeFlors sniffled and brought a handkerchief to his face; he had a cold.

"Jode Pierce was shot last night, he's nearly dead," Ray Teal said.

He saw LeFlors stiffen when he announced the news.

"Jode Pierce? That boy that goes about reading his Bible all the time?"

"Yes sir, that's the one."

"I don't understand."

"He was shot from ambush last night. Shot whilst riding along the road from Bozeman. Him and some of the other boys was coming home from town."

"Why would anyone shoot a boy like Jodc? The boy's as mild as milk; he couldn't have an enemy in the world."

Teal hunched his shoulders at the question. He told J.D. he didn't know.

"We thought maybe he'd pass before now," Ray said. "Hole clean through him, come out his guts. It was sometime early this morning when the boys brought him in. I had Old Pete put a poultice on the wound and we all sat up with him thinking every breath was going to be his last. Jimmy Jake read the Bible to him on and off, thinking that might comfort him. It didn't seem to do much one way or the other." The truth was, Ray had never seen a man shot as badly as Jode Pierce and stay alive so long afterward.

J.D. looked down at his open hands that hung by his side.

"I don't understand," he repeated.

"The boys thought maybe you'd come have a look at him, maybe say a few words before the end comes."

"Sure, sure." J.D. took his hat down off a peg by the door and followed Ray across the compound to where the bunk-houses were. It was a warm sunny day, but off to the north it looked cloudy.

"He's in here," Ray said, and they went inside one of the bunkhouses. There in the sunlight streaming through one of the windows, in a square shaft of light where motes of dust danced like fireflies, J.D. could see a circle of his cowboys gathered round one of the bunks.

They parted for him to approach. Some stood, others leaned back along one wall.

Teal said to Jimmy Jake: "Let Mr. LeFlors have your seat, son." And Jimmy Jake moved aside and stood along one wall with several of the others.

There was a pan of bloody water by the bed and a pile of bloody rags piled up on the floor. An old busted down cowboy everyone called Old Pete sat near the fevered head of Jode Pierce. Old Pete was glad to be the outfit's doctor and horse nurse. He knew more about fixing up sick horses than he did about people, but he figured one wasn't all that different from the other. Now gunshot wounds were a different matter altogether.

"I did what I could for him," he told J.D. as he sat down next to the wounded boy. "There's only so much I could do. He's in the Almighty's hands now."

A thin stream of crimson phlegm leaked from one corner of Jode's thin bloodless lips; the eyes partway open looked as though they were seeing something nobody else in the room was able to see. Louis Butterfield figured maybe Jode was seeing angels or the

Almighty himself. Louis firmly believed that a dying man was able to see into the spirit world.

"What's keeping him alive?" J.D. asked Old Pete.

"Nothing," the cowboy said.

J.D. laid the tips of his fingers upon the boy's cold forehead only to withdrew them as quickly as though he had touched something hot. Slowly he stood and looked at the faces of the others. Not knowing what he should say, he returned his attention to Old Pete.

"See that he gets a proper burial when the time comes. Jimmy Jake, I need to talk with you outside."

Jimmy Jake followed J.D. outside the bunkhouse, where they stood in the warm cleanness of the outside air.

Jimmy Jake had damp eyes.

"Did that boy have family?" J.D asked. "I know you two were close."

Jimmy nodded his head.

"I think he had a mother in Pittsburgh and two sisters there as well."

"Well, see that you go through his personals once he's passed, and if you can find me an address, I will write to them and tell them the news."

Jimmy Jake swallowed hard and fought off the tears that were burning his eyes. But before he could say anything, Louis Butterfield came outside and said that Jode had just died.

"Did any of you boys get a look at the man who shot him?" J.D. asked. It was a hopeless question.

Jimmy Jake wiped his eyes and said: "There has been an awful lot of killing around this valley lately, but I don't see why anyone would murder poor Jode. He was as kind a fella as any there ever was. Whoever did this sure is a no-good son of a bitch!"

J.D. LeFlors could think of only one man who fit that description, and the thought troubled him.

He had not seen John Henry Crow for almost two weeks. He did not know where the man was staying but suspected somewhere up on the ridges, where a man could hide himself if he kept moving around. He instinctively looked off toward the blue mountains and the low lying tree-covered hills preceding them.

The cowboys filed slowly out of the bunkhouse. Some went to get spades in order to dig a grave in the cemetery that lay a mile from the main house.

"What ya' plannin' on doin' about poor Jode, Mr. LeFlors?"

It was a question he had not prepared for but was already thinking about. He saw Ray Teal file out behind the young cowboys and called to him.

"Ray, I need to speak to you in private."

Ray had come up from Texas in the year after the big drives ended into Kansas. He had ramrodded a thousand head of cattle all the way from the Brazos and lost less than two hundred along the way.

Ray had always been a private man, but his son, Homer, one of the young hands, had openly spoken of his daddy's days as a lawman in Tascosa and how he had at one time done some bounty hunting and a few other things in that way. Who could say for sure what was a young boy's truth? But J.D. LeFlors never doubted for a minute that his foreman was a man with some dark history in his past.

They walked a little way off toward the corrals before J.D. spoke what was on his mind.

"I need to ask you to do something for me, Ray. Something outside what I hired you for."

Teal hitched a foot up on the lower rail of the corral and let his gaze fall upon the little herd of half-broke mustangs he had rounded up over the winter and spring. He took special pride in them.

"I'm listening."

"I think I know the man that murdered Jode Pierce."

Ray did not take his eyes from the wild, muscled horses, his gaze shifting with their every movement.

"I can't prove it," J.D. said. "I can't say a hundred percent that I know who it was, but I believe it's the man I hired — the stock detective."

Ray could feel it coming like a locomotive downhill.

"I never told anyone outright I'd hired a man. I figured it was my business how I took care of things. It was my cattle being stole, you know that!"

"Yes sir."

"His name is Crow, John Henry Crow."

Ray knew the name. Anyone who knew anything knew the name. And it pinched something inside his head to hear it mentioned.

"Something had to be done!" J.D. declared, his voice rising against his will. "Goddamn if a man can just stand around and watch his cattle get stolen!"

Ray fixed his stare on a small black mare clear on the other side of the corral, looking out at the vast landscape as though she missed it. He had caught her and some others by running them up a box canyon; now he was sorry he had.

"You've been a good hand to me, Ray, ever since you come up from Texas. You're not always going to be a hand, Ray. Sooner or later, you're going to want your own piece of ground and something to go on it. Maybe that south section down by Yellow Hat Creek. A place like that would be a good place for a man to live out his years, a good place to have a few wild horses and some cattle."

"You offerin' me that section of land, Mr. LeFlors?"

"Could be that I am."

Still, he watched the little mare, saw the way her velvet ears flicked at the distant sounds that only she could hear. Ray turned his head just enough to stare into the desperate eyes of J.D. LeFlors.

"What'd make you want to give me a piece of land like that?"

"Not give, Ray. There'd be a price you'd have to pay for it."

"You mean Crow?"

"I figured there was anyone who could take care of this business, it'd be you, Ray."

"What'd cause you to figure that, Mr. LeFlors?"

"It's not important. Let's just say I know a good man when I see one. I know a man that doesn't want to be a hired hand all his life when I see one. I know a man that wants something more than to have to draw wages from another man all his days. I know it in you Ray, I can see it in your eyes; you want the same freedom that little wild mare over there wants. Freedom means having something of your own and not depending on others. I'm offering you that, Ray."

"It's a lot to be asking a man, Mr. LeFlors, for me to go find that man and kill him."

"It's got to be done, Ray. I don't see no way around it. I could see another way, I would. I don't."

Ray was thinking that it was good grass and water, that section down along Yellow Hat Creek. He was thinking that a man could do well to own a piece of ground such as that. What other chance would he ever have to own something of his own? He was nearly fifty. If a man doesn't own anything by the time he gets to be fifty, it isn't likely he ever will. He thought of Old Pete — stove up cowboy reduced to rubbing liniment on horses and men and sweeping out the bunkhouses, barely hanging on to his pride, and someday he wouldn't even be able to do that and where would he be then?

All his life he had been someone's hired hand, just like Old Pete. Only he had been luckier than Old Pete so far.

"Crow's got a reputation as a man killer," he said.

"I reckon anyone is vulnerable if caught by surprise," J.D. said.

"It might could take awhile to find him and kill him," Ray said. The thought of owning that section of land along Yellow Hat Creek was growing on him.

"Of course. All the time you need. I'll get Jimmy Jake to handle things while you're gone. He needs the experience anyway. And once you've finished this business, I reckon you'll want to move on down to that south section anyway. I'll offer Jimmy your job as ramrod. You'll be a retired man."

They struck their bargain with a handshake.

The next morning, Ray Teal rose two hours before daybreak, gathered up his saddle and Winchester rifle, and went to the corrals. He tossed a wide loop of his rope over a buckskin gelding, a big, deep-chested animal built for the mountains and climbing. Then he selected a mule to pack with.

He fitted the description of the stock detective in his mind, the one J.D. LeFlors had given him: dark-eyed man with pale skin, rides a gray horse, "you'll know him when you see him."

Judith Valley was a big place to hide in, and there was no particular place to start hunting such a man. Ray figured he would just have to roam through the hills and across the ranges hoping to come across a dark-eyed man with pale skin.

He had hunted men before. Mostly it was just a matter of time, a matter of patience — sorting out all the ones who looked like they belonged and finding the ones who didn't.

The saddle creaked in the chill predawn air as he lifted himself into it. The lights in the bunkhouse windows were just now being lighted, soft yellow light that announced the hands were sitting up on the sides of their bunks, pulling on their boots and getting ready for another day of ranch work.

His own boy, Homer, was in there among them. Ray thought of the woman who had given birth to the boy and could barely remember anything about her, except that her name was Elmira Thigg. Life and time and the matters it presented a man seemed to have slipped away from him without his willing it.

He reined the buckskin's head around and headed toward Yellow Hat Creek. He figured it was just as good a place to start as any. And why not see that section one more time, only this time with the eye of an owner.

It's your time, Ray. It's your time to see that something good happens.

He rode off down the valley, thinking it was time something good happened.

CHAPTER FIFTEEN

How many days had passed? She seemed to be losing track of the days. Every day seemed like the one before; the numbness had not worn off. Every day she walked that stretch of land between the house and the far side of the meadow to where the grave was, her feet sweeping through the wildflowers, the hum of bees low in the grasses.

She asked herself why she stayed. The answer always was: where else was there for her to go? No answer, but a question. All of life for her seemed now full of questions.

She tried to sleep at nights but couldn't because she slept too much during the days. Cowboys from nearby ranches brought her their laundry, whether out of sympathy or need she did not know. But thank God they did, for the money helped to keep food on the table and grain for the shaggy horses.

With great effort, she made a trip to Bozeman, the first since Billy's death, and purchased flour and bacon and some salt and sugar. She also purchased a bottle of whiskey.

The whiskey didn't last long, not nearly long enough. But while it had, it dulled her senses and kept her mind from remaining too much on the lonely little grave out beyond the meadow.

It rained for three days straight, then the sun came out and everything looked fresh and green. It brought tears to her eyes to see how fresh and green everything looked. It brought a great emptiness, too. Like there was a hole in her heart and everything just keep leaking out — all her feelings and all her love and all her tenderness.

John Henry Crow returned on the twenty-first day, exactly three weeks to the day since he had last visited. She had nearly forgotten his name but not his face, not who he was.

He brought a sack of apples and held them out to her.

"I bought these from a man on the other side of the valley," he said. She could not remember when she had last eaten a fresh apple. It seemed a small delight, the sack of apples.

"Would you like coffee?" she asked.

"Yes," he said and offered her a dry smile. She thought him not a man accustomed to smiling, for it seemed an effort.

"It's all I can offer you," she said.

"Are you sure?" The question was strange and made her feel cautious toward him.

She did not know what she should think of his question.

He carried a small table out into the yard, and they sat there on chairs and drank coffee and watched three angry blue jays chase each other through the tops of some nearby pines.

"Have you found a place to purchase?" she asked.

At first, he seemed not to understand her question. He had nearly forgotten the lie he had told her about how he was in the territory to buy a ranch.

"No, not yet," he said. "But I have seen several that hold promise."

She went in the house and returned with more coffee. He seemed never to take his eyes from her. More reason, she thought, to feel cautious around him.

"Do you live here alone?" he asked.

She was reluctant to say. He smiled, assured her that he was not eager to pry into her privacy, assured her that his questions were merely for conversation's sake, innocent inquires.

"My son . . ." she began. "My son was murdered not long ago." She could not remember exactly the number of days. She wanted to say twenty-one.

"How?" he asked. "How was your son murdered?"

She looked as far into his eyes as their darkness would allow and could find nothing to tell her why he was asking such questions.

"He was shot and killed," she said, all the while watching carefully for some sign that would indicate the reason for his interest. There appeared none.

"Well, that is a terrible thing to happen," he said. She felt the wave of emotion lift itself up through her. But something within appealed to her not to cry in front of this man. He did not seem to her the type of man a woman should cry in front of.

His gaze did not give way, and he stared at her over the rim of his china cup until she lowered her own gaze.

"Yes, Mr. Crow. It was a terrible thing to happen."

"I'm sure it was. Do you enjoy riding?" he asked.

The question had been entirely unexpected, as were most things about him. Even the sound of his voice surprised her; it was a soft, delicate voice but without much emotion.

She shook her head slightly, the light of mid-day dancing through her russet hair.

"Why do you ask?" she said.

"It appears a wonderful day for a ride. There's a lovely spot not far from here by a copse of trees where a stream runs through. I discovered it when last I was here. Would you like to go for a ride with me?"

The answer caught in her throat.

"I hardly know you, Mr. Crow."

"Exactly," he said, then held up one finger, touching it to his lips. "There is secret joy in not knowing everything one will do. How long has it been since you've ridden a horse for the pure pleasure of it? How long has it been since you've known even one full moment of joy? I look at you, Mrs. Sloan, and I see a woman who has not known the small pleasures of life. Forgive me, but what do you have to lose?"

The wind touched delicately along her arms. His words and questions were like small knocks upon a door that she was standing behind. Should she open it?

"You are an unusual man, Mr. Crow."

He smiled.

"So I've been told. Will you ride with me?"

Maybe it was the sheer loneliness of having no man for so long a time. Maybe it was her need to escape the great sorrow that had tried to swallow her up since Billy's death. Whatever it was, she found herself saying, "Yes."

She changed into riding britches while he saddled one of the shaggy horses, then led it out and waited for her to come from the house.

"Do you need a hand up?" he said.

They rode at a walk through the tall grasses that the wind moved in undulating waves, and she found herself enjoying the ride. The shaggy horse seemed to enjoy it, too.

When they arrived at the copse of cottonwoods, he offered to help her down. She dismounted without his aid, and he suggested that they sit on a fallen log close by where the water trickled over a bed of polished stones. Frogs croaked unseen but stopped when they approached, then started up again.

"This is a good place," he said.

"I know. My son and I used to come here when he was young. It was one of his favorite places."

They sat there for a long time without speaking, listening to the wind flow through the trees. He, holding the reins of his horse, tapped the loose ends of them lightly upon his leg and craned his neck to the sky, where large clouds drifted.

"When I was a boy," he said, "I used to lay on my back on days like this and see what things the clouds made."

She had done the same as a girl, and so had Billy.

"Every child that's ever lived surely has done the same," she said.

"Do you really think so?" His look was quizzical.

"Yes. I do," she said.

It seemed to please him that she thought so.

Then he asked her to hold the reins of his horse, and when she took hold of them, he threw himself upon the grass, upon his back, and spread his arms wide and stared upward into the sky.

What he saw in the ethereal shapes of the clouds were the bodies of dead boys, but he lied and said: "I see the head of a lion, and over there is a sailing ship."

She did not know quite what to think of him.

"Do you want to try?" he said.

"Lay in the grass and look up at clouds?" she asked.

"Yes."

"No. I think I should be getting back."

"I'm an educated man," he said. It was yet another example of how quickly he could change subjects. She found it disquieting.

"I studied both law and medicine back east. Harvard," he said. "I could have practiced either profession."

She truly did not know what to make of him.

"Why didn't you?" she asked.

"They were the professions of my father and his father. I thought I would like to do something different."

She instinctively knew that he wanted her to ask him about himself, to ask him what it was exactly that he had chosen to become. But when she did not, he turned himself over on his elbows and settled that dark dark gaze upon her once more.

"For me," he said. "There was only one true attraction: the West."

"I must be getting back," she said. He feigned disappointment.

"Why?" he said. "What do you have to get back for?"

The truth was she had too much enjoyed the ride; her sense of guilt at finding herself enjoying anything so soon after Billy's death left her nearly shaking. She had trouble mounting the shaggy horse. John Henry Crow helped her.

"Then getting back is what we shall do," he said.

The return ride did not seem to her so joyful; her mind was filled with the tragedy of twenty-one days before.

A small herd of pronghorn antelope leaped from the brush ahead of them and zig-zagged their way over a ridge, and a little farther on, several grouse exploded from the grass, their wings beating the air as they disappeared.

"It seems like everything here is sudden," he said.

"Yes, sudden," she said.

There was still plenty of day left when they returned to her cabin. He took the shaggy horse and removed its saddle and bridle before turning it out into the corral. She watched him from the porch, not at all sure what to make of him.

"Well, I must go," he said.

"I could fix an early supper," she said.

He looked around at the small spare holdings and said: "You don't need to trouble yourself."

It was a strange offering, something she had not intended.

"In payment for the apples," she said.

He took a moment to look off into the surrounding distance. She could not help but feel that he was expecting someone to be out there.

"Well, perhaps a light supper would be just the thing," he said.

"Put your horse up, then. It'll be ready soon."

There was little to offer. She made clabber biscuits, fried slices of thick bacon in a black iron skillet, and pulled a few onions from the little square of garden along the cabin.

All the while, she noticed, he kept his attention on the distance as though watching for something, or someone. As though expecting someone. Unlike before, when he would not, or could not, take his eyes from her.

They ate in the yard, where he had earlier carried the table out from inside the cabin. He ate with deliberation. She noticed again, as he ate, the fine smooth hands, the long delicate fingers. He was no rancher; of that, she was certain. He paused now and again to sip from his coffee.

His hat hung on the back of the chair, his ashen hair hung in long locks nearly to his shoulders. She noticed the ridge of his jawbone, the thin unbroken line of his nose, the smooth wide brow. She wondered if this almost delicate man with the soft voice and smooth hands had it in him to murder boys, to murder her boy?

"Are you married, Mr. Crow?" She decided to try and find out, if she could. He looked up, the dark liquid eyes filled with mild surprise and the late glossy light of ending afternoon.

The first traces of a faint smile curved the edges of his mouth.

"No."

"Then you have no children?"

Holding his fork in mid-air, he lowered it and said: "No. I have no children, Mrs. Sloan."

"And do I remember you saying that you were from Nebraska?"

Placing both hands upon the table, he said: "Why the interest?"

"Well, we have gone for a ride together and now are sharing a meal. I feel as if I should know you better."

"Yes, I did say I was from Nebraska, among other places."

"And you are here seeking to buy a ranch?"

"Yes. I did say that, too."

"I couldn't help but notice your hands, Mr. Crow. May I say, they don't look like hands that have known the work of a rancher."

He looked down at his hands and laughed aloud: "You are quite observant, Mrs. Sloan. And it is true about my hands. But you see, I pay other men to perform the labor necessary. Me, I just enjoy the fruits of such endeavors. The true West, you know. What could be more Western than owning a cattle ranch?"

"It's too bad you couldn't have met him," she said.
"Who?" he asked.
"My boy, Billy."
His gaze did not waver, he showed no sign. She did not know whether to be relieved or disappointed. It had crossed her mind that if he displayed the wrong behavior she would excuse herself, go into the cabin, retrieve the old breechloader rifle left to her by her late husband, return to the yard with it, and murder him. The thought caused her hands to twitch.
"I'm sure your son was a fine boy," he said. "May I have more of your coffee?"
"He's buried out there, beyond the meadow," she said.
A soft, almost imperceptible shifting of his eyes, then he said: "It seems a pleasant spot."
He felt the low throb begin in his temples, the arching ache just behind the eyes. He touched two fingers to the side of his head. Why was she so insistent about talking of dead boys?
"Are you alright, Mr. Crow?"
He thought of the mute boy, Joshua. The throbbing grew steadily.
"I must go," he said.
His eyes closed momentarily. He must go and feel the near presence of the boy, must tell him of his meal with Mrs. Sloan and of the ride and of lying on his back and staring at the clouds. Joshua would enjoy hearing about such things, he was sure of that.
His eyes snapped open, and he saw her staring intently at him.

"Mr. Crow? Are you sure you're alright?"

He felt sick and dizzy from the torture in his head.

"Yes . . . yes."

She watched his halting step as he stood, walked to the corral where he had tied his gray horse, and mounted. She was sure that he would fall from the saddle before he rode a hundred yards, but he did not.

Afterward, she lay upon her bed in the waning light and listened to the great silence. Even the wind had died. It was as if all the strength had been borne from her with John Henry Crow's departure, and now she was too tired to think, to fear, to consider the meaning of his presence.

As he rode away from the cabin, these thoughts clouded his mind: *Why have you gone to the woman, John Henry? What can she change in you? Have you forgotten the mute boy upon the ridge? Eli McGregg was the first!*

And the gray horse bore him away.

CHAPTER SIXTEEN

When he looked around and saw Monroe Hawks sitting his horse, Nate Love was greatly surprised at just how old the man looked. Monroe smiled, nonetheless, and said: "Nate, you've lost your hair."

Straightening as far as he could, Nate said: "And all yours has turned white."

Monroe introduced Junius Bean.

"Reporter for the Denver paper," Monroe announced. "Wants to write stories about me, and maybe you, too."

Junius wondered, looking at the two of them, just how it was possible that men of such reputation had lived as long as they had. They looked for all the world a pair of old plug horses that didn't have much left in them. And yet, when he looked into their eyes, he felt a coldness pass through him; they were still dangerous men, the both of them.

"Mr. Love," Junius said, extending a hand. Nate took it, felt its softness, and released it.

Monroe stared out toward the pile of tin cans and busted glass, then down at the Schofield Nate was holding in his right hand.

"Ain't that the gun you shot Roy Thourgood and Slim Miller with down in the Nations?"

Nate looked down at the pistol.

"I believe it is."

"Well, it's good to see you keep in practice," Monroe said.

"I wasn't sure you'd come," Nate said. "I wasn't even sure you'd still be alive."

"Well, as you can clearly see, I am." The two of them allowed their gazes to rest on one another for a time, a flood of old memories filling their brains. Each was somewhat saddened by what time had done to the other.

"Might as well come on up to the house, you look like you could stand a good meal," Nate said at last.

"Maybe we ought to ride on into Bozeman and eat there," Monroe said. "I recall, your missus never was one glad to see the likes of me." Monroe had always found Suddy to be polite but distant whenever he was in her company. Why she was, he didn't exactly know, other than that women could be that way; they could turn a cold shoulder to you and not even know you. His own wife had been a little that way. Cold as an iced fish when she wanted to be.

"No, you'll eat here," Nate said. "Mr. Bean and you come on to the house."

She saw them coming back from beyond the house, where Nate had gone to kill cans. She had noticed when the shooting had stopped and had looked out the window and seen two men sitting on horses talking to Nate. One of them was Monroe Hawks. She didn't care to guess who the other was. Probably some killer he had brought along. Monroe was fond of hanging out with bloodletters and buscaderos.

Seeing Monroe Hawks again was worse than seeing a haint. It sent cold chills down her back and made her eyes flutter. He was old and bony. But it was him alright. Those cold eyes hadn't changed a bit — cold killer eyes.

She waited till they reached the front of the house before showing herself in the doorway. Monroe was surprised that she hadn't changed in looks all that much, except that she had grown large. But she looked about the same otherwise. He wondered how she had stayed nearly the same when Nate had declined so.

"Miz Love," Monroe said, shifting all of his weight in the saddle while she rested her gaze on him. He could see no joy in her face for his having come. He hadn't expected any.

"Mistuh Hawks," she said, sliding her gaze from Monroe to the squat man riding alongside him. Seeing him up close, she was relieved to see that he was no killer, or if he was, he was a mighty timid-looking one. Of course, killers came in all sizes and shapes and forms of dress. But what she saw sitting alongside of Monroe Hawks was no killer — even a blind woman could see that.

"This is Junius Bean," Monroe said. "Met him on the train to Denver. He writes for a newspaper." She nearly sighed from relief.

Junius touched his fingers to the brim of his bowler. "Ma'am."

"Suddy, these men have come a long way. I reckon they could stand to eat something," Nate said.

Suddy shifted her gaze from Junius Bean to her husband. Nate was still her man, still the man of the family, and she never would openly disobey him or show him disrespect. But it didn't keep her from giving Monroe Hawks another look before retreating to the kitchen of her cabin.

Monroe saw the look and scratched his beard.

"She wasn't expecting you," was all Nate said.

"I reckon not," Monroe said.

Nate worked the pump handle up and down, the mechanism groaning from dryness, and filled up a pan of fresh water for the two men to wash their hands and faces. Monroe shuddered at its coldness, then dried his hands and face and rolled himself a cigarette before strolling over to the pig pen.

"Hogs," he said after staring in on the Durocs and Chester Whites. Junius seemed fascinated by the size of some of the boars.

"They look well fed," he commented.

"I never figured you for raising hogs," Monroe said. "Somehow, it's something that I'd never have guessed of you." It wasn't a criticism on Monroe's part; it was merely surprise.

"It beats the hell out of picking cotton," Nate said with a slight show of teeth.

"I ain't so sure I'd rather pick cotton," Monroe said.

"When did you ever pick cotton enough to know what it'd be like?" Nate asked.

"A long time back in Mississippi. You ever heard of share-cropping?"

"Heard of it all my young life."

"Well my daddy and yours was probably the same when it came to being in the poor business. About the only difference was the color."

"Never knowed that about you, Monroe. All the years I knowed you, I never knowed that about you."

"I ain't one to tell ever'thing there is," Monroe said. "Some things ain't necessary. Where you got your boy buried at?"

"Up yonder," Nate said, pointing to the little rise beyond the rear of the cabin.

"Let's walk up there."

They did. Junius trailed along behind them, respectful of the common bond between the men ahead of him. He had considered staying close to the cabin, where the smells of fried pork were already coming from the kitchen. But then he saw Suddy's dark face stare out the window at him and he decided it was best he stuck with the men.

Wind swept down in a low rush from the blue mountains and tugged at their clothes.

"Planning on going to Oglalla soon's there's enough money to buy a carved headstone," Nate said almost apologetically. "Meantime, that's going to have to do." He pointed at the pine slab he had burned Efrim's name into and placed in the ground.

"Suddy wants a pair of angels carved into the headstone when we buy it," he said. "Wants an inscription, too. Something from Psalms."

The truth was Monroe Hawks had never met the boy lying beneath the grassy sod; he hadn't even known Nate to have a boy so young until the letter had arrived.

"You reckon you know who did it?" Monroe asked.

"Don't know the man's name," Nate said. "Except that he's more'n likely one of the stock detectives the big ranchers have brought in."

"Well, that ought to narrow it down to a few dozen men."

"There's something more," Nate said. "I believe the same fellow killed a squatter over on Yellow Hat Creek. His people said the man that done the killing had pale skin and rode a gray horse."

"Teddy Blue used to have pale skin and ride a gray horse. You reckon it could be him?" Monroe asked.

"Teddy Blue froze to death in the Chisos Mountains several winters ago," Nate said. It came as a shock to Monroe. Teddy Blue had once been a deputy U.S. marshal with him and Nate under Judge Parker's court out of Fort Smith. He had been a good man and a good friend until he found out robbing banks was a good deal more profitable than collecting a federal paycheck, and a good deal less arduous than tracking down lawbreakers. But just because Teddy Blue had become a bank robber didn't keep Monroe from liking the man, and it came as a shock to him now to hear he had frozen to death in the Chisos. It was a rare thing to hear about a man freezing to death as far south as the Chisos Mountains.

"Well, Teddy Blue is the only man I ever knowed that had pale skin and rode a gray horse," Monroe said, recovering from the news.

"I don't know who it is," Nate said. "But I think maybe I know who it was who hired him — a rancher name of J.D. LeFlors."

"Well then, that's the place to start looking for this fellow."

"Efrim was just one of them," Nate said. "He was just one of the boys murdered. He was with another boy name of Billy Sloan. A widow's boy. I reckon she's worse off than me over this thing. Least I've got Suddy."

"I've known stock detectives before," Monroe said, tugging his hat tighter against the growing wind. "They're mostly just gunhands, killers. Ain't never met a one that was worth a damn cent! I'd rather eat my supper with a bounty hunter than be in the same hotel as a damn stock detective."

Suddy saw from her kitchen window the three of them standing on the rise, the wind worrying at their coats. She saw too, how Nate and Monroe Hawks stood there talking to one another just like she had seen it a hundred times before back in Fort Smith, men talking among themselves in a private way like they were talking about the cost of land or the price of a good horse. Only they weren't talking about either. They were talking about more killing, talking about it like they used to in the old times.

She turned her gaze from the window and blinked back the tears that had been growing in her eyes ever since Nate had told her that he had sent for Monroe Hawks.

They ate their meal with little conversation. The air was thick with Suddy's regret at having to keep the company of a man that would most likely bring her more heartache. Junius tried being cheerful by engaging them all in discussions. They just looked at him like he was wearing centipedes in his hair.

Afterward, the men stepped out into the evening air, and Monroe smoked a cigarette. Junius offered to share his flask of whiskey with them, but only Monroe took up his offer.

The scent of the hogs drifted up to them, then the wind shifted and they could smell pine and Junius said, "Thank goodness for a west wind."

"It don't take a professor to see that Suddy's none too happy to have me here, Nate," Monroe said after a while of smoking and sipping from Junius's silver flask. He considered it too delicate to sip whiskey from a flask but had no choice since it was the only whiskey being offered. He had remembered Nate as being a teetotaller for the most part, although on special occasions, he had seen Nate drink with the best of them. He remembered the time they had chased Madam Cherry and Albert Fly into the Nations and Nate had nearly died of the chilblains and he'd had to feed Nate his Indian-bought whiskey just to keep him alive.

"She knows how you can be," Nate said. "She knows how you can be in a fight and she remembers all the old times when me and you rode out for Judge Parker. And she remembers all the killing we did together."

"I never backed away from a fight," Monroe said, his voice a little stiff. "A man ought not be held in low light because of that."

"She ain't faulting you, Monroe. She's faulting me for having sent for you."

"She figures bad is bound to come from it," Monroe said.

"Most likely."

"I guess she didn't ever understand the business of men," Monroe said. "Most women don't, or can't."

Junius found himself intrigued by such talk. The mere fact that he was privy to the musings of such men as Monroe Hawks and Nate Love was in itself a fairly fantastic thing to him.

"Suddy's filled with grief and loss, Monroe. All she can think about is what she's lost and what she might lose. Can't blame her for that," Nate said.

In the far distance, they could see a small herd of elk drift down from the treeline on the slope of a nearby hill to graze in the twilight, the edges of light now violet, the trees and mountains now jagged and black.

From far far off, a single gunshot. Both men traded looks but did not comment on it.

"I promised the other boy's mother we'd see justice done," Nate said.

"Well, that's why I've come," Monroe said. He was developing a sore tooth, the same tooth he should have had taken out a year ago. He reached for another sip of Junius's whiskey.

"You and Mr. Bean can bunk in Efrim's room," Nate said.

"You go on ahead," Monroe told them. "I'd just as soon stay out here awhile and have another cigarette. We'll plan leaving first thing in the morning if that suits you, Nate?" Nate wasn't sure that it did suit him, but he'd sent for Monroe, and now that Monroe had come, there was no turning back or rethinking the situation. They both knew what they were going to do.

Junius was grateful for the offer of a bed, a real bed and not a prairie bed.

"You might leave that little flask, you don't mind," Monroe said to the reporter. Junius held it forth and Monroe thanked him. All three said goodnight.

He rolled himself a cigarette and smoked it and sipped some of the whiskey and watched the night come on black and full, creating a great darkness that gave him the feeling that he was the only living soul left on earth.

It was there in that moment that her memory came to mind: *Cora McDuffy*. Ever since Harry Walker had thrown it up to him in front of the reporter, he had had a difficult time shaking the tragedy of her memory.

He wondered why he was thinking of her now, except for the fact that it was dark and lonely and quiet, the way it had been that night he had killed her.

She had been a townswoman. He had hardly known her or her husband or any of her children. He could not even remember if it was Abilene or Hays. Maybe it was Hays.

There had been a disturbance in one of the saloons; there was always a disturbance in one of the saloons when the cowboys were in town. Harry Walker, his deputy, had come pounding on the door announcing there was trouble down the street. Monroe had left the comfort of a warm bed, a bed he had not been alone in, and dressed hastily, taking up one of his pistols.

Harry Walker had kept talking in his ear as they'd hurried down the street about how the cowboys were drunk and threatening to kill one another, how there had been a woman involved, a prostitute. Harry's breath had been hot with whiskey.

"Going to be a killing, Monroe! Sure as hell them cowboys are going to kill each other!" Harry had kept saying.

He hadn't known where the woman had come from or what she had been doing out so late in the night.

The disturbance had spilled out onto the street. Cowboys, several of them, had tumbled out of the saloon, cussing loudly. He'd seen, in the faded light coming through the doors of the saloon, that all were armed and some had already pulled their pistols out and were waving them around.

The woman had been somewhere nearby, only he hadn't known it. She had been as caught up in the disturbance as he had, there in the dark, among the shadows.

The cowboys had spilled out onto the street, their number spreading into a widening circle. Harry, half drunk, impetuous, shouting epithets at them.

He'd knocked Harry aside, told him to shut up, to go on home. But it had been too late.

Several of the cowboys had turned at their approach, cussing.

The woman had been trying to cross to the other side of the street when one of the cowboys had fired his pistol with a flash of light. Then, Harry had fired his pistol into them, firing as rapidly as he could: *BANG! BANG! BANG!* And the cowboys' bullets had flown so close they'd ripped through Monroe's shirt, which had been hanging loose because he hadn't taken the time to tuck it inside his pants; the bullets had come so close he could hear them splitting the air around him.

And when he'd returned fire, it was as if the cowboys had parted in unison and he saw the woman being knocked backward into the street, her hands flying upward as she fell.

They'd all seen her fall. And the witness of her falling had been enough to quell their thirst for fighting.

He'd heard Harry say: "You've killed that damn woman, Monroe!"

And later, he'd learned that her name was Cora McDuffy and she had been out so late to buy a remedy for her child's colic from the local physician. The little blue bottle lay by her side unbroken.

It was something he could never undo, an old wound that would never heal.

He shook himself free of the memory, felt the black night enter his lungs, and knew someday he'd be laid in the same sod as Cora McDuffy and Efrim Love and all the others.

It was a thought that brought him no comfort.

CHAPTER SEVENTEEN

Ray Teal crossed Yellow Hat Creek and found a recent grave, not more than a couple of weeks old, he guessed, judging by the way the sod was sunk in. He found a rusty saw blade — it had been broken. He guessed the saw blade and the grave had belonged to squatters. There were signs of old campfires, little circles of blackened ground and fragments of charcoal. Squatters were not uncommon. They had moved on. Maybe it had something to do with the grave.

Well, it didn't mean anything to him, they were gone.

He stood for a time surveying the landscape, the soft rolling grass, the way the sun sparkled off the creek, the way the leaves of the cottonwoods trembled in the wind, the jagged peaks of the far blue mountains.

It would be his, he told himself in silent satisfaction, if he could catch the stock detective and put an end to the killing. J.D. LeFlors had described the man as sickly of skin and morose dark eyes and riding a steel gray horse, a man most dangerous in every respect. Ray had dealt with dangerous men before.

But it hadn't been a dangerous man who had earned him the most money. The most money he had ever gotten for his efforts was three hundred dollars for a man named Junebug Watts, a demented little man who had made the mistake of shooting the only whore in Saltillo, Texas at the time.

Her name was Fannie Smart, and she was the only white whore in a hundred miles, well liked not only for her obvious charms but for her willingness to nurse the sick and be charitable in other ways as well. Her supporters were mostly cowboys and widowers and a few of the more discreet citizens of that hamlet. It was bad enough having to live in a place like Saltillo, they all agreed, where there was little to do most days but listen to the wind blow and drink warm beer and play dominoes. Fannie Smart had been the only true entertainment the town had known, and she could play some songs on the piano and sing as well. Those most offended, which was most of the men in the town if a true and secret count had been taken, collected three hundred dollars among themselves to have her attacker brought to justice. On the surface, three hundred dollars seemed like a lot of money, but as one old widower put it: "What's money if we got nothing worth while to spend it on?"

Junebug Watts had shot Fannie in a most delicate area that had rendered her permanently incapacitated as far as her profession went. It might as well have been a plague of locusts that had visited the little town, as devastating as it was to have the only good whore wounded and put forever out of action.

Ray Teal was the only man with experience in tracking down desperadoes, although Junebug Watts could hardly be classified as a true desperado, having committed nothing more criminal than card-cheating and petty thievery up until the time he'd shot Fannie, which he had not done with intention.

He had actually been paying her a professional visit at the time of the unfortunate accident.

"What's that you got bulging in your pocket there, Junebug?" Fannie had inquired in a teasing manner when Junebug had arrived that day with a new Colt's Lightning he had purchased for ten dollars from a hardware store. He was planning on robbing the Del Rio stage the following Friday afternoon and had purchased the pistol for that purpose. He had grown tired of performing petty crimes that hardly paid enough to get from one day to the next. He figured it was time to move up in the world.

"Why that's my new six-shooter!" he explained with obvious joy. "Do you want to have a look at it, Sweetie?"

"You know I don't like guns in the bedroom, Junebug. Take that thing outside and leave it!" Fannie had declared.

"Well, I just can't leave a good gun like this lying around where somebody might find it and make off with it!" Junebug said. "It cost me ten damn dollars!"

Fannie had insisted that if she was going to conduct any business with Junebug that warm evening, he'd have to leave his pistol outside her bedroom door.

It had been better than a month since Junebug had been able to card-cheat and petty crime enough money for a visit to Fannie, and his need was great; but so was his desire not to lose the pistol.

"Well if you'd just let me show you the dern thing, it ain't nothing to be concerned with." He'd reached in his pocket to take it out and it had caught somehow and he'd dropped it. It had gone off and sent a bullet through Fannie's profit center — or the back portion of it.

Ray had caught Junebug Watts easily down in Juarez and returned him to Saltillo, and collected his three hundred dollar reward money. He hadn't stayed around long enough to find out Junebug's fate.

He squatted on his heels and surveyed the distant surroundings, the ridges and hills. *The son of a bitch has to be out there somewhere, and I'll find him*. Just like he had found Junebug Watts and all the other men he had ever tracked.

Jimmy Jake was the first to announce it to the others. Even Ray's boy, Homer, hadn't known.

"Mr. LeFlors has put me in charge for the time being," he said.

"Where's my old man?" Homer asked.

"Gone to do some business for Mr. LeFlors."

"What sort of business would it be that he wouldn't tell me?" Homer asked.

"Mr. LeFlors didn't say, but I believe he has sent your daddy to find that killer stock detective and take care of him."

Homer's soft mouth parted enough to show his buckteeth.

The others exchanged excited looks.

"Well, if anybody could do it," skinny Calvin Pruitt said, "it'd be Mr. Teal, ain't that right, Homer?"

Homer said, "Sure, sure. My old man's been a bounty hunter. Back in Texas he used to hunt men down for the reward money. He hunted down a man that shot the only whore in Saltillo once."

Louis Butterfield said: "Shit, he better be damn good to find whoever it is shooting everybody to pieces! I mean, he killed Billy Sloan and Efrim Love and poor ol' Jode like they was nothing but jackrabbits. Ain't telling how many of the others he's killed, either!"

Wayne Brazos said, "I believe Mr. Teal can do it." The others looked at him because he usually picked the right side in a fight and was himself a good prizefighter and ought to know about such things.

"Well, I ain't saying it's certain that Mr. Teal's gone off to find that killer," Jimmy Jake said. "But what else would be so important as to send him off so sudden?"

None of them knew.

J.D. LeFlors could see from his window his cowboys standing around in a circle talking, Jimmy Jake announcing his appointment as ramrod. He had no desire to go among them and explain the situation himself. He figured Ray Teal to be gone not more than two weeks. Such business should not take more than two weeks, three at the outside. He had no doubts as to Ray Teal's ability to handle the situation with John Henry Crow.

Crow was a killer, but then so was Ray Teal. And the element of surprise was in his and Ray's favor, for John

Henry would never guess that he had now become the prey and not the predator.

J.D. felt pleased with his decision.

Orna Sloan awoke with the light of morning fractured across her bed. She had been dreaming about Billy and Efrim Love. In the dream the boys had been crying out to her to come help them and she could not, for she was caught and held by some unseeable force — caught, she remembered thinking, possibly in the black branches of trees.

The boys were crying and she could not go to them, could not reach them. Over and over again, the dream had played itself in her head until she awoke in a fit of anguish only to discover that it was morning and that there were no boys to help, that her own boy was buried out beyond the meadow. And the reality of it was as cold and hard as a knife blade.

Ray Teal rode through the valley, stopping at every ranch to ask if a man with sickly skin and a gray horse had passed through lately. No one remembered having seen such a man.

When he rode to the cabin of Orna Sloan, he asked the same question he had asked of everyone: "Have you seen a stranger come this way, a man with sickness in his face and riding a gray horse?"

"Why are you asking?" she wanted to know.

Ray was reluctant to state his business but chose to say: "It is a personal matter."

Should she reveal that she knew such a man? After all, John Henry had proved no danger to her, and the man asking after him was shy about stating his reason for his interest.

"It's important that I locate him," Ray said, seeing that the widow Sloan was not wanting conversation.

She shook her head.

"He might know something about the killing of your boy," Ray said. He saw how that took hold, saw her reach out for the wall and steady herself.

"How would you know that?" she asked.

"Don't know for certain, just that he might."

If there was any chance that John Henry might somehow be involved with Billy's murder, she must speak what she knew.

"His name is John Henry Crow," she said, the words tumbling from her lips. "He has come to visit me twice. He said he was looking to buy a cattle ranch somewhere in this valley. I don't see how he would know about Billy's killing unless —"

"Well, I need to find him Miz Sloan."

"He rode off that way," she said, pointing toward the ridges to the north.

"Up there?" Ray asked, pointing toward the ridges.

"Yes, up there."

Ray touched spurs to his mount, and Orna Sloan watched him ride toward the ridges, the tall grasses sweeping at his stirrups as his big bay horse rocked along ever farther into the distance. A sickness overtook her.

* * *

The mute boy found John Henry sitting on a flat rock overlooking the valley. Ever since John Henry had returned several nights before, he had been unusually quiet. Joshua was not sure if it had been because of the particular camp he had chosen or if there was some other reason that had caused John Henry's change of mood. He picked at his meals and left plenty of food on his plate. He did not whistle or clean his weaponry, as was his habit. Once, he had simply stared across the campfire, the flames licking in his dark dark eyes, without speaking, and it had caused Joshua to look away and wonder.

When he found John Henry sitting upon the flat rock, he made sign with his hands that it was time to eat. A storm was gathering itself just to the west, over the blue mountains, streaks of black rain sheeting down in the distance. The winds picked up.

"I'm not hungry," John Henry said. "You have wasted your time in fixing a meal."

Joshua shrugged his shoulders and signaled that he did not understand why the loss of appetite.

John Henry could not explain his murderous mood since the night he had fired his rifle into the laughing cowboys. Usually the mood passed, but this time it hadn't.

Ray Teal climbed his bay up a steep slope onto what was known as Strawberry Ridge. He had once shot a bear nearby. He figured to have the advantage of surveying the surrounding landscape once on top. But partway up, he came across a single set of shod tracks, two, maybe three, days old.

Following the tracks through the stands of pine, losing them now and again, he worked his way up the ridge in a slow cautious way. An old heat coursed through his veins, and he remembered once more his days in Texas when he'd tracked men for a living.

The sky had turned slate and it was coming a rain. He did not look forward to more rain.

Joshua wondered at John Henry's mood. He found himself in a cheerless spirit because of John Henry's somber state of being. He knew of John Henry's headaches. Still, this was something different.

John Henry sat on the flat rock all that afternoon and watched the storm approaching over the blue mountains like a blackened sheet.

He thought of the woman and of the mute boy that prepared him meals he would not eat. Why he'd ever bought the boy off of that whiskey peddler to begin with he was not sure. It had been a mystery to him.

Ray neared the top of the ridge, paused to remove his Winchester rifle from its scabbard. Something told him that what he was looking for was atop the ridge: the sickly-faced man with the gray horse.

Caution caused him to remove his spurs and leave them on a fractured stump black from an old lightning strike, the carcass of the tree lay rotting not far away.

Joshua had gone to collect water from a rock depression when he heard the crack of a twig among the deadfall that lay scattered along the slope. He stared through the trees, his eyes alert and wet.

As soon as the horse stepped on the twig and snapped it, Ray decided to dismount and tie up. He'd go the rest of the way afoot.

Orna Sloan made haste in saddling one of the shaggy horses. She was determined to carry the news that Ray had brought her to Nate Love. She needed to tell someone; Nate Love would know what to do.

A storm was gathering.

As soon as Joshua saw the figure of a man working his way up through the trees, he retreated back toward the camp, to where John Henry sat on the flat rock.

At first, John Henry could not understand what the mute boy was trying to tell him, nor was he interested, his mind full of blackness. Joshua picked up a dead branch and held it to his shoulder, then pointed back the way he had just come.

A cold prick of reality pierced the disturbed thoughts of John Henry. *Something was desperately agitating the boy!*

Ray gained the top of the ridge, knelt a moment to catch his breath, leaned on the Winchester. He was out of the trees now and nearly out of breath. It offered him a chance to look in all directions, trying to determine which way to go.

At first, John Henry waved off the mute boy's efforts, but the wildness that filled the wet angelic eyes told him that something was amiss. He stiffened at the recognition.

"Go and scatter the ashes!" he ordered. "Then take the horses on down the far side where the water runs down."

He quickly checked the loads of his weapons, all the while fighting the blinding pain in his head.

Ray in his pausing caught the faint sound of voices, or what seemed like voices, catching in the ever increasing wind. Thunder rolled from the west, then several flashes of lightning followed by more thunder. The hour of the day was already late; in another hour; it would be dark, what with the storm's approach.

Ray listened intently, trying to determine from which direction he had heard the voices. It began to rain.

While the mute boy took the horses down a path of deadfall and loose rock where old water had spent centuries running off the ridge, John Henry snaked his way in the direction the boy had indicated.

Clucking to the horses to urge them to step over the fallen spiney trunks of dead trees, Joshua worked his way ever downward.

It was instinct that caused Ray to know that his quarry was within hand, old deep-rooted instinct. He felt the hairs on the back of his neck and arms prickle.

The rain slammed down from the swollen sky. The rain came in such ferocity that it blotted out everything more than ten yards in front of him. He cursed its timing.

John Henry paused on the ridge; the rain fell in silver sheets, driving, hard and cold and stinging. Whatever the mute boy had seen was out there somewhere. He had no doubt that whoever it was had come for him.

He knew it wasn't J.D. LeFlors because he had no heart for coming after a man. He reckoned J.D. had hired someone.

Retreating from the rain and the open exposure on the ridge, Ray worked his way down the slope until he was in among the trees again. There, the rain was slackened by the spreading pine branches.

He kept his sight upon the ground above him as he slowly crept along, moving in among the trunks of the wet pines.

John Henry sat in the rain and let it pelt down on him, its cold wetness a slight relief from the pain in his head.

He thought of dead boys and it was like an unfulfilled hunger.

"Don't move a hair, mister!" He barely heard the voice until it spoke again.

"I'd say you are the goddamn stock detective, judging by the looks of you!"

Then, stepping out of the silver rain, John Henry saw the weathered cowboy, the brim of his hat knocked down over his eyes, water sluicing off it. He held a Winchester in his hands, pointing it at him. He had nothing to lose.

Both men fired at once. The bullets knocked each of them backward. The smell of rain and nitrate gathered in their nostrils as they struggled against the clutching earth.

They lay not ten feet apart, John Henry feeling the throb and fire of his blood leaking from a jagged wound in his neck and tasting the warm salt of his blood, Ray struggling to regain his feet but unable to rise because of the boil of pain in his belly.

Ray realized that the bullet was still in him, buried in his guts, and he struggled desperately against it. Reaching for his rifle, he was determined, to finish the job he had started out to do. He was determined to own that piece of land on Yellow Hat Creek and to spend his days breaking mustangs and watching long orange sunsets over the blue mountains.

His fingers gathered in the Winchester and he pulled it toward him. Using it to push himself into a sitting position, he fumbled with the lever, trying to jack a second shell into the chamber.

Then, from the same silver rain, a shadow stepped forward, bent, took the pistol from John Henry's hand and aimed it at Ray.

Somehow, Ray could not get the lever of the Winchester to operate. He tried and tried and tried, but he couldn't make it work.

Coming toward him through the rain was the small slight figure holding John Henry's pistol. Ray cursed the failed Winchester, cursed the rain, cursed the approaching figure.

The mute boy raised the pistol, aimed, thumbed back the hammer, and slowly squeezed the trigger. And

Ray couldn't understand why such a soft-faced boy would come out of the rain to kill him.

The shot sounded like thunder, but only John Henry was able to hear it.

CHAPTER EIGHTEEN

Monroe Hawks and Nate Love saddled their horses in the predawn light of morning. Suddy had busied herself with fixing them a breakfast of corn dodgers, fried ham, molasses, and black coffee. Standing before the warmth of the iron stove, she knew she'd fixed breakfast for Nate and Monroe a hundred times before. Only it had been twenty years since the last time, and since the last time, she'd figured she'd never have to make any more breakfasts for the two of them; but she was and it broke her heart to do so.

Junius Bean was still asleep, the soft utterance of his snores could be heard from Efrim's room. It made her nervous to have strangers in her house, especially the strangers Monroe Hawks was prone to bring around. She remembered the old times when Monroe had been as likely as not to show up at their door with one character or another, men wearing plug hats or half-breed Indians. And once he'd even showed up with a one-eyed tracker who'd claimed he was a descendant of Daniel Boone, then had got them all lost up in the Ozarks. How anybody could get lost in the Ozarks was a mystery to her.

"How far to this LeFlors's place?" Monroe asked, tightening the cinch of his horse; he pushed a knee into the horse's belly as he did so.

"Clear the other side of the valley," Nate said. "It'll take us half the day to get there."

They finished saddling their horses and went around to the back in order to wash their hands and faces in a barrel of rainwater before going in and sitting down at the table. The room was warm and sweet with the smells of frying ham and corn dodgers.

Suddy shuffled about without speaking to either of them. Nate knew, and so did Monroe, the reason.

"Your friend, Mr. Bean," Nate said. "He ain't got up yet."

Monroe looked back toward the room where he and Junius had shared the bed the previous night.

"It's the first bed he's had a chance to sleep in since we left Denver," Monroe said. "I reckon he's fond of it."

Suddy poured them coffee and set plates of food in front of them, and without another word, they began to eat with the earnestness of men who get up early of a morning knowing there is serious work ahead of them.

She stood at the window staring out into the dark, off toward Efrim's resting place. She couldn't help but think: *Soon, your poor ol' daddy'll be joinin' you, child. Now that Mistuh Monroe's come, I don't see no way round it. More grief is what he brung me*.

"You think maybe your friend would want to come with us, Monroe?" Nate asked. Nate's fondest hope was that Junius would not be accompanying them, for he was a poor rider without sidearms and would only slow them up or get in the way in his estimation.

"We've no time for reporters," Monroe stated matter of factly.

Nate nodded, relieved that Monroe had made the right decision.

They swallowed the last of their coffee, stood to the sound of chairs scraping across the plank floor and the ringing of Monroe's big Spanish spurs. Monroe said he'd wait outside for Nate, figuring he'd want to say good-bye to Suddy in private. Suddy was somewhat surprised by Monroe's sensitivity. He sure had never had any before.

Outside, Monroe crossed over to the saddle horses and made himself a cigarette and smoked it. Suddenly it felt like old times again, standing in the predawn darkness, the sky off to the east breaking clear and the smell of horses and leather and the air so chill. Standing there waiting like that, waiting to go on a manhunt. *Damned if it wasn't like old times!*

Nate stood at the table across from Suddy, whose arms were crossed in front of her. "I don't know exactly how long I'll be gone," he said. And Suddy looked at him with bereaved eyes and said, "I don't believe you are ever comin' back."

"No," he said. "You're wrong. I'll be coming back as soon as my business is taken care of. Our business."

She said, "It ain't no business of mine, far as I'm concerned. And I am too old to be lied to."

"I'll be alright," he told her. She had her doubts but didn't voice them openly; spatting and fussing was something to be done in private, not in front of company and strangers.

Then, she turned and looked out the window once more. This time she saw Monroe standing by the saddle horses smoking a cigarette, and a coldness ran through her head to heel. He was like an old hound waiting to go off chasing rabbits one more time. *Staring off at what?* she wondered. *Staring off at the emptiness*.

Nate kissed her on the cheek and was surprised that her skin was so cool, smooth and cool like porcelain. He turned to the door, and she threw her arms about his neck and said, "It ain't too late to let this thing go, Nate Love. It ain't nevah too late!"

But how could he explain that it was too late?

She felt, when she kissed him, the hard bulge of the Schofield pistol beneath his coat. Then, she saw him take up his Spencer carbine from where he always kept it leaning in the corner by the door. Just like she'd seen him do a hundred times before, only it had been a long time since. A very long time.

She heard them ride off into the deep black velvet of that hour of morning and then sat heavily upon a chair until she could hear only silence and the uneven guttural snore of Junius Bean.

By the time Junius awoke from dreams of Denver and Earnestine, his plain-faced wife, he had thought for a long full moment that he was in his own bed and Earnestine was somewhere in the next room in hers. Then, looking about him in the strange room filled with the gray light of dawn, he realized he was lying in a spring bed in the Montana Territory. He could smell the warm sweet smells of food coming from the kitchen and his hunger caused him to sit up.

As he dressed, he saw no evidence of Monroe in the room: no boots or hat or coat.

"Where is Mr. Love and Mr. Hawks?" he asked Suddy, who he saw sitting at the table alone, her face a mask of lonely sorrow.

"They gone off," she said without turning her gaze toward him.

"Where?" The thought was troubling to him, for he had hoped to ride along on whatever adventure the two men were bound to create.

"Mistuh J.D. LeFlors's place I reckon," she said, her words a mumble of regret.

"Oh! I must catch up with them!" announced Junius.

Suddy shook her head. "You'd be catchin' up wid trouble!"

"No matter," he replied. "It's what my newspaper has paid me to do write about the adventures of Mr. Hawks!"

Suddy finally placed her round, white-eyed gaze on him.

"Is tha' newspapa' of yours gonna pay fo' your *funeral* too?"

Suddy's inquiry caused him to blink twice.

"Well I don't see . . ."

"You seem like a nice peaceful little fellow," she said. "Why you wantin' to be keepin' the company of Monroe Hawks? Don't you know that man is a bloodletter and a haint-maker?"

"Haint?"

"Ghosts!" she declared. "Man's set mo' ghosts to walkin' 'bout than most anybody. When Monroe Hawks is 'round, they's bound to be killin' goin' on!"

"You know Mr. Hawks's reputation well?" Junius asked with warm interest.

Suddy shrugged her large round shoulders at the same time she let out a "Huuuumph!" of derision over the question.

"Knows it all too well," she said. "Mistuh Love and Mistuh Hawks rode all ova' the Nations together. Hunted down the worst of the worst for Judge Parka', bless his ol' soul."

"Yes, I know," Junius said. "Monroe told me of the time he and your husband were in a gun battle with a fellow name China Jim and some others."

"Whole lot of otha's, truth be known," Suddy said, finally turning her attention to Junius; she saw that what few strands of hair he had left on his round bony head were all askew from having slept.

"I'd like to hear more about it," Junius said. "More about your husband and Mr. Hawks's adventure in the Indian Nations."

"What I could tell you 'bout them would stain your soul, Mistuh Bean. It did my husband's. It would yours, too."

"I'd be willing to pay you for your trouble, for your time," Junius said, and she could see the eagerness dancing behind his eyes. It wasn't that there hadn't been other reporters who had sought them out over the years — dry little white men wearing paper collars who wanted to hear stories about Monroe Hawks and *The Nigger, Nate Love!*

That's what they'd called Nate back then: Nigger Nate. It caused her heart to burn hot to hear him called that. But Nate never seemed to mind it all that much: "It scares people to hear Nigger Nate's after them," he'd laugh whenever they discussed the subject. "Especially white people. It's like they're being chased by the bogeyman." But still, she didn't care to hear him called that name.

And for a whole three or four years after Nate had quit the business of lawman, reporters would show up asking after Nigger Nate and Monroe Hawks and all the two of them had done together. They came often enough so that Nate said they should move up to Montana and get clean away from it all. And they did, but still, even then for a time afterwards, a paper fellow would show himself at their door, asking the same questions. Finally, it had stopped and the years had turned peaceful. When Nate had suggested they try raising hogs, she did not even bother to object, for she was just glad all the rest of it had ended.

Until now.

"Naw," she said to Junius's request to pay her for remembrances of the old times. "I ain't got nothin' to say 'bout them days! They's been ova' a long time now, and they'll stay ova' fo' a long time mo'."

It was a disappointment for him.

"I understand your son was killed most recently," Junius said, hoping to take a different tack with her.

"Mr. Hawks stated it as the reason he was coming here, to help find your son's murderer."

He saw the pain flash through her eyes and was immediately sorry that he had been so blunt.

Suddy lifted her chin with great effort and stared directly into his small brown eyes.

"Yas suh, he was." And the plain and painful declaration caused Junius to lower his gaze for a brief moment.

"My condolences," he said. "It must be terribly hard for you."

Her hands lay atop the table and she stared at them.

"No need you playin' on my sympathies, Mistuh Bean. No use a'tall."

"No ma'am, I wasn't meaning to."

"Yas suh, you was. You hungry?"

"Yes ma'am. For some reason, I am famished."

"Well then, I reckon you should eat somethin'." She stood and moved to the stove. He wasn't but a poor little white man who'd come a long way for nothing. She couldn't turn him out, even though she wasn't happy Monroe Hawks had brought him in the first place. She couldn't see him hungry though. She couldn't see anyone hungry as long as there was a spare biscuit or a slice of meat. She sat and watched him eat with a zeal she had not seen in a man for quite some time. Nate himself did not eat very much these days, hardly enough to keep him alive.

Watching Junius eat reminded her of her nephew, Woodrow, back in Barks County, who could practically eat an entire roasted hog by himself. Woodrow was a string bean of a man, tall as a pine tree and just as skinny; but he could eat like no one else she'd ever seen in Barks County, or anywhere else for that matter. She served Junius a second helping and then a third, until there was nothing left in the pans, and still, she thought, looking at him, he'd have eaten more if there had been more. *Just like Nephew Woodrow*, she thought.

Later, he followed her up the hill to the grave so she could pull weeds off it. Junius noticed the homemade marker and commented on it. Suddy said that Nate had fashioned it from a piece of siding on the hogs' shed and then burned Efrim's name into it with an old piece of iron. She told him how they planned to go to Oglalla and buy a granite headstone from a man who specialized in them and would carve Efrim's name into the stone and maybe a pair of floating angels, too.

"That'd cost some money," Junius said.

"No price too big to let our boy be lost to weeds and grass and rain," she said, now down on her knees, pulling at stalks of thistle.

"No ma'am, it sure is not," Junius said. "What do you reckon a stone marker with a name and angels carved into it would cost?"

She said she didn't know.

"Could be a lot," he said. "What with angels and a name and all."

"Reckon so," she said.

"Maybe forty, fifty dollars or better," he said.

The thistles had bloomed a soft purple and had strong roots.

"Well, whatever it is, we'll come by it sooner or later," she said.

"Could be sooner than later," Junius said.

She stopped pulling at the thistles.

"You mean I was to tell you somethin' about the ol' times, about Nigger Nate and Monroe Hawks?"

"Yes ma'am, that's exactly so."

She looked at how in just a few weeks the board marker had weathered and leaned from where the wind was always pushing at it. It wouldn't be long before Nate'd have to be putting up another — that is, if he and Monroe didn't get themselves killed first.

She couldn't just go on and let the grave be lost. The idea expanded itself in her mind, and it seemed like the right answer to some of her worries.

"I'll tell you," she said suddenly, pulling hard on the bull thistles. "I'll tell you things about Monroe Hawks and Nate that'll make you sit up and blink your eyes and wish you'd neva' heard such things. But it'll cost you three stone markers, and not jus' one!"

He looked at her in complete surprise.

"Three?"

She nodded, yanked the last of the thistles from the soil and heaved them aside.

"Yas, suh. Three!" She held up three fingers and brushed dirt from her bare knees as she stood.

"One fo' Efrim, one fo' Nate, an' one fo' me!"

He hesitated in his response.

"It's three or nothin' a'tall," insisted Suddy. She'd made up her mind right then and there that if she was going to talk about ugly things, unwanted pasts, she was going to do it for a reason, a real good reason, something that would pay her and Efrim and Nate for all the ugly times.

"I'd have to wire my paper," Junius said. "I'd have to get approval for the additional expenditure."

"You do what you have to, Mistuh Bean. I ain't goin' nowhere."

"Sure, sure," Junius said eagerly. "I could ride to town and know in a day or two."

"I'd want them deliva'd," she said.

"Huh?"

"They'd have to deliva' them tombstones up from Oglalla and deliva' them the way I wanted them — have all the names right and the angels carved in, too."

"Yes ma'am, I reckon that could be arranged if my paper approves the expense."

"Good," she said and started back down the hill toward the cabin.

"You can take Mistuh Love's wagon and that black hoss into town if'n you care to. Tha' ol' saddle hoss of yours looks plum wore out."

"Yes ma'am, I'll do that."

"You do know how to hitch a wagon, don't you?"

He had to admit that he didn't. She sighed greatly and went to get the harnesses.

CHAPTER NINETEEN

John Henry couldn't believe that he wasn't dead, but somehow, he wasn't. The mute boy had bound his neck with a red kerchief he had pulled from his pocket and some mud he had daubed from the wet ground. Through the numbing pain, John Henry tried to speak but couldn't.

Joshua squatted beside him, staring in earnest at the wound as he bound it with the poultice of mud. The rain beat down on his face and he blinked his eyes against it. Somehow the bullet had passed through his neck without killing him. He thought wryly that he had dodged death, but he wasn't sure that he might not die in the very next minute. He had seen men mortally wounded who took up to three days to die. He wasn't sure that he wouldn't be one of them.

He offered his mute benefactor a wan smile, and Joshua answered with silent thoughts that John Henry could not decipher. He was, instead, content to rest his head upon the boy's lap and allow the ministrations to take place.

It was then that John Henry felt the coldness creeping into his fingers. A coldness that tingled as though his blood had stopped flowing to his hands. He raised one hand to the bandanna that held the mud poultice to the bloody wound in his neck and touched it lightly. It was very hard to swallow, but he managed. And when he did, he tasted his own blood — a thick saltiness that was not, to him, completely distasteful.

The rain slackened, and John Henry used the tip of his tongue to swipe some of it from his upper lip; it had a harsh flat taste, the rainwater, but it helped relieve his parched mouth.

Joshua helped him to sit upright, and when he did, he nearly fainted. Finally, he saw the dead man lying nearby, the top of his head blown open, the lifeless legs and arms flung apart. Steam rose from the body through the mist of rain.

He searched the eyes of the mute boy and saw in them the distillation of light he knew came from the unleashed secret of what it is to kill a man for the first time. It was a thing that one man could not describe to another: what it is to kill someone for the first time.

Then, in a curious and cautious effort, Joshua left him sitting there, went to the body of the dead man, and began to remove his boots. They weren't very good boots, but Joshua tried them on anyway and found that they did not fit him, being too small. He laid them aside, disappointed — his own shoes were falling apart, the soles tied up with pieces of twine.

Ray's one great pride in life was the smallness of his feet. It now became a point of consternation for the mute boy, the smallness of Ray's feet.

He searched one of the dead man's pockets and found a Barlow knife, a twist of tobacco, and three

Indian-head pennies. In the other pocket, he found a liberty dime. Joshua took these as his own.

John Henry watched with interest the stripping away of the dead man's possessions. *Why not?* he thought. *They are rightfully the boy's: to the victor go the spoils*. The boy was proving to be resourceful in his newly discovered talent as a cold-blooded killer.

Joshua turned from the corpse content with what he had found, but John Henry indicated with a painful nod of his head that the boy should search further. When Joshua hunched his shoulders and held up his hands to show that there was nothing more to be found, he saw John Henry staring at the bloody hat. And when Joshua picked it up and examined it, he found nearly thirty dollars creased inside the sweatband.

He offered John Henry a beatific smile, and John Henry did his best to offer one back.

The rain came to a halt, the storm having swept its way to the east, but the light was dying, dead — the color of a fish eye.

Joshua indicated with several hand gestures that he would go and bring back their horses from where he had left them tied. John Henry shook his head, the rain and terrible wound to his neck causing him to shiver with cold. The boy was at odds as to what he should do next. John Henry reached for his arm, and the boy understood and lied down beside him to offer his own warmth against the wet chill of John Henry's being.

Sometime in the night they heard an owl hoot.

* * *

Nate and Monroe met Orna Sloan on the Bozeman road.

"Mr. Love!" she said breathlessly, for she has been riding the black shaggy horse too hard. "I was just on my way to your place!"

Nate took time to introduce Monroe Hawks. She saw a man with clear colorless eyes settled beneath frosted brows. There was something in the way he looked at her. She had not been looked at by a man in such a way in a long time — in a very long time. Such a look caused her to avert her gaze for an instant.

"Apologize, Miss," Monroe Hawks said, realizing that he had taken too much liberty with the woman. "It's just that you remind me of someone I once knew. The truth was the woman reminded him of someone named Charlotte Rose, whom he had known down along the Cimarron several years ago. Charlotte had been young and pretty with ringlets of auburn hair and he had been very much in love with her. He had first laid eyes on her one lazy afternoon in the Golden Cage Saloon, where she sang and recited poetry for the collected. She had become the object of every cowboy's affection. She was everything his wife had not been."

This fair woman on the sweated shaggy horse reminded him of Charlotte Rose, who was later known as the Rose of the Cimarron. She died of the yellow fever the year following her arrival, and Monroe had never gotten the opportunity to know her as well as he would have liked.

When she at last returned his rainwater gaze, she remembered where she had heard his name before.

Monroe Hawks. It was the name that Mr. Love spoke of weeks before when he'd come to visit. It was the name of the man he said he was sending for to help him bring justice.

She felt sudden joy and relief.

"You are Mr. Love's friend, from down in Texas."

"Yes'm. I reckon I am. At least I'm from Texas," Monroe said with a slight grin that lifted his hoary moustaches.

"Then I owe you a debt of gratitude."

Monroe thought she had been attractive at one time, before the wind and hard work and lonesomeness had gotten to her. *She could be again*, he thought. *Like Charlotte Rose was*. He wondered if she had ever sung or recited poetry for cowboys.

"No, you don't owe me anything," Monroe said. "Nate's explained to me the situation. I came because he asked me and because we're old friends. That ought to be enough."

She thought him at once noble. She had not thought of any man as noble for a long time. He did not take his eyes from her, nor did she from him.

Nate wondered aloud why she was on her way to see him.

"I have news," she says.

"Of what sort?"

"A man came past this morning inquiring after another man. He was dressed like a drover but was well-armed. He said the man he was looking for might have something to do with Billy's murder."

"Who was the man doing the asking?" Nate asked.

"He didn't say his name."
"Did he say who it was he was looking for?"
"He said the man's name was John Henry Crow."
She saw them trade looks.
"Do you know him?" she asked.
Monroe was the first to speak.
"We know him," he said.
Nate said, "Hard to believe he's come this far north. He must have run out of people to kill in Nebraska and all them other places he's ever been."
"Do you reckon it was this LeFlors that hired him on?" asked Monroe.
"Don't see why he wouldn't. J.D. LeFlors has never done anything weak-handedly. If he was going to hire a killer, it'd be someone like John Henry."
"I'm thinking so, too," Monroe said. "John Henry Crow's about the best damn man-killer I know of."
"Then he's the one?" Orna Sloan asked.
"Can't say he is for certain," Monroe said, once more engaging the woman's gaze. "But it sounds like John Crow's work, ambushing boys and squatters."
"It does," Nate agreed. "There was a time in Wyoming he was rumored to be doing the same sort of work, only nobody could prove it one way or the other."
Monroe had heard about the nasty business in Wyoming, too. John Henry Crow had been an on-and-off topic of conversation over the years. Such men as he and John Wesley Hardin and John Selman proved to be killers of the first rank. Monroe wondered if there wasn't something in the name of John since it seemed to him a great number of killers carried that

name. Monroe often thought about such things as the first names of killers and why women were so mysterious in their natures and what, if anything, did horses think about. He figured it was a good thing for a man to keep his mind active.

Orna Sloan wanted to confess but couldn't bring herself to say that the man now suspected as being responsible for the killings had visited with her on two occasions. On one of those occasions, she had gone on a picnic with him. She felt a knot settle just below her ribs.

Both men's gazes fell to the surrounding distance before Nate said: "If it is him, if it is John Henry, me and Monroe will find him and kill him." Then, turning his head slightly, he said: "You ought to ride on to my place and let Suddy fix you something to eat and rest that horse of yours. He's nearly sweated out."

She felt awash with guilt that she had spent even a minute with her son's killer and not realized it. She should have realized it, she told herself.

Monroe walked his horse close to hers; the shaggy black tossed its head.

"You okay?" he asked. And when she did not answer, he said: "It'd be best you listen to Nate. Your pony is about all in." But his true concern was for the woman and not the horse. "Walk him the rest of the way, and let him stop to blow now and then, and you'll be fine."

She swallowed back the confession that was caught in her throat and lowered her eyes so as not to let either of them see the tears brimming in them.

Nate said, "It'll be alright Miz Sloan." And she watched as the two of them continued on the road to Bozeman.

J.D. LeFlors sat that evening in his parlor watching the storm through the large bay window set in the north section of the house. He had paid a carpenter sixty dollars extra to build the bay window so he could look out at the blue mountains. He could not know that as he watched the storm a mute boy named after an old biblical prophet had just blown out Ray Teal's brains.

He had not heard from Ray since having sent him after John Henry. He had not expected to hear from him until the matter was taken care of. The fact was that not hearing anything was a comfort to him.

He drank his whiskey in the comfort of a horsehair rocker and watched the storm march through the valley on the long legs of blinding flashes of lightning, followed by the deep and ominous rumble of thunder — a thunder that sometimes crashed like cannon — like the noise of war. Like the noise of the day he had lost his nerve for the first time at a place called Cemetery Ridge. He refused to think about the war. He had killed men, but it had weakened him to do so; it weakened him to even think about it.

His thoughts turned instead to the barren wife lying in the back bedroom; he thought now of when she had been young and beautiful and promising, a Southern belle wearing white gloves and a nosegay about the waist of her peach dress. She had been lovely and light and delicate, more delicate than magnolias. But, in the ensuing years, she had proved as hopeless as dust and borne him no sons, no children of any kind. Because of it, or in spite of it, she had become an embarrassment to him, a woman who had fallen prey to opium and depression. He often thought, regrettably, that he should have never left Virginia with her.

They never spoke more than a word here or there, whatever was necessary to acknowledge the mere physical appearance of the other when occupying the same room or the same dining table on those occasions when they would eat a meal together.

Mostly, he took his meals in Bozeman, both lunch and supper.

He took other things in town, too — his carnal pleasure with the Bozeman whores. She was aware of such things, the woman sleeping in the other room, whose silver tintype sat upon the spindle table next to the horsehair rocker. He refused to look at her, even the frozen image of her youth, of her magnolia delicacy.

From the far corner, where a Regulator clock stood, he could hear the steady *tock, tock* of the timepiece's movement, like a heartbeat spilling out of the silence, a sound that beat through the flocked wallpaper and wainscotting and crept along the polished tile floors, over the Brussels carpet, and clear to the closed door of his wife's bedroom.

He did not miss Virginia and its great civility, although he did miss its tobacco. He had gone to war a young man, leaving behind the white porticos and massive oaks, the sweeping lawns and stables of thoroughbred horses. He had gone to war with a light heart and a handmade scarf wrapped round his neck, given him by his sweetheart, the woman who now slept in the back room and to whom he rarely spoke anymore.

He had gone to war, certain that it was his glory and duty to do so, just as other young men of Virginia had gone to war, riding their fine thoroughbred horses with garlands perched upon their heads, their high-stepping mounts heading down the roads toward Manassas and Bull Run, their fine new sabers rattling at their sides, glinting under the hot Virginia sun, their manservants and footmen going off to war with them. *Happy as coons*, he thought.

But they had died horribly, many of them. And those who had not died had been mangled and defeated. Mangled and defeated in every way a man could be. Defeated in a bloody and terrible way that could not be talked about. And when it was finally, finally over and he'd returned home, the porticos were blackened from fire and the oaks were split from shot and shell and the lawns were grown to weeds and brambles. The thoroughbred horses had all been confiscated. The slaves had all fled north.

So there was nothing after the war, and he had married the woman in the far back room and gone West — first to Texas, and later to Montana. But like tainted water, the war never fully washed out of his veins; it had weakened him in immeasurable ways. Even now, years later.

He drank his whiskey, not from fancy cut crystal decanters but straight from the bottle. *A man ought to drink his whiskey while alone and with the intention of getting drunk, straight from the bottle*, he told himself.

Sometime during the night, the bottle fell from his hand and sounded empty as it thudded on the Brussels carpet.

He awakened to the clattering knock upon his door, rose sluggishly from the horsehair rocker, stumbled, regained his balance, and moved slowly through the room. Minnie Bluefeather met him before he could enter the foyer.

"Two men have come to see you, sir." Minnie always referred to her boss as Sir. It was something he did not discourage in her.

He moved past her without speaking and went to the door. One of the men he recognized, the Negro. Nate, he thought his name was. The other man was unfamiliar to him. He looked like a bandit with bandit eyes and bandit dress, especially the large pistol revealed through the parted coat. He saw, too, that the Negro was wearing a sidearm. An unusual and disturbing sight to him, a black man carrying a gun.

"I'm not hiring," he said. "Got all the cowboys I need. Don't you live somewhere in this valley?" The question was directed at Nate.

"The other side," Nate said. "I live the other side."

"You're the hog man!" J.D. said with sudden recognition.

It seemed to Nate like someone was always having to call him something other than what his name was. He leveled his gaze on the rancher.

"My name is Nate Love, Mr. LeFlors. You can call me that, Nate Love."

"Sure, sure. What's your business here, Love?" He had not yet recovered from the whiskey and was in no mood to be disturbed so early in the morning. Anyone who disturbed a man before he'd eaten his breakfast was a man without good manners in his book. It bothered him greatly that he was being disturbed now.

"Come to ask about John Henry Crow."

They both could see it, Nate and Monroe, the flinching of the eyes, the way a man who's been stung with the truth or a secret revealed will do.

"Don't know any such man."

The other man, the tall thin one with the snowy moustaches and the bandit eyes, stepped forward, so close that J.D. could smell the sweat and leather of him. He was an imposing figure standing so close.

"Didn't come for lies. Didn't ride all this way for nothing just to be lied to. I won't tolerate it," Monroe said.

The whiskey was pounding through his veins, beating against his temples. Old pain, sharp as though his skull had been cracked, flamed behind his eyes, pulsated down into his jaws.

"You're not from around here," was all that J.D. could manage to say in response.

"No goddamn it, I ain't. Now tell us about John Henry Crow!"

"You're too late! I already sent my man after him! My man will find him out and see that he quits this valley!"

"You're admitting you hired him?" Nate's dark face was a storm of anger.

"No! No!" J.D. LeFlors said, his hand holding onto the jamb of the door to steady himself.

"Then why'd you send your man?"

"Sent him because he killed one of my cowboys. Shot one of my drovers in the back. Just a boy that read his Bible and gave no one any trouble." It was an admission he hadn't been prepared to make to strangers, or anyone else. But his head hurt and his patience had worn out and he couldn't see that it mattered any more.

"The blood's on your hands," Nate said.

"No!" protested J.D. "I was protecting what was mine! I have a right to protect what is mine! Thieves and trash stealing from me won't be tolerated! And you are a goddamn nigger and can get off my porch!"

Nate pulled the Schofield from his belt, thumbed back the hammer, and the clicking it made could be heard clear to the corrals.

"You're nothing more than trash yourself for hiring a man that would murder boys!"

Monroe took a step backward, made it clear he would not interfere.

"You're going to let him shoot me?" LeFlors cried out.

"Hell mister, I reckon he has a right! Might just as well stand up and take your medicine!"

The Schofield's bore was inches from the forehead of the rancher. Flies buzzed in his ears, and there was a sick smell coming up from his own flesh.

Nate Love wanted to kill the man; more than anything, he wanted to kill the man who had helped to murder his boy. But he had lost something in the years between the old times and now. He had lost his taste for killing, at least killing in that way — a man unable or unwilling to defend himself, no matter that he might deserve it.

"You tell me where he's at," Nate said. "You tell me where John Henry Crow is at!"

J.D. LeFlors shook his head slowly and sadly like an old bull about ready to collapse. He had survived a war and a barren wife and the Indians. He didn't know whether he could survive another minute.

"I don't know. I never have known where he keeps himself other than somewhere out there." He motioned with an out-flung arm to the vast valley.

"He comes and goes whenever he chooses. I haven't seen him since he shot my drover! I sent my best man to find him and kill him."

Several of J.D.'s cowboys had gathered before the house, having been drawn by the loud voices of the strangers. Monroe cast his gaze upon them, saw that they were but boys, green as apples, fuzzy-cheeked drovers, and said: "They may know how to ride a horse and chase cows through the brush, but you ain't got a man here that's good enough to find John Henry Crow and kill him!"

Nate lowered the Schofield and said, "I'll be damned!" Then strode from the porch and mounted his horse.

Monroe leaned even closer and said, "You are lucky that man didn't kill you. He might still do it. I wouldn't be surprised."

"I almost wish he would," J.D. LeFlors said, his voice full of resignation.

"Well sir, you might just get your wish if we don't find John Henry Crow, for I reckon ol' Nate there will have to take out his vengeance on somebody."

CHAPTER TWENTY

It was hell and damnation to sit a horse, but John Henry Crow gritted his teeth and swallowed back the throbbing pain in his throat. It was as though he had tried to swallow a hot coal, only it got stuck. Morning was announced on the voices of several birds that trilled as they perched on the tips of tall trees. Some of the birds had blue heads and brown bodies. Drops of dew clinging to the grass sparkled under the morning sun like shattered glass. A few leftover clouds drifted as harmless as angels in a crisp blue sky.

Overhead as well was a wheel of turkey buzzards, whose sense of tragedy and keen sight had drawn them to the ridge of death. Ray lay like an open invitation, his life's blood staining the grass around him.

John Henry took notice of the buzzards, then pointed to a distant ridge, and Joshua understood they must leave quickly or have their presence known by others who would see the wheel of ugly black birds and be drawn to the destruction.

John Henry remembered there to be an old line shack over beyond a distant ridge. He had skirted it on several occasions while searching for cattle thieves. They mounted their horses and rode for all of two hours, resting here and there to allow John Henry to tend to his swollen neck. When they reached Yellow Hat Creek, Joshua removed the bandage from John Henry's neck and rinsed it in the creek before reapplying it. The wound was purple and puckered from where the bullet had passed through; John Henry could barely sip water and get it to stay down.

After another two hours of crossing east to west, they began their ascent to the far ridge, where John Henry knew the old shack stood in among a stand of lodge pole pines.

The old man had been cutting corns from his feet with a pocket knife. Sitting on an upside down wash tub, he whittled at his feet. He looked to be as old as some of the rocks cropped up out of the ground. Whenever asked, he couldn't remember exactly how old he was, nor did he care.

His eyes weren't so good anymore; everything he looked at had a cloudiness surrounding it. He had to bring his feet up close to his eyes to see to cut the corns for fear of cutting off one of his toes. He had already, a long time ago, cut out the sides out of his shoes so that they wouldn't rub up against his corns. But it didn't seem to do any good; his feet constantly hurt him anyway and caused him to waddle like a duck.

He had lived a long time in Montana. He'd hunted beaver when nothing but a young man and the Blackfeet were still around to cut a body's throat. He had stood so long in icy cold ponds pulling out the heavy corpses of drowned beaver that the bones in his legs and hands still hurt even after fifty years.

Goddamn Montana, and goddamn everything about it, he thought every time he thought about it. Why he'd ever come in the first place and why he ever stayed was a mystery to him. Except that he remembered Montana as having once been a free and wild place to roam, with nothing but a handful of white men in it. Now, it was nothing but white men. The Indians, even the Blackfeet, had all but vanished or become like white men.

Well, he reckoned he'd be vanished, too, before much longer.

He cut away at his corns with the pocket knife and thought maybe it was time he went to California before it got too late. He'd heard good things about California. He'd heard about the warm weather they had there and about the blue ocean and about the Spanish señoritas. Every winter he promised himself that as soon as spring came, he'd leave and go to California. Why he hadn't gone yet, he didn't know. It just seemed that once winter got over, it was too far to go.

Once or twice a year, he walked to Bozeman. It was brutal, but then so was the long loneliness of his existence on the ridge. He thought about going to Bozeman now as he cut away at the corns on his feet. He wondered if he could still walk that far with his feet so bad.

He had run out of whiskey during the last big blizzard to hit the valley; snow clear up past the windows — a time when a man most needed not to run out of whiskey, he had run out. He had run out and had marked on his calendar the day he had. Every day thereafter he had spent a minute or two staring at the date: April 14. He would never forget April 14, the last big blizzard and the day he had run out of whiskey. And some of that last blizzard still lay up on the blue mountains, where it would remain until winter showed up again.

There were other things in Bozeman he could use as well. A woman, for one. He was never certain of the exact date he'd had his last woman; he had not thought to mark it on the calendar as he did most major events in his life. Why he had forgotten to mark the date on the calendar the last time he had had himself a woman he couldn't remember either. At the time, it hadn't seemed all that important. It seemed, though, that it had been sometime in the autumn of the previous year, for he remembered riding home along a stream where the aspens were quaking golden in the sun and being in a high old mood, having spent a day or two in Bozeman. He liked it when the sun danced off the aspen leaves and the creeks. The whore's name had been Maybelle and she was fat and jolly and could drink as well as him. He had at least remembered her name, and it caused him to smile to have remembered that much.

He had a pan of water that he soaked one foot in while working on the other. And after he'd cut on a corn for a while, he'd trade feet in the pan of water; pulling out the one and sticking the other in. It struck him as how his feet looked like bony fish — white and long and floppy.

He gave off on trimming his corns for a time because it could get as painful as pulling a tooth, another thing he had had to do that last winter. He'd had to first loosen the tooth by tapping on it with a cold chisel, which had made it feel like most of the top of his head was coming off. Then, using a pair of nail pullers, he had yanked it out.

Feet and teeth! They could be more worrisome than a nagging wife — something he'd never had, but he had known plenty of men who had been married and they all seemed to have been married to nagging wives.

He ate a handful of wild onions while resting his feet in the pan of water. He looked about him, at the leaning shack, at the tall weeds and the heap of rusted cans that had collected from a thousand meals of beans. It seemed he had eaten so many beans he could fart his way to California if he ever chose to go. His wood supply was nearly gone. Every year seemed to get a little harder. Bozeman seemed to get a little farther away, and so did California. And so did all the dreams he'd ever had about seeing the world and getting rich.

He laughed thinking about seeing the world and getting rich. And when he laughed, the few teeth left in his mouth showed like rotted spikes and the spittle dribbled down his chin until he found no more humor in it and his laughter sputtered and failed like a broken steam engine.

Well, hell, he determined, he might just up and go to town first thing in the morning. Why not? Go, stay two, three days maybe, see the pretty girls, drink some mash, maybe fat Maybelle was still in the territory. The thought bolstered his mood.

He hoisted one of his feet out of the pan and began once more to whittle away at the corns, renewed in the promise of what tomorrow might hold for him.

Then his half-blind mule brayed.

He looked up from whittling his feet. A man and a boy came riding through the trees. It caused his skin to crawl, seeing strangers come riding through the trees.

He stomped over the water pan trying to get his other foot out.

The man was tall and wore a bloody bandanna 'round his neck. He had hardly any color to him except for the eyes, which were as dark as the inside of a well. The boy looked sprightly, large innocent eyes caught up in his young face, eyes like a woman's or a young girl's.

"What you want here?" he asked the two of them.

Neither spoke, but the man pointed toward the cabin. The old man looked around, not understanding. The boy laid his hands up against the side of his face.

"You wanta go to sleep in my cabin?"

The boy nodded.

"What the hell would I let you do that fer?"

The boy smiled, pulled John Henry's pistol from his belt and aimed it at the old man. Joshua saw the rheumy eyes roll white.

"Been chased by Blackfeet Induns and shot in the arse with arra's!" spat the old man. "Been grabbed by a grizzled bear and had half my hair ripped off. I got to cut corns off my feet ever six months and I been outta whiskey since April fourteenth. Shootin' me would be a favor!"

Joshua looked toward John Henry, a half-smile touching his mouth. John Henry nodded for Joshua to lower the pistol from where it was aimed at the top of the old man's head.

John Henry pointed to his neck, then reached in his pocket and pulled out a silver dollar and flipped it in the air so that it landed at the old man's corns.

The old man clucked his tongue, bent down, picked up the coin and examined it.

"Cost you two," he said. "Two dollars you wanna sleep in my cabin."

The smile left John Henry's lips, but nonetheless, he pulled out a second coin and tossed it to the old man, then motioned that he should find the boy something to eat. Those dark eyes said he wasn't fooling and the old man had better not hold out for more.

"Hell, might have a can or two of beans left yet," he said, putting both coins in his pocket. "You want 'em hot or cold, boy?"

The swelling had subsided considerably in John Henry's neck, but the wound had become infected.

"I need to borrow your pocket knife," John Henry whispered.

"Huh?"

"The knife you've been using to cut the corns off your feet."

The old man was reluctant to give over his knife for fear they'd use it to cut his throat. They looked the type.

"What you want it fer?"

John Henry made a gesture toward his neck but gave up trying to explain. Even whispering was laborious. "Give it to me."

The old man did. John Henry held it over the fire until the blade blackened. He stripped off the bandanna from his wounded neck and handed the blade to Joshua. "Cut open that pus bag and drain it out," he instructed.

"Good Gawd!" the old man said when he got a look at the infection. "Yer neck is full of poison!"

Joshua eyed it with a great deal of curiosity. Then, with a fine smoothness, he drew the tip of the knife blade across the infected area and a sound escaped John Henry that caused the old man to look away.

The smell caused the old man to lose his appetite for the beans that were cooking over the fire.

"Christ and tarnation!" he bellowed. Men shot through the neck and mute boys and no whiskey since April 14 — to him it was like raining frogs or a prairie full of locusts, the visitation on him of such tragic circumstances.

"Job had it better," he muttered as he stood and moved off into the night.

John Henry felt the tightness leave his neck the minute the knife blade stung him. He felt the great gush of something awful leave him, and it nearly took his breath away.

Joshua inspected his work in the fire's light, seemed pleased, and laid the knife aside in order to wash the bandanna in a pan of rainwater and retie it round John

Henry's neck. The wet cloth was like cold fire and John Henry gasped but allowed the ministrations.

Joshua had had his thoughts on other matters, however. For three days, he had had his mind on other matters.

Now, having finished tending the wound and redressing it, he stared into John Henry's dark dark eyes.

John Henry could not help but wonder what the boy was thinking; surely he was thinking something the way he stared after the old man's every move.

The boy uttered a noise, pointed off toward the darkness, where the old man had gone, away from the camp's fire.

"What? The old man?" whispered John Henry, his hunger so severe from not having eaten in four days that he was having sharp pains in his ribs.

Joshua nodded.

"Kill the old man? Is that what you want to do, kill the old man?"

The boy's eyes reflected the camp's fire — glowing liquid, like moonlight on water.

John Henry felt the headache grow inside his brain, felt it flare and fan out through his skull.

"Angel . . ." he whispered, and placed a hand upon the boy's arm.

Joshua stared off into the dark, where the old man had gone.

"Then go on and do it," John Henry whispered. The boy stood and moved away from the fire, into the gathering darkness.

His name was Walter and he had been born Walter Josiah Parker nearly eighty years before in Oak Grove, Ohio to Irish immigrants Clara and Carver Parker. He had left home when he was fifteen and struck out for the Stoney Mountains to trap beaver and live wild as the Indians. He had married an Arapaho woman, who'd borne him two sons, but all three had been lost to the cholera. He had a tintype of himself taken in a St. Louis photographer's studio. He was wearing beaded buckskins and a beaver hat. He kept the tintype on a shelf over his bed in the cabin and would often stare at it for hours on end, as though by staring at it he could bring back that time of his life.

Time was a mean son of a bitch in his book. Sometimes it caused him to weep, thinking about where it had all gone and how quickly. It wasn't fair that a man should wind up with corns all over his feet and his teeth all but rotted out and bones that stayed cold even in the summer. Sometimes, thinking about these things made him weep openly.

Now, he sat on the fallen trunk of a jack pine, gathering new air into his lungs while trying to quell the stench that had filled his nostrils when the boy had cut into the man's neck.

Nothing smells as bad as death, a fact he had long since known as the truth. And what he had smelled coming out of the man's neck had sure smelled a lot like death.

Why did it have to come and visit him, death? Weren't things bad enough? Wasn't being without any whiskey since the fourteenth of April and not having any woman since way last year sometime bad enough? Why'd a dead man with a mute boy have to come riding into his camp and hold pistols on him and make him cook up his beans for them and give up his bed and have him sleep out on the ground?

It didn't make any sense to him, not after all these years, and he was growing tired of it. He figured he'd wait until it got late before he busted them over the head with his shovel. Bust them both over the head and bury them! Why not?

Then, as he was sitting there drawing fresh air into him and thinking about busting them over the head, he heard the footfall of someone behind him.

"What — ?"

The boy was standing there in the half-moonlight pointing the pistol at him.

"Why'd you come all this way to kill me?!" cried the old man. "What'd I ever do but be hospitable and cook you my beans and let you sleep in my bed?"

The old man must have forgotten that the boy couldn't tell him the answers to his questions.

Staring into the dark innocent eyes of the mute boy, Walter Parker knew he was never going to see California and was sorry as could be that he had not gone to Bozeman the week before.

John Henry heard the crack of the pistol beyond the camp's fire, and he felt suddenly weary.

CHAPTER TWENTY-ONE

She had been busy cleaning her kitchen, working around the pensive little white man who sat in her kitchen and stared after her with large expectant eyes. He wanted her to tell him a story about Nigger Nate and Monroe Hawks and what they had done in a mean and bloody way back in the old times. But she wasn't ready to talk just yet, not until she was sure he could get the money for the three gravestones. He said he was waiting on a wire from the Denver newspaper.

Junius Bean watched her work; he thought she worked with an uncommon energy as she scrubbed and cleaned every pot and pan, every shelf, every nook and cranny. She reminded him of his Earnestine in that way. Earnestine had a deep and abiding aversion to any sort of dust or grime and an equal passion for keeping it out of her house. If only her interest in him had been as great, he mused with much regret.

"You'd be so kind as to 'scuse me while I clean around where you is sittin'," she said at one point, standing over him with a broom.

He was reluctant to leave the warm coziness of the kitchen, but she stared at him until he did. He went outside and stood on the porch, then wandered out to the corrals and stood staring at the horses. They were large creatures, creatures that he did not trust completely, but he was attracted to them nevertheless.

He wished he had an apple or a carrot to feed them, but given some thought, was just as glad he did not; he had heard that a horse bite was about as painful and terrible as anything that a horse could do to a human, worse even than a kick! He couldn't imagine being bitten by a horse.

He stepped away as the horses became curious of his presence and came over to where he had been standing with one foot on the bottom rail of the corral.

The wind tugged at his bowler, which he had used both hands to fix tightly down on his head because the wind was blowing so hard. He'd had the misfortune on several occasions of having to chase his derby down various wet and muddy streets of Denver. It was always a humiliation to have to chase his hat.

He felt suddenly alone, lost in the great vast Montana landscape with its valleys and far blue mountains still covered in snow even though it was summer. Some of the grass was nearly as high as his waist, and the sky seemed to go on forever. He wondered why anybody would ever come here, or once they had, why they'd ever leave.

Suddy checked on the man every now and then from her window. He seemed a speck against the light, a little man in a black suit and a round hat, lost and out of place. A part of her felt sorry for him, but not so sorry that she wanted him underfoot while she cleaned her kitchen or made the beds or swept the eternal dirt from the floor.

She knew sooner or later she would have to tell him terrible things about Nate and Monroe. She didn't mind telling terrible things that Monroe had done but was not eager to speak of her husband in such a poor light. But then the thought of their graves being lost to the wind and rain and weeds tugged at her heart, and she knew what she had to do in the end and was willing to do it.

She was sweeping the doorway when she saw the white woman riding toward the cabin. She knew without knowing that it was Billy Sloan's mother, the widow.

Junius saw the woman, too. The wind came up and tried to take his hat, but he grabbed it with both hands and held on.

The shaggy horse seemed to shudder its relief when Orna Sloan brought it to a halt.

"Tha' hoss looks like he's 'bout ready to keel ova'," Suddy said with great concern.

"Yes, I'm afraid I rode him too hard. He's never been ridden much and isn't used to it, I guess."

Junius was fairly smitten by the woman's looks. The cascades of her auburn hair had come loose during the ride and tangled wildly about her fine face. He had never seen such a narrow waist on a female. Her feet were small and delicate, and everything about her seemed to take his breath away. He found himself quickly going to assist her down from the horse, but she dismounted on her own before he could reach her.

She turned with surprise to see the man walking briskly toward her. He seemed a funny little man with his derby hat pulled down tightly over his ears and his ill-fitting suit straining at the buttons.

He grinned hopelessly at the embarrassment of having failed his self-appointed mission of helping the woman down from her horse.

"How . . . do," he managed to stutter, stopping just short of where she stood, then struggling to remove his hat in a display of gentlemanlike behavior. The thin strands of his remaining hair fluttered in the wind like gray ribbons. Realizing the mistake, he quickly plopped the bowler back upon his skull.

She half expected him to remove his coat and lay it on the ground for her to walk on. She did not know quite how to respond to him.

"Come on in outta the wind," Suddy urged. Orna offered Junius a weak smile and turned toward the house before he had time to properly introduce himself, which he wanted to do more than anything. Instead, he simply followed her up the steps and into Suddy's warm kitchen.

"I reckon you must be Mizzus Sloan, Billy's mama," Suddy said once they had closed the door against the hard wind.

"Yes. But call me Orna, there's no need that we stand on formality."

Suddy offered her a warm smile and said, "I'm Suddy Mae and this here is Mistuh Junius Bean. He's visitin' for a short while."

Orna wondered if it wasn't a mistake that she had come, for she felt out of place, didn't know quite what to say, and yet she felt the need to be there, to be near this woman who had also lost a son.

Junius pulled a chair from the table and offered that she sit, and when she did, he felt greatly relieved that he had managed at last to do something right.

Suddy heated coffee and put a plate of warm biscuits before them and some comb honey she kept in a mason jar. Junius could barely contain himself at the thought of fresh honey poured over warm biscuits. But he managed to allow the women to serve themselves first.

"You go ahead an' eat an' fresh yourself up a bit," Suddy said. "Then we'll talk." Suddy knew a hungry person when she saw one, and she saw one in Orna Sloan. She had heard through Efrim that the Sloans didn't have much at all, that they were about as poor as people could get, yet they weren't trashy in their behavior, just poor. She remembered Billy as always having been a skinny boy, too skinny in her book. And now, looking across the table at his mother, she saw that Orna suffered the same thinness as her son. A person skinny because she never got enough to eat looked different from any other kind of person there was. Some folks were just naturally skinny even though they had plenty to eat.

She remembered a man who had been a neighbor back in Fort Smith, a deputy like Nate and Monroe. His name was Dick Durbin, but everyone called him "Skinny Dick" because he was as tall and thin as a flagpole. But she had never known a man to eat the way

Skinny Dick Durbin could eat. She recalled one time when he had eaten an entire turkey by himself at a Thanksgiving dinner that Judge Parker had put on for some of his favorite deputies. Fortunately, everyone knew about Skinny Dick's massive appetite and the judge had ordered three turkeys prepared. Even Nate had remarked it was like watching someone throwing quarters down a well to see Skinny Dick Durbin eat a meal.

With a touch of sadness, she remembered that Skinny Dick Durbin had been shot in the stomach by a Cherokee gambler and had lingered for two weeks before dying. All he could complain about in that time upon his death bed was the fact that he couldn't have a decent meal anymore.

"I might as well die," he'd finally said, "as to never be able to eat another meal." And then he'd immediately closed his eyes and breathed his last.

Junius was trying desperately to make himself noticed by offering to pour Orna more coffee and smiling broadly enough to show some of the gold caps on his teeth. But the thing that Orna noticed most about him was the fact that he was sweating profusely. Little beads of sweat glistened on his high forehead as well as on his upper lip. Even the backs of his hands were damp with sweat, she noticed, when he poured her more coffee.

Suddy noticed Junius's efforts to make himself obvious to the woman and wished that he would go back outside so that the two of them could have a private conversation. No woman could talk certain things with another when there was a man underfoot, even a little man wearing a jug hat.

Orna wished, too, that she and Suddy had a private moment to talk about their sons. She felt that the deaths of their children was a great burden that they privately shared and one that the man, Bean, could not possibly understand or appreciate. She did her best to not encourage his attention.

Finally, Suddy said, "Mr. Bean, I could use your help with a few matters."

Junius blinked at his name being announced.

"Oh, yes. Of course, Mrs. Love."

"Since Nate's gone, there ain't nobody to slop the pigs. I'd do it myself, but as you can plainly see, I've got company. An' judging by the sound of them pigs out yonder, they is ready to be slopped." It was true, the pigs had been raising a ruckus for the last twenty or thirty minutes. They were used to Nate bringing them their slop at a certain time of day and that time had already come and gone. Everybody who knew pigs knew that they were more intelligent than most people gave them credit for.

Reluctantly, the reporter rose from his chair. He wasn't happy about leaving the company of Orna Sloan for the company of a pen full of hungry pigs.

"Might just as well grain the horses while you're out there," Suddy added. "An' I could stand some more firewood to be chopped for the stove — that is, if you is plannin' on eatin' any more meals."

He figured he should hurry and attend the chores she gave him rather than linger and allow her time to think up more for him to do.

"The slop buckets is on the back porch wid the slop already in them," she said with a bright smile.

He tried hard not to breathe in the aroma of the slop buckets as he carried them out to the pigs. They saw him coming and quickly gathered before the trough. Without trying to look at the contents of the slop buckets, he reached over the top of the fence and poured them into the troughs. He himself was never fond of the taste of pork, and now, as he watched, the slab-sided creatures jostle and snort and stick their heads down into the slop, he knew that he never again would eat so much as a slice of bacon.

He nearly shuddered watching them.

Several times in the process of doing the chores Suddy had assigned him he found reason to pass by the kitchen window and steal glances at Orna Sloan. He wished she would take some sort of notice of him. But not once that he could see did she even so much as look his way.

He grained the horses, including the shaggy one that was the widow's. He took special care to give it extra grain. He was just finishing when the wind came up and took his hat in spite of the fact that he thought he had screwed it down on his head as far as it would go.

The hat was built perfectly for rolling along the ground, and the winds carried it across the yard and out toward the open prairie. He started after it in hot pursuit. And it was then that Orna Sloan finally took notice of him.

"What is Mr. Sean doing chasing his hat?" she laughed aloud.

Suddy looked, too, saw the comical scene as the wind kept the bowler yards ahead of the little fellow, who was running along bent over trying ever so hard to snatch his hat from the greedy clutches of the playful wind.

"I swear," Suddy said. "I ain't asked that man to do hardly nothin' at'all fo' me exceptin' to slop them ol' pigs of Nate's and to chop up a little kindlin' wood, an' all he can do is chase his hat around the yard!"

Both women watched and laughed until they had tears rolling down their cheeks.

"Well, I guess he was wantin' you to take notice of him," Suddy said, finally plopping herself into a chair because her sides ached so from laughter. "I guess he done figured out how to get your attention."

"He may not catch up to his hat until he gets to Bozeman," said Orna. And they both burst into laughter again.

All Junius could do was to run as fast as his short stubby legs could carry him, which was for all purposes a losing cause considering the strength of the wind that day.

After awhile, Orna looked across the table at Suddy and said, "I've not laughed in such a long time." And Suddy understood instantly how the woman felt, for she felt the exact same way. It seemed like the laughter had lifted out the old dead pain and swept it away just like the wind was doing with Junius's derby hat.

"It's good that you come an' visited me," Suddy said. "I surely can use the company."

"I'm glad I came, too," Orna said. "I'm glad I came, too."

And for a long time they talked about their sons and their men and life without them. And once in a while, they took time to laugh at the sight of Junius still chasing his hat in the wild Montana wind.

CHAPTER TWENTY-TWO

From J.D. LeFlors's ranch, they rode to Yellow Hat Creek, where Nate pointed out the recent grave.

"It was squatters," Nate said. "John Henry Crow come by and told them they was to move on, and when they didn't fast enough, he shot one of them, a boy about the age of Efrim."

They allowed their mounts to drink from the creek, the water riffling over smooth rocks and glistening under a slanting sun.

"Well, we'll catch him soon enough and kill him," Monroe said, rolling a cigarette between his fingers as his horse dipped its muzzle into the cold stream.

"It's getting late, maybe we ought to cross over and camp for the evening," suggested Nate.

"You don't want to keep riding?" Monroe asked.

Nate hated to admit it, but he'd had about all the riding he cared to for one day.

"Just thought maybe you was getting tired," Nate said.

"Well sir, I believe I could ride another ten or twelve hours, but I doubt that this old horse could. He's been breathing hard for the last mile and seems a bit gaunt." Nate was glad to hear it, even if he knew that Monroe was using the excuse of the horse being tired and gaunt rather than lay that burden on himself. It didn't matter, not to him it didn't.

"Well then, let's go on over the other side and toss down our bedrolls and get a little fire going."

"You still a good hand at catching fish?" Monroe asked.

Back in Arkansas, Nate had prided himself on his ability to catch fish and would often go fishing and come back with several large catfish that weighed thirty or forty pounds apiece. But Nate's fishing abilities paled in comparison to his ability to make a meal of them. There was never a finer hand at cooking fish than Nate Love.

Thinking about it now, Monroe's mouth began to water for the sweet taste of freshly caught fish.

They unsaddled their horses and let them graze freely nearby. "Them horses feel even half the way we do," Nate said, "they won't even consider running off." Then, taking a line and a hook from his saddlebags, Nate wandered down to the edge of the creek near a spot where the brown water slowed and eddied into a deep pool and the bank was undercut on the far side.

"Reckon there's any fish in this creek, that's where they'll be," he said, uncoiling the line. He went along lifting several rocks until he found a few grubs, which he used for bait. All the while, Monroe sat on the grass and smoked his cigarette and watched Nate casting out his line to the far side where the deep hole was then slowly dragging it back toward himself. Monroe pulled off his boots and rubbed his feet and enjoyed the respite.

On the third cast, Nate yelled: "I got one!" and even Monroe got a little excited. It turned out to be a trout that sparkled silver in the sun. It was nearly as long as Nate's hand but narrow in the body. After twenty more minutes, Nate had caught four more fish of about the same size, then the hole proved empty.

"Guess that'll have to do us," he said.

"Maybe there'd be some more down farther," Monroe said.

"Maybe," Nate said, "but these'll do us."

Nate ran a knife from their gills to their tail fins and threw the guts into the creek, where they drew the attention of a large snapping turtle.

"A snapping turtle is about the ugliest creature I know of," Monroe said, watching the turtle snap up the fish guts.

Nate cut and sharpened a pair of cottonwood switches from a nearby tree and ran them through the trout so that they could be held over the little campfire.

"I reckon the snapping turtle would have to be the second ugliest creature I have ever laid eyes upon," Nate said, handing over one of the sticks holding a trout.

"What'd be the first?" inquired Monroe, for he could not imagine anything uglier than a snapping turtle. He believed he had seen most creatures there was to see, and to him none could beat the snapping turtle for ugliness.

Smoke rose in little wisps from the fire and the smell of frying trout was truly a blessing.

Monroe waited patiently for Nate to tell him what he thought was uglier than a snapping turtle. When Nate seemed to lose his thoughts as to the subject, Monroe said: "Well, what is it? What in hell could be uglier than a snapping turtle?"

Nate grinned until all his teeth showed.

"I'd say it'd have to either be a mugwump or that little gal you was seeing in the Nations that one time. I remember her as having been Choctaw, or at least some of her kin was."

Monroe flushed embarrassed at the memory. It was true, he had been seeing a part Choctaw woman in the Nations for a short spell, a relationship he'd tried desperately to keep a secret. But there were few secrets that a man of his reputation could keep, and seeing the Choctaw woman proved to be one of them. He reckoned, often thinking back on it, that every man sooner or later could find beauty in a woman where no other man might. His just happened to be the Choctaw woman.

Now that it had gotten started, Nate couldn't keep from chuckling over the incident.

"What the hell is a mugwump, anyway?" Monroe asked, hoping to divert the conversation down another path from where it was headed.

"Mugwump is a creature about as long and ugly as that there foot of yours," chuckled Nate, turning his fish in the fire. "Only it lives on river bottoms and hides itself down in the mud, and ain't nobody could eat one even if they was starving because they're so dern ugly and nasty tasting, worse than a dogfish in every way!"

"Well, whatever would that have to do with the Choctaw gal I was seeing in the Nations?" Monroe asked as though innocent of the obvious answer.

Nate was beginning to laugh so hard he nearly dropped his fish into the ashes.

"Nothin', I guess. It's just that as human beings go that gal had a leg up on being homely."

"Well, I'd be the first to admit that she wasn't the prettiest woman in the territory," Monroe said, sensing that his reputation as a ladies' man was open to question.

"Hell, she wasn't even the prettiest in her family," laughed Nate. "Fact is, if she and those ugly sisters of hers had been in a beauty contest, nobody would have won and they'd all been tied for last place!"

"I think maybe you're being unfair to that girl and her family," grumped Monroe, concentrating on his own fish, which was nearing ready to eat.

"Maybe so, but I have to admit, at the time it surprised me that a man with your reputation was so caught up with a homely gal."

"She had her good points," argued Monroe, wishing that Nate would drop the subject.

"She surely must have had," laughed Nate. "What were they anyway?"

"Well, I don't believe I care to discuss my personal business right at the time," Monroe said, retrieving his trout from the flames and pulling off bits of the warm sweet flesh and plopping them in his mouth.

They ate pretty much in silence, concentrating mostly on picking out the small bones of the fish and sucking the sweet juices from the tips of their fingers.

"I don't remember her name," Nate said after having eaten his second fish.

"Who?" Monroe asked.

"That Choctaw gal."

"Oh, no," Monroe said with a shake of his head. "I thought I said I wasn't interested in discussing the subject." Monroe remembered then that Nate could be as persistent as anybody when he got his mind on a particular subject that interested him. It seemed the subject of the homely Choctaw girl interested him now.

"Well, we don't have to discuss it," Nate said. "I'd just like to recall what her name was now that I'm thinking about it. A thing like not being able to remember a person's name will keep me awake tonight."

"No it won't."

"It will. What harm would it do for you to tell me her name. Least I'd be able to get my sleep and be fresh and ready to go first thing tomorrow."

"Monroe knew that Nate wasn't going to let up until he told him the Choctaw girl's name."

"I hope I ain't come all this way just to be reminded of things I'd just as soon forget," Monroe said, wishing that the subject of the Choctaw woman could be dropped from the evening's conversation but knowing that it wouldn't until he gave up and told Nate the woman's name.

"Why be so touchy over a gal's name?" Nate said.

Well, the last thing Monroe wanted after having ridden all day long was not to get any sleep. He was dog tired.

"Her name was Anna Rainwater," Monroe said, his manner resigned to Nate's persistence. "Now, are you happy?"

"Yes, I am happy to be able to remember that gal's name," Nate said. "Anna is a pretty name."

"You can drop the topic whenever you've a mind to," Monroe said, for in the fading light he didn't have to see to know that Nate was grinning like an egg-eating opossum.

"What was it that ruined the relationship?" Nate asked.

"Are you going to pester me all the night long so that neither of us can get any rest?" Monroe asked, eating the last fish then slipping down into his bedroll, where he rested his head on his saddle. The sky had turned a deep purple and the far blue mountains had disappeared in the encroaching darkness.

Nate had retired to his own bedroll across from the little campfire, now nothing more than glowing embers that seemed to have a breathing life of their own.

"Well, I was just wondering what it was that caused you to lose interest in her?" Nate said, unwilling to let the subject drop.

Monroe muttered something from his blankets, and Nate said: "What?"

"She had a dern husband," Monroe said loud enough for everyone still awake in Judith Valley to hear.

"Husband?" Nate said, trying hard to contain his mirth.

It did sound somewhat humorous now, even to Monroe, to remember that a woman as homely as Anna Rainwater would have a jealous husband and a lover when so many prettier women had no suitors at all.

Monroe said with a lighter tone to his voice: "Yes, it seems I sure wasn't the only one that appreciated her particular charms — and they was plenty and they was ample, believe me!"

"Well, ain't that something!" declared Nate. "A husband!"

"Yes, and a big son of a buck he was, too," Monroe said, finding himself now grinning over the memory. Falling out of married women's bedroom windows was something he had done more than once, but it always seemed that he had been the last one to find out they had been married in the first place. And as homely a woman as Anna Rainwater had been, he never would have guessed or suspected her to have been married. It was after that, after having fallen out of Anna's bedroom window, that Monroe swore off such activity and took a wife and settled down for a time.

"Nate, do you remember Charlotte Rose, the Rose of the Cimarron?"

"Yes. I do remember her," Nate said, half asleep from the deep exhaustion of an all-day ride.

Then Monroe didn't say anything more about her and Nate knew, even in his half sleep, that Monroe was still carrying a heavy heart for the young woman who had sung songs and nursed cowboys and recited them poetry when they were well. She had died of the yellow fever way too early in life. And of all the things that Nate had witnessed Monroe as having suffered, there was nothing to compare with the suffering he had gone through over the death of Charlotte Rose, a woman with whom he had barely been intimate.

Nate remembered her as being exceptionally pretty, with russet hair that the sunshine danced in and large blue eyes. Nate fully thought that Monroe should have remained a married man or that he should have married Charlotte Rose at the time. But Monroe had remained aloof from the woman, for whatever reason no one who knew him seemed to understand. Nate had figured that maybe it was just because Monroe admired her so much he couldn't bring himself to present his case openly to her. Whatever the reason, the opportunity had passed with Charlotte's early and unexpected death. Nate never saw Monroe act the same way around another woman again.

As soon as he knew that Nate couldn't see him, Monroe felt inside his coat pocket for the little filigreed locket pinned there. It was a trifle, but he kept it pinned on his inside pocket nonetheless. The light was nearly gone except for what emanated from the glowing embers that breathed brighter with each stir of the wind. Monroe snapped open the locket and leaned toward the campfire, holding it in the soft light so that he could see her image as taken by a St. Louis photographer on one of her singing tours. The photographer's name was Otis Fly, and he later became quite well known and was commissioned by the president to take his portrait while sitting in a horsehair rocker.

He studied the photograph until the light gave out completely, and even then he did not close the locket but simply held it in his hand and imagined what he could no longer see.

In a way, it seemed to him that she had never really existed, for their time together had been so brief and twenty years had passed since. Finally, he leaned back against the saddle again, repinned the locket inside his coat, and gazed up at the stars. She had given him the locket as a gesture of appreciation for taming the ardors of a wild cowboy one evening in the Golden Cage as she recited a poem entitled "Ode Unto Thee." Her smile had nearly taken his breath away.

His thoughts slowly turned to what lay ahead of him and Nate the next few days. Nate was old and not so keen of eye or step. He concerned himself with Nate's welfare. What if Nate were to be killed in a gunfight with John Henry? It troubled him greatly.

All his life, he'd never thought about his own death, had never been afraid — not even during the war or the whole time he'd been a lawman in the Nations or any other time he could recall. But now, lying there looking up at the stars, he thought about dying and what it was going to be like when it happened. He wondered if dying was going to be an easy thing to do and if he was going to be able to get through it with some dignity. He'd known plenty of brave men who'd broken down at the end, men who'd cried and called for their mamas. He thought it must be a powerful thing, death, for it to break brave men down like it could.

He realized just how sorrowful his mood had become. He heard Nate snoring and wished he could be snoring, too, instead of wide awake and thinking about such things as death. He wished he had thought to bring a bottle of whiskey, something to take the chill off the night air, but was left instead with only his blanket.

He figured this business of finding John Henry Crow and killing him could not take all that long, and once it was finished, he'd ride to Bozeman, get himself a tall glass of whiskey, a good steak, and some female companionship. Maybe he'd ask Orna Sloan to accompany him into town and maybe there would be a dance they could attend. He thought that a buggy ride on a moonlit night might be just the thing to set him right again.

She seemed like a handsome woman, steady in every way, except she didn't know much about horses or how hard to ride them. But such things were small matters in the ways of the world, and he could teach her if it came to that.

Happily, he realized that his mood was quickly becoming brighter again now that he realized all the potential there was to be had, even in a place like Montana.

He punched his old hat down over his eyes and let the deep tiredness finish its work.

CHAPTER TWENTY-THREE

Once it had ceased being speculation and been confirmed that J.D. LeFlors had hired John Henry Crow to end the rustling of his cattle in the Judith Valley, public sentiment quickly turned against him. A delegation led by Ev Windlass, the second largest cattleman in the valley, came to state their feelings on a warm pleasant day at an hour near noon.

They stood in his front yard wearing black suits and holding their hats in their hands in a gentlemanly fashion: Ev Windlass, Jake Childress, Al Freemantle, and even the foreigner, Karl Swensen. *Like ravens looking for scraps*, J.D. thought, *the way they stand around in their black suits and won't enter my house*.

"Come to tell you, J.D.," Ev Windlass said, it being obvious that he had been appointed spokesman for the group, "that we ain't on your side in this affair. Ain't none of us in favor of what you done in hiring a killer like John Henry Crow. It wasn't necessary! There were plenty of other men of less murderous reputation that could have been hired."

J.D. had been well past drunk already. Now, he stood there searching their faces, looking for a sign of support. He could see none and turned his attention first to what he considered the least of them.

"Knowed you when you didn't have but three, four little scrawny cows and a mangy bull," J.D. said to Jake Childress, a wan little man who had prospered since his arrival from Missouri twenty years before. "Was me that helped you find a range and allowed you first water rights. Now look at you, standing there like some stiff little easterner. Wasn't that you married Flora Hampton and got into her daddy's money, I doubt you'd have a pot to piss in or a window to throw it out of!"

Jake shifted his gaze from that of J.D. LeFlors to the toes of his new shoes. The shoes had been bought by way of catalogue along with several dresses his Flora had ordered. Her money was a comfort to him, but it wasn't any of J.D. LeFlors's business.

Then, J.D. turned his attention to Al Freemantle, a large slump-shouldered man who wore a hat as big as any ever seen in the entire territory. Al Freemantle could be spotted a mile away just because of the big hat he wore.

"You was nothing more than a busted down cowboy when you come to the territory, Al," declared J.D., spilling some of the whiskey from his bottle. "First time I laid eyes on you, you was walking down the Bozeman road carrying a saddle with a broken cinch and a Winchester rifle and everything else you owned in life strapped to your back. You forgot who it was took you home to supper that night and gave you a job the next morning? You forgot it was me? You forgot it was my say so at the bank later on that got you the loan to buy that little spread you still live on now? How many cows you own now? How much money you got saved up in that bank I helped to get started? How's that plump wife and those fat children of yours?"

Al wasn't by nature a man who spoke much; words were difficult for him. He'd rather wrestle with cows or mean horses than words. He thought for a brief moment of saying something to J.D., but then thought better of it — more words would only make things worse and not better between them.

Then, not getting the satisfaction of an argument from Al, J.D. turned his ire on Karl Swensen.

"Well Swede, you in on this, too? I'd expect you to be."

"It's not right, J.D.," Karl said. "It's not right that those boys was murdered in cold blood. Even your own hand, Jode Pierce, was murdered in cold blood and you let it happen. Jode Pierce, he read the Bible and was a good feller. Everyone feels pretty bad that such a good feller as Jode Pierce was murdered!"

Karl Swensen had great flowing moustaches that were like corn tassels, and when he spoke they rose and fell in great sweeping movements.

"Damn foreigner!" declared J.D., for how could he withstand the accusations of such men but to declare their heritage invalid.

Karl swept his forefinger and thumb over his moustaches but did not comment further.

"You brought this to my door!" J.D said, his anger growing great with them as he stared down from the porch at Ev Windlass. "You never could stand the fact that you was number two in this valley! This is your way of bringing me down!"

"You've always had to have things your way, J.D.," Ev said. "I guess we never figured to stand up to you. But this murdering business is more than any of us will stand for."

"You'd have your cattle stolen, your stock run off?" declared J.D. "What next? You going to let the sons of bitches come in here and steal your wives and children? Why not just pack up and leave it to them, the thieves and the rustlers? It'd be the same as if you don't do anything about it, don't put a stop to it where you can!"

"Jode Pierce wasn't a thief or a rustler," Karl Swensen said. "He was a good feller who read his Bible!"

The whiskey burned Jipson LeFlors's brain so that he could hardly speak sense. His anger was as hot as flames.

"You don't understand a damn thing! None of you! I already sent one of my men to put an end to it!"

The announcement seemed to have little effect on the small delegation.

"It's too late for that, J.D.," Ev said. "What's done is done. You brought this trouble to our valley."

Then they turned, climbed into their buggies, and rode away. He watched them until the dust along the road settled again and they weren't but specks against the horizon.

Then he looked over toward the bunkhouses and saw that Jimmy Jake and Louis Butterfield and Homer Teal and Wayne Brazos and Calvin Pruitt had witnessed the confrontation.

Their slow approach into the yard replaced the emptiness left by the ranchers.

"Is it true that you sent my daddy to kill that stock detective?" Homer Teal asked. He looked as though he might cry.

"Your daddy is the best man I knew to see the job done," J.D. said. "And when he has seen to it that Crow is cared for, he will be rewarded for his troubles."

"But that fella killed Jode. Shot him from ambush. Shot him in the back!" skinny Calvin Pruitt said, his Adam's apple bobbing up and down in his neck. "And he shot all them others, too. What would keep him from shooting Mr. Teal in the back like he done the others?"

It was something he did not care to explain to such a dull boy as he considered Calvin Pruitt to be. The boy was a good roper and could ride a horse with the best of them and was an all around good hand, but he was dull in all other ways.

"Don't you have work to do?" he asked of them. "I guess any man that don't have work to do ain't needed around here anymore!"

Jimmy Jake hung behind as the rest of them drifted off toward the bunkhouse, for he had more personal reasons for being angry than any of the others.

Ever since Nate Love and Monroe Hawks had appeared at the house, J.D. LeFlors had taken to spending more and more of his time in Bozeman and not even bothering to come home at night. The talk had that J.D. was spending most of his time at the Valentine House with Bess Beauford, Jimmy's own sweetheart.

At first he didn't believe it when Louis Butterfield told him. But when Wayne Brazos confirmed it after a return trip to buy fence posts, he felt his anger hot and nearly unbearable toward his boss.

"Jimmy, saddle up the roan," ordered J.D. as the other cowboys slowly dispersed. "I'm going into town and the roan needs riding."

"I'll go along with you," Jimmy Jake offered in an attempt to see the truth for himself.

"No need, boy. You've got plenty to do around here. See to it that the herd is started up to the north range come morning!"

"You shouldn't have done it!" blurted Jimmy, his anger spilling over into the grief he still carried for Jode Pierce.

J.D. had started to retreat into the house for a clean shirt to wear into town when the accusation stopped him.

"Done what, boy?" he said, turning slowly to face the young cowboy.

"You shouldn't have hired John Crow to come here and kill Jode!"

"You let go of them notions, boy! My business ain't none of your business!" He turned toward the door.

"You've been seeing my sweetheart, Bess!"

The accusation nearly staggered J.D., for he had not expected to have his business at the Valentine House publicly announced by a hired hand.

"You let off with your loose mouth, boy! I mean now!"

"No sir, I won't! She's my sweetheart, Bess is, and I'll not having you see her!"

"She a goddamn whore! And I reckon she'll see whoever pays her!"

The rebuke was stinging, like a slap. Jimmy Jake blinked back angry tears, tears that threatened to slide down his cheeks, tears that would shame him if seen.

"Now go saddle the roan and be quick about it or pack your bedroll and be gone!"

He found he could hardly breathe from the anger that constricted his chest and throat. And yet he would not allow J.D. to see him cry.

"Reckon I'll collect my pay," he said stiffly. "Reckon I don't need the work so bad."

"Fine, suit yourself!" Then J.D. called out to Louis Butterfield that he'd be the new ramrod until Ray Teal's return and to saddle up the roan and bring it round to the front door.

The rest of the boys tried talking him into staying, but Jimmy Jake said he'd had enough and that he'd been insulted and, worse still, that J.D. had insulted his sweetheart by calling her a whore.

"Well, she is a whore," skinny Calvin Pruitt said. "That ain't no reason for you to be quitting us." All the anger Jimmy Jake had in him burst like a small dam, and he swung his fist into the side of Calvin Pruitt's face, knocking him backward over a bunk. The others grabbed hold of Jimmy and held him back from inflicting any more pain on Calvin. Calvin's dull nature made it impossible for him to understand why a friend would hit him in the face and knock him over a bunk.

He sat on the floor touching the spot on his face where Jimmy had struck him.

"I guess things has gone to hell ever since Jode was murdered," declared Wayne Brazos. "Jode was the most decent one among us. I always thought we'd be forever happy and working for Mr. LeFlors."

It was a declaration of forlornness that had its effect on all the boys at once. They were all saddened by the loss of yet another friend. Even Calvin Pruitt felt the loss more than the pain in his face.

"I guess we won't ever go swimming together in the pond again," Homer Teal said. "Or race our ponies like we used to."

Jimmy put his things together, wrapped in his bedroll, then shook hands with all the others, even with skinny Calvin Pruitt.

"I'm sorry I had to hit you," he offered. Calvin said, "That's alright, I know you didn't mean anything by it."

They watched Jimmy go off toward the house, where Minnie Bluefeather met him at the door and gave him his pay and a small sack of sandwiches, which she had made for him to take along.

"You take care, Minnie," Jimmy Jake said, his eyes unwilling to meet hers.

"Don't take up card playing or sinning ways," Minnie said. "You are a fine boy and I will miss you."

He nearly cried over the show of her concern. He'd never known the love of a mother, having been raised by an uncle in Minnesota until he'd run away at the age of fifteen. Minnie Bluefeather's display of concern for him was as near to a mother's love as he had ever known.

"Yes, well I will miss you, too," he told her. "And I'll miss your cooking."

Homer Teal had to walk a little ways off in order not to be seen crying, and so did Wayne Brazos.

J.D. was drunk and being mean all at the same time. Several times he had cursed Bess Beauford and threatened to strike her, and once he came close to doing so but fell over a chair in his attempt to reach her. His anger was still boiling over from the encounter with his neighbors and then with his own cowboys earlier in the day.

"It's nobody's business what I do!" he declared.

"Sure, honey," Bess had said several times, trying to mollify him. She was determined to keep J.D. LeFlors a contented man. For ever since he had begun coming around to see her, to purchase her services, she had allowed herself to dream of the possibility of a future. J.D. LeFlors was the biggest cattleman in the territory, which meant that he was also the richest. And even though he had a wife at home, he vowed that he was not in love with her, and on several occasions in the throes of his passion, he had declared his love for Bess.

She had known of other whores who had married well and lived the "charmed" life of respectability and social standing. Why couldn't it happen to her as well? All she had to do was read his thoughts, make him feel special and desired. It was a trick any woman worth her salt could perform on just about any man who ever put on a pair of boots or rode a horse. J.D. LeFlors, she reckoned, was no different from any other cowboy in that way.

So, when he ranted and stood on the bed in his union suit and waved his fists in the air and talked about the enemies that were all around him, she could only assure him that everything he said was the truth.

Then he did something she had never expected to see him do: he sat down in the middle of the bed, crossed his legs like an Indian, and cried. Big tears rolled down his cheeks and he said, "My life has come to this! No one respects me and I'll probably never be governor because of John Henry Crow's bloodthirsty ways."

"Now, now, honey," Bess said, summoning up all the false sympathy she could. "You ought not to talk that way. It's only upsetting."

He flung his hands above his head as though beseeching the peeling wallpaper ceiling.

"No! No! I'd be better if God should strike me dead for all the future I have in front of me!"

Then the door burst open and Jimmy Jake stood there with a pistol in each hand.

"It ain't God that's gonna see you dead, J.D. — it's me!"

Bess sprung off the bed and flung herself in a corner, all the while yipping like a dog with a broken tail.

Jimmy Jake tossed her a sorrowful look and said, "I am greatly disappointed in your behavior."

J.D. stopped crying long enough to begin laughing.

"Well, I seen some goddamn sorry sights in my time, but you are among the sorriest! Come to defend the honor of a whore!" he declared. "And not a very damn good one at that! Well, have at it, boy! Shoot me if you will, but I don't think you can stand the thought of having your neck broke by a hangman's noose."

"I reckon I don't have much reason to care!" announced Jimmy, his lips quivering, his eyes tear-stained. "Now that you have stolen my sweetheart and had my best friend murdered. This is for Jode," he said, firing one of the pistols into J.D. "And this is for stealing my gal!" He fired the other. Both shots hit J.D. square in the widest part of his body and flung him over backward. His blood stained through his union suit and onto the sheets and then soaked down into the corn shuck mattress.

"Lord God!" screamed Bess Beauford. "You've killed him!"

"It was the purpose of my coming," declared Jimmy. "I came here to kill him and I reckon I did."

Bess blinked several times and Jimmy said, "I reckon you better go and get the sheriff."

CHAPTER TWENTY-FOUR

He had sent the boy to Bozeman to buy sulfur powder and iodine and fresh bandages to dress the wound in his neck. It had become reinfected and he'd had the boy lance it with the old man's knife again, which had nearly caused him to faint.

He had written out the list of items he wanted from Bozeman on the back of a piece of calendar the old man had hanging on a wall above his bunk. The calendar was old and yellowed and featured a portrait of a cherubic, pig-tailed maiden holding a can of Bull's-eye evaporated milk.

"The old man probably wore his eyes out staring at her," whispered John Henry as he tore the calendar from the wall. "I reckon as homely and unappealing as that old man was, it didn't stop him from wanting what most men want."

"Get me a bottle or two of whiskey, bourbon blend, and take the gray stud. He'll get you there and back a lot faster," he added, his voice husky from the soreness of the wound. He had also added some stores to the list: salt pork, beans, flour, coffee, and eggs. The old man had nothing left to eat in the cabin, and in spite of the pain in his neck, John Henry's appetite had grown steadily each day.

Joshua caught the gray horse and rode off toward Bozeman as casually as if he had been on his way to a picnic. John Henry sat on a chair in front of the cabin, where the sun warmed the walls and himself, and watched the mute boy ride away until he was lost from view amid the tall grass and then the trees.

The need for supplies and medicine was only part of the reason why he had sent the boy off. There was something else, too. The boy had become dangerous. John Henry knew one thing for certain: he knew about killing men, and he knew about men who killed other men. Some did it because they thought it was necessary. Others killed because they enjoyed it. The mute boy enjoyed it.

The truth was troubling.

The sun made him drowsy, but he fought to keep his thoughts clear. He needed to sort out exactly what he should do about the boy before it became too late. And it would become too late. If there was one thing John Henry was certain of, it was that sooner or later, the boy would want to kill him, or at least try. It was a natural evolution among men who found killing to their liking. It would be a test of the boy's capacity; his taste for blood would require it. There would soon come a time when shooting defenseless men would not satisfy him. He would be compelled to pit himself against a greater challenge, and the greater challenge would no doubt be against John Henry himself.

He'd have to be cautious from now on around the boy. If the boy smelled fear in him, he surely would try to kill him. The sun's warmth seeped through his flannel shirt and absorbed itself into his flesh. Ever since having been shot, he was cold most of the time. The sun grazed the side of his face, the side where he had been shot through the neck, and it felt good to be warm for once.

He could not help but close his eyes and feel the weight of deep exhaustion, an exhaustion that was nearly numbing. For the first time, he felt a stab of fear penetrate his brain. If he were to fall asleep, the boy might return and kill him outright, just as he had shot the old man from behind, without warning.

He had bought the boy from a whiskey peddler camped near the Platte on a day when it was cold and spitting snow and the river looked black under the gray swollen clouds. He had come upon their camp late one evening, journeying from Ogalalla to Montana.

The boy had appeared greatly abused by the whiskey peddler, and there appeared something tragic and beautiful in the mute boy's eyes that had appealed to the deepest part of him.

He felt himself sliding deeper into a drowse as he remembered that time.

The whiskey peddler had been typical of his lot: dirty and profane in every way a man can be dirty and profane. He'd bragged how he ran whiskey up to the reservations, how the Sioux traded their women and young girls, even, just for a jug of the whiskey.

"Them red sons of bitches will do practically anything for a taste of ol' Tose!" the whiskey peddler had declared. "Fact is, that's where I picked me up this boy, from the Sioux. Don't know where they stole him from, but they was using him up pretty good and pretty regular. Paid three jugs of corn liquor and a gaunt mule fer him. I need me a boy to assist me in my bidness, don't you see!" The boy had been as dirty and unkempt as the whiskey peddler — barefooted and his clothes not much more than tattered rags.

"Well, I can see where a boy like that would come in handy," John Henry had remarked, being careful not to reveal his true intentions toward the situation.

"Yes sir and goddamn! The only trouble is, the little bastard ain't able to speak a lick. Make's it mighty boring as fer as conversation goes. But he serves me in other ways that don't call fer no talkin', if you catch my drift." The whiskey peddler's raucous laugh had been louder and more ear-splitting than the braying of a mule.

John Henry had decided then and there he would purchase the boy from the whiskey peddler if for no other reason than to deny the man the privilege of abusing the boy further.

"How much you take for him?" he asked. They had been eating mutton stew that the boy had cooked in a black iron kettle. "I could use me a good cook to make the trip with me up to Montana, where I'm headed on business."

The grizzled man blinked and ran greasy fingers through his shaggy beard.

"Waugh, I don't believe I'd take anything fer him!" he'd announced after several seconds of thinking about it. "What'd I want to sell a good boy like him fer?"

"You could always get another, I suppose . . . one that talked, maybe," John Henry had said with cold casualness. "Why not sell him to me?"

"Boy's a good cook alright, better'n a woman, stronger, too. And like I said, they's other things he's good at, too. Reckon I don't see no reason to sell him."

John Henry had set his plate of mutton stew on a rock and stood, walked over to where Joshua had been squatting on his heels, eating from his plate with his fingers.

"Go pack your things, son. I'm buying you from this fellow."

Joshua's gaze had darted from the dark half-lidded eyes of the stranger to those of the whiskey peddler.

"Go do it now," ordered John Henry.

"Say, wait a goddamn minute!" protested the whiskey peddler. "I said he ain't up fer sale!"

John Henry had parted his coat enough to show the crossdraw holster holding the Walker Colt on his left hip.

"It ain't a matter of whether he's for sale, friend. It's just a matter of terms."

The whiskey peddler had turned his attention to the twelve-gauge shotgun leaning against one of the wheels of his wagon.

"Too damn far to even think about," John Henry said. "But then I reckon you already know that."

A look of great and bitter disappointment clouded the whiskey peddler's crusty features.

"I reckon . . . he'd be worth at least two hundred dollars!" declared the whiskey peddler.

"I reckon ten dollars is more like it," John Henry said.

"Ten goddamn dollars!"

"Ten and throw in that paint mustang and a saddle. The boy needs to have something to ride if he's going with me all the way to Montana. Montana is a long ways off in case you didn't know."

"Waugh, mister! You might as well rob me and gouge out my eyes and take all my mash as to offer me ten goddamn dollars fer that boy and a good horse and saddle."

"Well, I could just shoot you," John Henry said. "That'd be easier than robbing you and gouging out your eyes and hauling all that rotgut liquor across country."

The whiskey peddler's eyes had jiggled in his head as though he had been struck a blow by a pick handle.

"Oh, Sweet Jesus! You invite a feller into yer camp fer dinner and he winds up taking advantage of ya! Go on ahead, take the boy and leave me ten goddamn dollars! What difference can it make and what choice do I have except to be less trustin' the next time!"

His last thoughts sitting there in the chair were of the boy hurrying along behind him on the trail far enough from the whiskey peddler's camp to not have to worry about being followed and shot at with the man's twelve-gauge shotgun. Now, he'd have to kill the boy. A strange and bitter irony, he thought.

His head dropped down and his chin rested on his chest. He was glad to be warm again and welcomed the deep sleep he was sliding into.

They found Ray Teal upon the ridge.

"Reckon that's the man J.D. sent to find John Henry?" Monroe asked.

"Reckon so," Nate said. "It's mighty grim seeing a man that's been left to the elements and the critters. It looks like he's been here for a few days, judging by the condition."

They both held their bandannas up over their noses because the wind was right and the smell of death was strong. The horses smelled it, too, and were skittish.

"I didn't believe that LeFlors had a man good enough to find John Henry and kill him," Monroe said. "I guess this proves it."

Nate dismounted and carefully approached the body.

"What's your intentions, Nate?" Monroe asked.

"Reckon we owe it to him to bury him."

"With what?" Monroe asked, for he was in no mood to bury people. "We didn't bring any shovels."

"Could gather rocks, I reckon," suggested Nate.

"That sounds like work I hadn't counted on," Monroe said.

"It's only decent," insisted Nate. "The man was trying to do the same job we are. He died because of it."

"He died because he wasn't good enough in the first place," Monroe said. He reached for his cigarette makings.

"No matter," Nate said.

Monroe gave up on the idea of rolling a cigarette and reluctantly dismounted.

"Don't know where it was in that letter you sent me that said anything about being part of burial parties," Monroe said, his voice edged with irritation.

"It'd go quicker if we was just to see it done rather than stand around and argue about it," Nate said.

It took the better part of an hour to gather enough rocks to cover the body of Ray Teal sufficiently to end the depredations wrought on him by hungry wolves and coyotes and the several ravens that had flown off a short distance when they had first topped the ridge and seen the dead man.

The work tired them and they took time to sit atop the rock grave and catch their breath and wipe the sweat from their eyes and the backs of their necks.

"I suppose next you'll want me to build a house," Monroe said.

"What would I want you to build a house for?" asked Nate.

"Well, I reckon you just love to see me work so much, you'd want me to build a house so you could see me work for a long time."

"You mind my asking when it was you got so blamed cranky?" Nate asked.

"Ain't cranky," replied Monroe. "I just don't see no reason to work when it ain't necessary. A man my age is wise to conserve his energy for more important things."

"By important you mean gals and such as that? Whiskey-drinking and card-playing? Them sort of important things?"

"Well, I'd sure like to know what things would be more important to a man than his own pleasure?"

"You know something, Monroe? When I turned around and saw you that day I was out there shooting cans with this old Schofield, I was nearly shocked at how you'd changed on me. Truth is, you was probably shocked, too. I looked at you and saw an old man and felt sorry I'd asked you to come all this way because I reckoned time had taken its toll on you, just as it had me. But sitting here on this pile of rocks, I'd have to say, you ain't changed one blamed bit. You are still the same old rascal you always was. Do you think there'll ever come a time when chasing after the ladies and drinking and gambling will be something you lay aside?"

"Yes," Monroe said. "When I am where this fellow we're sitting on is. Dead and buried."

Monroe laughed in that mischievous way that Nate had all but forgotten and said: "Hell and damnation, let's go catch John Henry. All this talk about my vices has got me het up to attend to them just as soon as possible. How are the whores and whiskey and gambling in Bozeman?"

A slow grin spread slowly across the dark face of Nate Love.

"Well sir, I hope you live long enough to find out for yourself. I personally would not know about the whores in Bozeman, nor the whiskey nor gambling neither."

CHAPTER TWENTY-FIVE

Junius Bean finally caught up with his hat a quarter-mile from the cabin; the hat had become snagged on a lone stand of bull thistles that grew in abundance along the Bozeman road. If it had not been for the bull thistles, the hat might have been blown clear into the next county. Junius sank to his knees with relief when he finally caught up to his hat. He was nearly out of breath and sweat dripped off his bare head. His few remaining strands of hair lay in frazzled streamers across his brow.

He had never felt quite so foolish or embarrassed as he did now, knowing that the widow had seen him chasing his hat from the window. He had looked up once and seen Suddy and the widow holding their hands across their mouths when the hat went rolling across the yard. He imagined them to still be laughing at him even now.

"Danged wind!" he cursed with one great heaving breath, for it was all he was able to manage, his sides hurt so from the long chase.

"Danged Montana anyway!" His sweat had soaked through his shirt and his coat and he had burrs caught in the cuffs of his trousers. His shoes were sorely scuffed from rocks.

He took a handkerchief from his pocket, wiped his forehead, and used his fingers to replace the strands of hair to their rightful place — directly across the crown of his scalp.

He wondered, kneeling there, how he could return to the cabin with any dignity now that the women, especially the widow, had seen him chase his hat.

He was still wondering when a sloe-eyed boy approached riding a gray stud horse. The boy was barefoot and poorly attired. Whorls of auburn hair glinted on his cheeks. The boy halted the horse there on the road and stared down at Junius, then stared at the hat snagged on the bull thistles.

Junius offered an inane grin and said, "I've had to chase my hat. The wind took it."

Joshua stared at the man's scalp. There were only two or three little strands of hair covering it. They were uncommonly long, reaching from one side of his head clear to the other. Practically ear to ear. They looked like little dead garter snakes. Joshua's laughter was a series of sharp utterances that startled the reporter.

"Well, there's no used to make fun of a man just because he's had to chase his hat in such wind as this," Junius said. "I'm sure it happens all the time in this country, the wind being what it is."

The boy nodded toward the hat hanging in the thistles.

Junius did not understand.

"What is it?" he said.

The boy pointed — first at the hat, then toward his own head.

"What's the matter, son — cat got your tongue?"

Junius saw the flash of anger in the boy's eyes, then saw as quick as anything, the boy pull a pistol from his waistband and point it at him.

"Whoa up!" declared Junius. "That thing looks loaded!"

The boy waved the barrel of the pistol toward the hat.

"What? You want my hat?" Junius uttered, his surprise and alarm great.

The boy nodded.

"Well, it's my only hat!" pleaded Junius. "How would it look if I had to go around bare-headed?" It was bad enough having been seen by the widow chasing his hat without having to go around bare-headed in her presence.

The boy thumbed back the hammer of the pistol, and the sound it made almost made Junius Bean's heart fail him.

"Lord! Don't shoot me over one blessed hat, son!" Then, he scrambled to retrieve the bowler, which had suffered little more than a few dirty smudges and one or two cockleburrs sticking from it. He took the hat in hand and held it out to the boy, who reached down from the gray horse and promptly snatched it from his hands before placing it atop his own head.

It was too large and slid down to the top of Joshua's ears. He could barely see out from under the brim.

Junius had to keep from grinning at the foolish way the boy looked wearing his hat.

Then the boy pointed to the reporter's shoes.

"You want my shoes as well?" cried Junius.

The boy nodded.

Reluctantly, he pulled off his shoes while the boy dismounted, still aiming his pistol in the direction of Junius.

"You're taking my wardrobe one piece at a time," Junius moaned as he sat on the ground watching while the boy tried on his shoes. They were much too small and the boy showed his displeasure by tossing them as far away as he could. He wondered if everybody in Montana had small feet.

It was obvious to the both of them that the man's trousers were too large in the waist and too short in the legs for them to be of much use to the slender boy. However, Joshua indicated his interest in Junius's coat. It was a plain broadcloth coat with three buttons down the front. Junius had purchased it, along with the trousers, from a Denver haberdasher for twelve dollars. Still, he didn't care for the idea of the boy stealing off with his clothes. It would only make him less presentable to the widow, being only partially dressed.

"No hat, no shoes, no coat!" wailed Junius. "I guess I am going to seem a sight to anyone who sees me." It didn't seem to matter to the boy that the coat's sleeves came several inches above his wrists or that it was damp with sweat. It was the first real coat he could recall ever having owned. It suited him just fine.

It struck him as an interesting thing that he did not have to shoot the man to get him to do what he wanted. Just waving the pistol around had been enough to get the man to give him his coat and shoes and hat. He felt terribly pleased with his newly found power.

Why kill the funny little fellow with hardly any hair on his head and no shoes or coat or hat? He laughed that strange utterance of a laugh as he rode off toward the town of Bozeman.

Junius sat heavily upon the ground trying hard to catch his breath once more. He'd nearly been murdered by a boy who couldn't even speak. He was as out of breath as he had been chasing his hat.

"Dang Montana and everybody in it!" he shouted, but only long after the boy had ridden out of sight. It was bad enough that he'd had to chase his hat, now he had to go chase his shoes.

CHAPTER TWENTY-SIX

"You have killed my only chance to get out of this horseshit town!" declared Bess Beauford as Jimmy Jake stared down at the two bullet holes leaking blood from the front of J.D. LeFlors's union suit.

"I reckon the sheriff will come and put you in a cell and in three or four days, the circuit judge will come and order you hanged. And in the meantime, I will have to go back to being a whore just to make ends meet! I reckon you've gone and ruined everything!"

"I'm sorry you feel that way," Jimmy Jake said, his tone apologetic.

"There ain't nothing dumber than a lovesick cowboy," said Bess Beauford. "Not in my book there ain't. I guess you just proved it!"

"Do you mind if I was to smoke a shuck while I wait for the sheriff to come get me?" he asked.

It seemed to Jimmy Jake that the sheriff ought to have come by now, that the two pistol shots he had fired into J.D. were loud enough to wake up everybody in town, including the sheriff; but so far no one came, and Jimmy felt like a smoke would calm his nerves some while he was waiting.

Bess had regained some of her composure now that she was sure that Jimmy Jake was not going to shoot her with either of his pistols. For that, she was relieved and especially grateful. For being left with little more than the prospect of staying a whore, she was less grateful.

"He was my future," she said, "and you've gone and put an end to that."

Jimmy Jake's hands shook as he used his makings to roll himself a cigarette.

"I didn't mean to put you in a bad fix, Bess. I always considered you to be my sweetheart. I guess I was overcome with jealousy."

"Well, I guess your foolishness has cost you your life," Bess said. "I'm sorry for you in that regard, but you have to know that what you did to me was wrong."

Jimmy had to strike two matches against his boot heel to get one of them to light so that he could smoke the shuck.

"Do you have some whiskey?" he asked. "I could stand at least one little drink of whiskey before I'm arrested."

There was still half a bottle of J.D.'s bourbon left and Bess poured them each a drink.

"I don't know why ol' Sheriff Peters hasn't come and put the manacles on you yet," Bess said, feeling more her old self, in spite of the lifeless body stretched out in his union suit across her bed. Only an hour previously he had been alive and randy and whispering sweet sentiments in her ear.

"I don't know why, either," Jimmy Jake said. "Those shots of mine were loud enough for the whole world to hear."

"Well, maybe you ought to make a run for it," Bess said. "While you still can."

Jimmy blinked at the suggestion.

"I thought you wanted to see me arrested and hanged," he said.

Looking at his long innocent face and stuck out ears, she knew he was no more vicious than a calf. It was true that he had come in and shot J.D. to pieces, but he had done it to protect her honor, even if it had been the biggest mistake she'd ever seen. And it was plain as white paint that he was head over heels in love with her. She didn't know why she was being so mean to him except that all the future she could ever imagine was lying dead as a keg of nails upon her bed.

"No, Jimmy," she said, tossing down the whiskey as if it were little more than warm water. "I guess you don't deserve to hang just because your jealousy made you crazy. I reckon I can understand how something like this can happen, how a feller like you can be head over heels in love with a pretty gal like me. But you ought to run while you still can. Ol' Sheriff Peters wouldn't bother to chase you much farther than the blue mountains was you to make it that far. You could go to Texas or maybe California and never be caught and remain a free man, though you'd have to forego your desire for me."

"Why, Bess, I swear, it sounds to me like you care about what happens to me," Jimmy said, the hazy gray smoke of his cigarette ringing his face.

"Well, maybe I do," Bess said. "Lots of cowboys have come and gone in my life, but none ever killed a man over me in a fit of jealousy. At least none that I know about. I guess that's got to account for something. I'd hate to see you hanged because of it."

"Oh, Bess." Tears had filled his eyes.

"Go on and climb out the window before they come and get you!" she ordered.

"I ought to stay and take my medicine," he muttered sadly.

"Don't be a damned fool!"

She kissed him once, hard on the mouth, and shoved him out the window.

Jimmy Jake galloped away with the wind and his own tears stinging his eyes.

CHAPTER TWENTY-SEVEN

John Henry woke from his slumber still sitting in the chair in front of the line shack. The sun had slid round to the far side and now he was sitting in the shade, which brought him a chill.

Judging by where the sun was in the sky, he guessed the hour to be late afternoon.

He'd had horrible dreams and now his mood was agitated, as dark as it ever had been. He thought of the boy, and the thoughts frightened him. In the dreams, the boy had returned to murder him. In the dreams, he had turned into the old man with corns on his feet and Joshua had stepped out of a mist and fired his pistol over and over again and he couldn't even defend himself because his movements were slow, like an old man's movements were slow.

His mouth was dry, his throat sore and burning. He went to the old man's well and slowly pulled up the water bucket from the bottom, then took the tin dipper hanging from the windlass and sipped the cool mossy water. His tongue felt swollen, and the drinking of the water was a near labor for him.

He could see his reflection in the bucket of water. He looked gaunt and sickly, more sickly than ever before.

His head felt feverish. Surely if he did not treat the wound properly and soon, it might take his life. Having studied medicine, he knew what an uncontrolled infection could do to a body. His troubles seemed great; they seemed to surround him. There was the infection, then there was the boy who would most likely try and kill him before all was said and done. Then, too, he did not know how many men LeFlors had sent after him.

Perhaps it had been a mistake to send the boy in for such meager supplies. Perhaps he should have gone and sought a doctor. Surely, Bozeman had a doctor. But then he realized his strength, or lack of it, would not allow him to travel far on horseback. He carried the bucket of water and the dipper back to the chair, his efforts labored.

He thought he might get sick and vomit, but there was nothing in him to throw up. He and the boy had eaten the old man's last can of beans the day before, but he had not been able to eat much because of the soreness in his throat, even though his appetite had increased.

Now, all he could do in the way of eating was to sit and stare at the rusting heap of bean cans the old man had tossed outside his front door over the years. He thought he could surely eat a lizard if one would come by and make the offer.

But in spite of his hunger and thirst, weariness ruled and soon his eyes drooped and fell shut again. And again, the dreams came. The terrible dreams of the boy coming out of the mist and firing the pistol at him.

He started awake several times, fighting off the fevered exhaustion.

He pulled his own pistol from its scabbard and laid it in his lap. He would not let the boy come out of the mist and shoot him. He believed that as soon as the opportunity presented itself, he would kill the boy. The boy had been a bad investment all the way around and he should have left him with the whiskey peddler to begin with.

"It was a mistake," he muttered.

Now he'd have to kill the boy. It was the only way.

CHAPTER TWENTY-EIGHT

They carried J.D. LeFlors's bloody remains over to Barber Bill's. Barber Bill did undertaking as well as haircutting; in fact, he preferred the former to the latter as a profession.

"A dead man don't complain as much," he took great pleasure in saying. Some people didn't get the joke and those who did, didn't appreciate it. Barber Bill was a rather pleasant man in spite of his dark humor. He gave himself his own haircuts, though how he was able to was anybody's guess.

Barber Bill was a Missouri man, and his great secret was that he had rode with Bloody Bill Quantrill during the depredations along the border. He had seen butchering at its worst and had finally run away to Indiana, where a sister lived in relative harmony with a husband and several small children. His sister had been a practitioner of Phrenology and had spent one afternoon reading the bumps on Bill's head. She'd feared for his state of mind, which was a prolonged melancholy over his past days with Bloody Bill.

"You are not meant to be a murderer of innocent men, women, and children," she had told him within the first few minutes of his reading. Bill had confessed to her Quantrill's heinous policies along the border and his own reluctant participation.

"Well, I kinda figured that out already, Maybeth," Bill replied to Maybeth's statement of the obvious. "Could you tell me what it is I am meant for?" Bill's mood was as blue as the sky.

"Well, remembering you as you was when we were children," Maybeth said, "you wasn't no good at much. I remember when you tried to draw pictures and how terrible you was at it, so I'd forget about becoming an artist. And I don't know you to possess any mechanical ways about yourself. And I've heard you sing and know that is not your calling."

Bill grew impatient with Maybeth telling him all the things he ought not to be and finally said: "Well, exactly what is it that you read in my head bumps? What does my bumps say I ought to do?"

"Not much that I can make out. You've got lots of bumps — more than the average feller — but they seem to read to an absolute commonness," was Maybeth's blunt answer. "Bill, I'm afraid you are cast only to perform lowly positions and that greatness is not to be yours. Now, I sure would have liked to have read ol' Bill Quantrill's bumps because I bet they were something else again, a man that would rape innocent women and burn down entire towns!"

However, Maybeth did teach Bill to cut hair, using her several small children and husband to practice on. Maybeth lectured, "A good barber is hard to find; there are, however, plenty of poor ones." He looked upon it for what it was — a way to earn a meager living. He had just about resigned himself to barbering as a lifetime profession, when he'd read an ad in the *Fort Wayne Journal* advertising the "Mortuary Sciences for Young Men Seeking A Future!" The ad went on to bestow the virtues of such a solemn yet necessary profession and did not attempt to understate the obvious: that there would always be a need for such services as the mortuary scientist could provide. "Never A Shortage of Clientele," the ad had stated boldly. "Plenty of Work for the Industrious Soul!"

To Bill, it had seemed a more dignified profession than cutting hair. He borrowed the fifty dollars it cost to attend the classes from Maybeth and received a diploma upon completion. The only complication was that there were already too many mortuary scientists in practice in Fort Wayne. But that was okay by Bill, who had always held the dream of moving west. So it was he took his talents somewhere they were more likely to be employed, the wild and wooly and murderous frontier. Fate, or something near to it, landed him in Bozeman, where the previous mortuary scientist had been no scientist at all but rather an alcoholic blacksmith who'd charged ten dollars to bury the dead without benefit of embalming or other funereal finery.

In fact, when asked about such things, the blacksmith, a man named Ned Shoefly, would laugh louder than a train whistle and say: "The only thing gets embalmed is me on this forty rod whiskey!"

In the end, Ned lost all desire to be in the funeral business and ran off to Santa Fe with the town librarian, who also happened to be the only school teacher in the entire valley.

Yancy Farragut, the town's newspaper editor, had editorialized that the illicit lovers had left the town bankrupt of several needed and necessary services and that the practice of such requited love in the future should be considered undemocratic by the participants, which had given Yancy's readers a great belly-laugh, but not Eliza Shoefly, the blacksmith's wife, who wore a black dress for nearly a year after and often wept openly.

Bill had settled in quickly and begun the practices of both haircutting and undertaking because there was not enough of either business alone to make a living. He soon was called simply Barber Bill, choosing not to take a chance that anyone would associate his real last name (Cripps) with the bloody slaughters that took place along the Missouri-Kansas border.

But, for a long time, the common and preferred gossip was that of Bill's predecessor: "Ol' Ned, he got tired of shoeing bad horses and planting folks. Drank so much he'd sometimes fall down in one of his own graves stone cold. Guess he didn't think much of his life, or why else would he've run off with such a plain-faced woman as the school teacher? His wife was plain-faced, too, but I guess Ned thought the school teacher was younger and therefore a whole lot more interesting than his wife! HAR! HAR! HAR!"

If Bill had heard the story once he'd heard it a hundred times.

When the lifeless form of J.D. LeFlors was carried into his establishment, Bill couldn't believe his good fortune. J.D. LeFlors had been the richest man in Judith Valley and the most well-known. J.D. LeFlors was as close to being a celebrity as you could get in Judith Valley.

"Better put him on display in your front window, Bill," Sheriff Peters suggested. "Sheriff Peters had short silver moustaches that danced up and down when he spoke. Lots of folks will want to pay their respects and make sure he's really dead. He'll probably attract more attention than a circus."

"What do you fill the bullet holes with?" Red Peters wanted to know. Red Peters sometimes worked as a deputy for his brother, the sheriff, on certain cases.

"Putty," Bill said. "I fill bullet holes with putty."

"Well, ain't that somethin'," declared Red Peters. "You mean like putty that's used around winders?"

"Yes," Bill said. "Exactly. It's something I learned in mortuary school."

"Well ain't that somethin'," Red Peters repeated.

"I'll have J.D.'s widder bring by some clothes fer him," Sheriff Peters said. "I'm sure she'll want him laid out in a fancy suit or somethin'."

The widow did not come until the next morning, and she brought with her the Indian housekeeper, Minnie Bluefeather, who carried in a black broadcloth suit, a white shirt, and a silk cravat while the widow waited in the cabriolet.

"Missus wants to know if you want to put shoes on him," Minnie Bluefeather asked.

"That'd be her choice," Bill said.

Minnie went out to the buggy, where the widow was waiting, and spoke to her. The widow reached down inside the buggy and held up a pair of black shoes. Minnie brought them inside the barber shop and handed them to Bill.

"She says put them on."

"Okay," Bill said. "I'd be happy to do whatever Mrs. LeFlors wants."

"She says she don't have no use for his shoes," Minnie Bluefeather said.

"I understand," Bill said.

"She says he sent all the way to Chicago for these shoes and never even wore them one time, that they are brand new and she has no use for them at all."

Bill nodded and admired the new shoes.

"She says she will come by later when he is ready and have a look at him."

"Yes, of course," Bill said.

"She says that you shouldn't think you can charge her an arm and a leg just because he's J.D. LeFlors and one of the richest men in the valley."

Bill nodded, sorely disappointed, for he had hoped for a very fancy funeral, one that would cost a great deal. He had recently purchased a new glass-sided hearse from Chiggam & Sons Hearse Company out of Denver. He figured to charge extra for a ride in it.

"She says that it's her money now, and she ain't gonna be charged an arm and a leg just to get him buried. She says that he ain't the rich one no more; he's the dead one and she's the rich one. She says she's the one paying the bills."

"Yes . . . hmmmm. Yes, I understand. Tell the grieving widow that there will be no gouging on my part."

"Good!" Minnie Bluefeather said, then turned without further inquiry or orders and climbed in the wagon next to the widow. Bill watched as the buggy disappeared down the street.

The sun was beginning to set under a brassy light when Joshua rode the gray stud down the main street. He saw a crowd gathered in front of the barber shop. He couldn't read, but he knew a barber's pole when he saw one. There was a large plate glass window that everyone was staring through.

He wondered what could be so interesting about a barber shop and so reined in the horse and found a place to tie it up.

After some little effort, he managed to work his way through the crowd and see what it was people were staring at in the window. It was a dead man laid out on two large blocks of ice.

Why would a dead man be lying in a barber's window? he wondered. The man looked like he had just laid down on the ice and gone to sleep in his good suit. Joshua's attention was drawn immediately to the new pair of black shoes the man was wearing on his feet.

Why would anyone put such good shoes on a dead man's feet?

He stared a long time at the man's shoes. They looked like they would cost a lot of money. They were as good shoes as he had ever seen.

J.D.'s cowboys came to view the remains. All but Jimmy Jake who had fled south thinking that Texas might be a good place to begin a new life, even though his heart was broken from having to leave Bess Beauford behind. He had romantic notions that he would someday return for her, notions that brought tears to his eyes. In the meantime, however, he figured there was plenty of work in Texas for a fellow who could rope and ride as well as he could.

Louis Butterfield said: "He don't seem so much laying there on them blocks of ice."

Wayne Brazos had tears in his eyes in spite of himself. Death seemed to him such a sad and final thing.

Skinny Calvin Pruitt said: "I don't know why you'd be broke up over a man that had a hand in Jode's killing."

"It ain't that," sniffled Wayne. "It's just that I never thought I'd see the day that a man as rich and powerful as J.D. would himself be killed. It sorta mortifies me to think of what could happen to a feller like me who don't own nothin' more'n a saddle and an extry shirt!"

"Well, that don't make hardly no sense at all," Homer Teal said. "What sort of sense does that make? Money ain't got nothing to do with whether someone walks up and shoots holes in you. I reckon there ain't no money that can stop bullets!"

"Well, I vote we go over to the saloon and have ourselves a drink, raise a glass to ol' J.D. and to Jimmy Jake, too, who is probably halfway to the border by now," Louis Butterfield said. "I'm sure Jimmy had his reasons for dusting J.D., but the plain truth is we need to give some thought as to where our next paycheck is going to come from. I doubt the widder will keep the ranch or none of us cowboys neither."

The other boys knew Louis to be the most practical-minded one among them now that Jode Pierce was dead.

"Any occasion to have a beer is fine with me," Calvin Pruitt said. "I believe I could drink two or three beers as dry and hot as it is today."

Wayne Brazos wiped the tears from his eyes with the bandanna tied round his neck. "Well, I guess this means we'll all wind up drifting away and never seeing one another again. It makes me sad to believe so."

Homer Teal said: "Hooray for Jimmy Jake! He's a wild cowboy now!" and the dark mood among them instantly lifted itself.

"I reckon he is," Louis Butterfield agreed.

"Damned if he ain't!" Calvin Pruitt said.

Even Wayne had to smile.

Darkness found the cowboys still leaning over the plank bar at the nearest whiskey tent.

Barber Bill had gone home to his wife, a woman named Myrtle, and had her put drops of camphor under his nostrils in order to quell the stench of death and embalming fluids.

Joshua had waited until after dark before returning to the barber shop window. The deceased still lay in plain view and still wore the new black shoes.

"The thought of the shoes had worn on his mind the whole day, and he could think of little else, not even the list of supplies John Henry had written on the calendar that was folded neatly in his side pocket."

He stood there for a long time more staring at the shoes, judging their size, than studying his own bare feet. He reckoned the shoes to be just about the right fit for his own feet. What would a dead man need with shoes?

He pitched a brick he had found through the plate window, and it shattered in a great silence, the shards of glass falling like sharpened rain drops.

Sheriff Peters heard the sound of glass busting. So did Barber Bill, who lived just a block away. Myrtle was busy washing Bill's hair in a basin of cold water. His hair smelled like embalming fluids.

The cowboys heard the sound of glass busting, as did everyone in the saloon and in that end of town.

It was an unusual sound to hear that time of night, glass busting. It was the sort of sound that drew their curiosity enough to make them stop whatever they were doing and go see why there was glass being busted on such an otherwise quiet night.

J.D. was still lying on half-melted blocks of ice amid a rainfall of busted glass.

"It looks like someone was trying to steal him!" Sheriff Peters said.

"No," Barber Bill said, his hair still full of wet suds. "They only wanted to steal his shoes. Look there at his feet!"

"Shoes!" said several of the cowboys at once.

"It looks that way," Barber Bill said. "They busted my winder just to steal his shoes. That winder cost me forty dollars! Whoever did this must have been a desperate thinker!"

For a long moment, there was little more than silence and the sound of winded men breathing.

"I don't reckon I ever seen the shoes stolen off a dead man before," Sheriff Peters said. "I reckon now I've seen everything there is to see."

"I saw a pig that was trained to laugh once," skinny Calvin Pruitt said. "It was in Abilene and a man there that owned a saloon owned the pig. The man would tell a joke and the pig would laugh."

"I saw it rain frogs once," Louis Butterfield said. "In Nebraska. It started out as hail and ended up as frogs all over the ground."

"I saw a whore that had six toes on each foot!" declared Wayne Brazos. "That was in Cheyenne and she charge extry for the privilege of looking at them."

One of the men who'd been drinking with the cowboys in the whiskey tent said, "Was her name Anna Trueblood?"

"How'd you know?" Wayne Brazos asked.

The man laughed like a mule. "Ain't it a small world," he said when he caught his breath.

The cowboys drifted back to the saloon, talking about the amazing things they had seen. Sheriff Peters couldn't wait to get back home and eat his pork chops and tell his common-law wife what he had just seen. Barber Bill was sorry he'd ever got the privilege of burying J.D. LeFlors. It was turning out to be a financial loss.

Joshua had misjudged the shoes by an inch or two, for they pinched his feet. But seeing how they looked, he figured he could ignore the discomfort. Overall he was pleased to have come across a dead man wearing brand new shoes.

CHAPTER TWENTY-NINE

John Henry was sitting in the privy a hundred feet from the shack, killing time by studying what was left of an old catalogue with half its pages gone, when he heard the approach of the riders.

He leaned forward and squinted through a crack in the weathered door. Through that seam of sunlight he could see two men ride up to the front of the shack. They were old men. One black, one white.

"'Lo in the cabin!" called the white man.

John Henry knew they were trouble looking for trouble. He wondered again where the mute boy had gone. He had left the day before and had not yet returned.

"Don't look as though nobody's home," Nate said.

Monroe was eyeing the paint horse staked out on a long lead rope.

"Man wouldn't leave a horse like that around so's somebody could just ride by and steal him."

"Maybe we ought to get down and look around," Nate suggested.

"Maybe so," Monroe said.

John Henry saw the men dismount and pull pistols from their belts and knew instantly they had come looking for him.

He hadn't finished his business, it'd have to wait. He pulled up his drawers and put the barrel of his pistol to the long crack in the door. If they came toward the outhouse, he'd shoot them. Otherwise, he'd let it pass because he was in no shape for a prolonged gunfight.

"You slip around back," Monroe said. "I'll go in the front. I'd be damn careful. John Crow is nobody to take chances with."

"I reckon I know how to take on dangerous men," Nate said, a little chagrined at Monroe's advice. "I reckon I ain't forgot who it was that shot China Jim and Roy Thourgood while that puny gal of theirs was shooting holes through you!"

"Well, that was a long time ago," Monroe said, "and neither of us has shot a man in twenty years. Our aim might be just a little off is all."

"I reckon we ain't so old or that it's been that long a time that even a dangerous man like John Crow would get more than one of us before we got him," Nate said. "Is there anybody special you'd want me to contact in case it's you he shoots?"

Monroe could have done without the humor.

"Maybe a woman friend?"

"No. There ain't no one you'd need to contact in case I get shot!" Monroe said. "And if it's you instead of me, I sure ain't gonna be the one to go tell Suddy. I'd write her a letter instead, a letter from a long ways off."

John Henry watched as the black man went around back of the cabin and the white man went in the front door, his pistol ready to fire.

In spite of their ages, they appeared to be professional men; he could see that plain as anything. J.D. LeFlors must've hit bottom, though, to have sent such old men after him. He thought about trying to escape the heat and stench of the privy for somewhere cooler and more refreshing from which to fight if it came to that. But the hinges on the privy door were rusty and screeched like scalded cats whenever the door was opened. It surely would give him away if he tried to open the door.

He cursed the fact that the mute boy had not yet returned. It would have afforded him another gun.

The cabin was unoccupied. Nothing more than a table and a single chair and a rope cot. Motes of dust danced in the shafts of light pouring through the glass-less windows. Then Monroe saw the stocky ten-gauge leaning in the corner.

"Look at this," he called to Nate through the open back door. "Whoever was here has left a good shotgun." He picked it up. He had seen a marshal in Laredo shoot a drunken cowboy with a ten-gauge. It had cut the man nearly in half. He knew it to be a destructive piece of equipment.

"Left his horse and his shotgun," commented Nate. "Maybe he was in such a hurry to leave this pile of trash he just forgot all the important things he owned."

"This is low living for sure," agreed Monroe.

“I never wish to be so poor as to have to live in a place like this.”

“Well, you might if you don’t get married again and settled down,” Nate said. “A good woman means everything. This is what happens to bachelors.”

“Nobody here, that’s for sure,” Monroe said, ignoring Nate’s comment about marriage and good women and bachelors. He stepped outside joining Nate’s search.

“I still can’t figure why someone would go off and leave a good horse like that staked out on a rope,” Monroe said. Old instincts told him something was adrift in the lay of things.

“Does seem unusual,” Nate confirmed.

“Well, I guess there’s no accounting for some things,” Monroe said.

“I reckon I’ll take use of that privy, however, as long as we’re already here,” Nate said.

“A natural man would use the great outdoors for his business,” Monroe said. “I reckon you’ve gone and got civilized.”

Nate ignored the comment and started for the privy.

John Henry cocked back the hammer of his pistol.

Monroe heard it like a man hears the buzz of a hidden rattlesnake, only a second too late.

“Nate!” he called out just as the bullet struck Nate high in the hip.

Nate’s leg went instantly numb and gave out from under him. The ground rose up and struck him a blow.

A great roar sounded from above his head; it was the sound of the ten-gauge being fired.

The buckshot struck the privy and blasted chunks of wood and splintered boards. Several pieces of the heavy buckshot ripped through John Henry and slammed him to the back of the privy, his pistol dropping down one of the holes. He was barely aware of being alive, except he could still see the sunlight streaming through the cracks and the newly splintered hole in the door. He struggled to right himself, to fight off the death that was smothering him. Blood seemed to leak from every portion of his chest and arms.

Suddenly, the door, or what little was left of it, flung open to a galling shaft of white light, then a figure stepped within the frame, blocking out most of the light.

"It's a poor way to have to die, in a shithouse!" Monroe said. "But I reckon in your case, it's a befitting tribute. You were one terrible son of a bitch!"

The boy rode out of the nearby trees and fired his pistol several times at Monroe as he stood there in the blasted door frame of the outhouse, the ten-gauge pointing downward at the dying John Henry Crow.

Nate was still on the ground, struggling to hold back the blood flowing from his hip. The second of the boy's shots spanked up dust from the back of Monroe's shirt and caused him to stagger. As he was hit by the bullet, his finger instinctively pulled the second trigger on the ten-gauge and John Henry Crow was forever lost amid the blast and smoke and carnage that such a weapon can exact.

The kid was off his horse now, running toward the man staggering from the outhouse and firing wildly, rapidly. Nate shot him as he ran past, shot him in a manner that caused him to take several sidesteps before falling over. Joshua crumpled and did not move.

For a long full moment, the blue smoke of gunpowder hung in the air before a soft wind came and carried it away. And for a long moment more, there was no sound other than that of the feathering wind and the labored breathing of two wounded men.

"Nate — !"

"Monroe — !"

The kid's bullet had punched a hole in him that made it difficult to take in a deep breath. He coughed several times, then gained his composure before walking over to Nate, who had managed to sit upright and was making an effort to regain his feet.

"Was it John Henry?" Nate asked.

"It was," Monroe said.

Nate looked over to the fallen boy.

"I wonder who he was."

Monroe stood, slightly tilted from the wound.

"I ain't never seen him before," Monroe said.

"Probably just another wild-eyed kid come to make a reputation for himself. He fell in with bad company when he fell in with John Henry Crow."

"Then some," Monroe said.

"Lord, that boy is poorly dressed, but look at them new shoes he's wearing," Nate said. The new shoes stuck out like sore thumbs on the raggedy boy.

"I reckon they're fitting enough to be buried in," Monroe said. "It's about all the good they'll do him now."

CHAPTER THIRTY

By the time they reached Nate's cabin, Monroe knew he was dying. The kid's bullet had hit a lung, maybe worse. It was hard to tell. Monroe knew enough about doctoring to know that a man who coughed up his own blood was a man in bad trouble. He had seen enough men shot to know.

Suddy held steadfast at their appearance, at Nate's bloody limb and Monroe's poor condition, his shirt stained red and him coughing up bloody fleck.

"Miz Sloan, you don't mind, heat some water up on the stove," Suddy requested of her guest. "Mistuh Bean, you helps me get these gentlemens undressed."

Junius Bean found that by the time he had helped both men off their horses, what few clothes he had remaining to him were soaked with blood.

It had been an unusual twenty-four hours, he thought. A time in which he had had to chase his own hat in front of the women, only to be robbed of it and his coat and nearly his shoes by a strange boy who did not speak. Now, what little he owned was soaked with the blood of two famous old gunmen, Nate Love and Monroe Hawks!

He did not know whether to laugh or to cry.

Suddy asked the widow Sloan to tend to Monroe, while she treated Nate's wound.

"You gone and done it this time, Mistuh Love," she said as she bent to the task, although the wound was not nearly as severe as she had first suspected. Once the blood was wiped away, there was but a small puckered hole through the flesh covering his hip bone. She could not feel the lead slug below the skin.

"Must've bounced clean off you," she said, adding a fresh bandage to the wound.

"Knocked hell out of me," Nate said. "Knocked me clean off my feet!"

"I reckon so," Suddy said.

"You go on in and look after Monroe," Nate said. "I don't care for the way he's been spitting up blood the whole ride back."

"I best stay here wid you, you my husband. Miz Sloan's lookin' after Mistuh Monroe."

Nate shook his head.

"No. You best see to it," he said. "Ain't nobody around here that can doctor like you can. Ol' Monroe could use you."

She started to protest but Nate raised his hand.

"He saved my life out there, Suddy Mae. Hadn't been for him killing John Henry with a shotgun, I might not be laying here now."

With a great sigh that trembled through her large bosoms, she raised herself from the bed and went to the other room, where Junius and Orna had Monroe stripped down to just his bottoms.

He was propped up with pillows behind him so he could breathe easier, a pan of bloody sputum set on the nightstand next to him. He coughed at her appearance. She could hear death rattling around inside him.

Junius and Orna gave way to her approach.

"How you gettin' on, Mistuh Hawks?" Suddy asked him in a gentle voice.

He watched her the way a cowboy watches a brush steer, with a great degree of caution.

"Getting on fine, Miz Love. Just fine." Then he coughed a great bloody hawk and spat it in the pan, and she knew that the last thing Monroe Hawks was doing was getting along just fine.

She examined the wound in his back; it was high up but not so high that it might not have struck a lung. She knew from experience that bullets had funny ways of traveling inside a body. She'd seen bullets go in one way and come out in a totally different place. Unexpected places. Only looking at Monroe, she didn't see where the bullet had come out at all — it was obviously still inside him.

Finishing her examination, she eased him back onto the pillows that propped him up.

"Well, I reckon you'll need to be restin' easy for a time," she said.

"I reckon soon," Monroe said, "I'll be resting for a longer time than I care to."

"The bullet's still in you," Suddy said. "Maybe down inside your lungs or maybe worse."

"I know," Monroe said. "I can feel the damn thing in there rattling around. You'll excuse my language."

"No need to concern yourselve wid your talk 'round me, Mistuh Monroe. I've heard lots worse, you know that."

"Yes," Monroe said. "It's just that being shot has made me irritable."

"I can see how that would be," Suddy said.

She let her gaze rest upon the man who frightened her more than any other she'd known in her lifetime. He looked old, propped up against the pillows, the gray hairs of his chest revealed in his partial nakedness. Old and thin and wounded as he was — frail. She tried to think what it was about him that had always caused her such deep fear. It went way beyond the fact of his and Nate's friendship, which she always had found threatening. And it went way beyond their fighting days together. Some men could fight with a fury and when the fighting was done, so was the fury. But Monroe Hawks always seemed to have the fury in him, buried deep beneath a rather quiet southern drawl and those watery blue eyes. A fury that was buried deeper than his very soul, she thought, and yet seemed at times to lie just below the surface of his being. Surely he had been born with it, and surely he would go to his grave with it.

For the first time, she wasn't able to sense the fury in him and that somehow disturbed her even more.

"I'll require a few minutes of privacy with Mistuh Hawks," she said to Junius and Orna.

They silently slipped from the room.

"Do you still like to drink your whiskey, Mistuh Hawks?"

He lifted his eyes, which had partially closed. The need to close them felt great to him.

"Yes, Miz Love, I still enjoy the privilege."

"Well, Mistuh Love keeps a bottle for medicinal purposes only, and I have brought it along." She took a small pint bottle from the folds of her apron.

He watched as she poured him some in a glass and then handed it to him.

"You sip it slow," she cautioned.

She waited until he finished before taking the glass from his hand.

A cough took him and shook his whole body, and a trace of red foam appeared in the corner of his mouth. She wiped it away with a fresh handkerchief.

"I reckon you know that your time is near?" she said.

He nodded.

"Near enough."

"Might just as well settle things then before it's too late," Suddy said.

"What sort of things we talking about, Miz Love?"

"Like where it is you goin' to be buried and is there anyone you want me and Nate to let know of your final restin' place?"

He felt the tug of great exhaustion pull at him. The need to close his eyes and surrender begged him.

"Well there is no one special," Monroe said. "And where it is I'm planted won't make too much difference to me." She could see he had not said all of what he was thinking by the way his eyes looked out to the blue mountains through the window.

"Is that all of it?" she asked.

"I reckon so," he said.

"It ain't enough," she said.

"What ain't?"

"Just to be buried in the ground and forgotten."

"Well, I ain't sentimental about such things, Miz Love."

"No, I can see that you ain't."

"Did Nate tell you that we killed the man that killed your Efrim?"

"He did, and for that I am grateful to you, Mistuh Monroe."

"No need to be. It was something that needed doing."

"Well, I guess it has cost you dearly, this business."

"Yes, I reckon it has. But I always did want to see Montana, and now I have. I've done just about everything else."

"Mistuh Monroe?" Suddy said, her voice barely audible, for she could see how death was taking hold of him, causing him to close his eyes only to fight them open again. His breathing was more difficult than it had been when she'd first entered the room.

"Mistuh Monroe?" she said again, and he opened his eyes once more.

"I want you to know that Nate and me will keep you here wid us. We'll see that things are taken care of."

He smiled and she thought he might say something, but he didn't. Then his head lowered, his eyes closed again, and his breathing finally came to an end.

She brought the sheet up over him and said: "I neva thought you'd die at home in a bed, but I reckon that was the one thing I was wrong about." The tears stained her cheeks as she sat with him for a time, knowing he needed her kindness while his soul passed on. She sat and held his hand, the long bony fingers still warm, and she wept.

Junius volunteered to dig the grave, and Orna washed and ironed his clothes. Suddy washed his arms and legs and face and shaved him with one of Nate's bone-handled razors. Then she combed his hair into place and trimmed his moustaches.

Between them, they loaded him in the wagon that carried him up the slight slope next to where Efrim was buried.

Nate sat in a chair because of his wound and watched as Suddy and Junius and Orna lowered Monroe into the grave on ropes.

Then Suddy read some from her Bible, a chapter from Revelations, before they all returned to the house.

Nate stayed quiet the whole time; Suddy knew he was chewing on old memories, old times. This time, she didn't mind.

"Mistuh Bean, may I have a word wid you outside?" Suddy asked.

"Surely, Mrs. Love."

When they had stepped into the yard, Suddy said: "I asked Nate to tell you about what happened to him and Mistuh Monroe and the shootout they had with John Henry Crow and his murderous assistant. I think it would be good reading, a real sensation for your newspaper in Denver, don't you?"

It raced through his mind like a wildfire: "The Last Fight of Monroe Hawks!" Of course it would make a whopping good read and he would have the exclusive story.

"Oh, yes indeed, Mrs. Love. Yes, indeed!"

"Then it will just cost you one thing more!" Suddy said with calm equanimity.

"Oh, what might that be?" Junius said.

"Another headstone . . . for Mistuh Hawks."

"Another headstone?"

"Yes suh, tha's the deal."

When the headstones arrived from Ogalalla, they were already inscribed. Two men unloaded them and set them up in a row.

"Will they do, missus?" said one of the men, an older man with dark hair and moustaches.

Suddy stared down at them, saw that the names were right and that the angels were delicately carved on each just as she had requested. She read each one, but troubled herself only to read the last of the four for a second time.

Monroe Hawks. A Fighting Man.
Died Montana Territory.
Friend.

And she bent and touched the stone face of one of the angels.

ISIS publish a wide range of books in large print, from fiction to biography. Any suggestions for books you would like to see in large print or audio are always welcome. Please send to the Editorial Department at:

ISIS Publishing Limited
7 Centremead
Osney Mead
Oxford OX2 0ES

A full list of titles is available free of charge from:

Ulverscroft Large Print Books Limited

(UK)
The Green
Bradgate Road, Anstey
Leicester LE7 7FU
Tel: (0116) 236 4325

(Australia)
P.O. Box 314
St Leonards
NSW 1590
Tel: (02) 9436 2622

(USA)
P.O. Box 1230
West Seneca
N.Y. 14224-1230
Tel: (716) 674 4270

(Canada)
P.O. Box 80038
Burlington
Ontario L7L 6B1
Tel: (905) 637 8734

(New Zealand)
P.O. Box 456
Feilding
Tel: (06) 323 6828

Details of **ISIS** complete and unabridged audio books are also available from these offices. Alternatively, contact your local library for details of their collection of **ISIS** large print and unabridged audio books.